# California Waves

## The Davenports, Book 2

### ~ Mila and Herschel ~

Bella Andre & Nicky Arden

CALIFORNIA WAVES
The Davenports, Book 2

*Meet the Davenport family! Six brothers and sisters who call picturesque Carmel-by-the-Sea home. Successful, brilliant, and passionate, the only thing they all still need is the perfect partner in love and life.*

When Herschel Greenfield achieved his dream of becoming an astronaut and going on space missions, he thought he knew the risks—but he never expected his splashdown would go wrong and he'd nearly drown. He tells everyone he's fine, but if that's true, then why can't get into the ocean? Somehow, some way, he needs to conquer his fear so that hc can continue going into space.

When pro-surfer Mila Davenport suffered a career-ending accident that almost cost her life, she had to adjust to an entirely new life where she spent more time on land than in the sea. While she loves her new career as a realtor, nothing makes her feel more alive than riding the waves. Certainly, no man has ever come close to giving her that same rush that the ocean does.

But after meeting Herschel, when she learns about his emotional fallout from his crash landing, she wants nothing more than to help him learn to love the sea as much as she does, despite his harrowing experience. The only problem is that she also thinks he's incredibly sexy and can't help but want him. More than she's ever wanted anyone. And when it seems like he feels the same way about her, that's when things suddenly feel truly dangerous. Far more dangerous than any surfing accident or crash landing. Because this time around, Mila isn't just risking her body—she's risking her heart.

But is Hersch willing to risk his heart, too? Or once he gets over his issues with the sea, will he be on the next spaceship out of town...and she'll be left with nothing but the memories of being with the most incredible man she's ever known?

# A note from Bella and Nicky

Thank you so much for being so excited about the Davenport family! Your messages about how much you loved the first book in the series (*California Dreaming*) meant so much to both of us!

Many of you mentioned having been to Carmel-by-the-Sea and how much you loved the small town, which truly does look like a fairy tale town come to life. In fact, one reader even told us that she had her honeymoon in Carmel-by-the-Sea. What a perfect place for a honeymoon!

Now we can't wait for you to read about Mila Davenport and the amazing hero that she falls in love with. And please keep sending us emails and messages on social media about the Davenports. We love to read them all!

Happy reading,
Bella Andre & Nicky Arden

P.S. Please sign up for our New Release newsletters for more information on upcoming books: BellaAndre.com/Newsletter and nickyarden.com/newsletter

# Chapter One

The sun smiled down on the plein air art show at Devendorf Park in Carmel-by-the-Sea, where Herschel Greenfield couldn't stop staring at Mila Davenport. She was tall, blonde, and fearless. A surfing goddess of the waves, and he'd just said the clumsiest thing to her, implying he wouldn't want a painting of her on his wall precisely because of that. Truth was, he couldn't imagine anything he'd rather look at all day than Mila, but preferably on dry land, so he wouldn't have to look at crashing waves and be reminded that the sea had very nearly killed him.

However, she couldn't know that was what he'd meant when he'd implied he didn't want to buy a picture that featured her surfing. Mila was stunning. Tall, statuesque, with long sun-kissed blonde hair and sea-witch eyes that seemed to see right through him. As she walked away, Hersch felt as though the breath had been knocked out of him. Not only was Mila gorgeous, she was strong enough to ride those treacherous waves. He couldn't imagine what it would be like to be able to walk into the water without fear.

And with that single thought, his near-death experience came rushing back, as intense and terrifying as the very day it happened, more than a year ago.

The mission to space had been successful. Everything had gone as planned, and re-entry to Earth's atmosphere was smooth. Even the splashdown itself was textbook. But within minutes, the seas turned, the waves roaring up with a sudden squall. The capsule, tough as it was, didn't stand a chance. Unable to orient itself upright, it was hit by a wave and knocked onto its side. Water began to gush in, freezing and frothing, swirling around their feet.

Hersch didn't panic—there wasn't time for that. Instead, his training kicked in, and he knew that the most important thing was to get every astronaut out safely. Hersch insisted his team exit the flooding capsule ahead of him into the flotation collar to await rescue. He was single. If he perished, he wouldn't leave behind a spouse or kids to mourn him.

With everyone out safely, Hersch left the capsule, but as he crossed the threshold, a huge wave grabbed him and swallowed him whole.

It happened so quickly he was robbed of a last breath before he plunged into the icy water and was pulled down. Survival instincts took over, something innate in him that screamed *live, live, live*. He managed to kick his way to the surface, desperate for air.

When he managed to get his head above water, the relief was only momentary. He began to flounder. Despite the regimented two hours of daily exercise while in the space station for so many months, his muscles had begun to atrophy, and his legs and arms were jelly, useless against the fierce waves.

He was left struggling in the ocean for what seemed like an eternity, spluttering as salt water filled his mouth, his nose, his eyes.

Rescuers almost didn't get to him in time, and he very nearly drowned. To make matters worse, it was filmed by media, so the whole excruciating episode was reported in minute detail worldwide. His near-death experience was viewed, discussed, written about, and retold repeatedly. He could never escape it.

Only when he heard his name spoken in a tone that suggested someone had been saying it multiple times did Hersch snap out of his dark memories. In front of him was a tall man in chinos and a polo shirt. His shaved head lent him a tough edge, but there was a warmth in his steely gray eyes that Hersch noticed immediately.

"You looked light-years away," the man said, not unkindly.

Not a bad guess, Hersch thought, wrenching himself back into the present. Thursday afternoon, third week of May, in Carmel. His heart was still pounding, but he pieced the fractured parts of himself back together until his breathing regulated and a smile could form on his face.

"Lost in thought," he replied.

"I'm Jay Malone," the man said, extending his hand. "And you're a man who needs no introduction. Herschel Greenfield, astronaut hero. I've been following your stellar career since the beginning."

Hersch swallowed. Since his accident, his relationship with the media had changed. Where once he'd been happy to give interviews or take photos for the press, now he would do anything to sink into anonymity and be spared retelling his story. He began to thank Jay, asking which newspaper or magazine he wrote for, when Jay cut him off midsentence.

"I'm a Hollywood agent," he explained. "I've got an eye for a story. And boy, do you have a good one. Have you ever considered turning your life story into a movie?"

Hersch was stunned. "A movie?"

Jay grinned. "When you sang 'Happy Birthday' to your mom on her sixtieth birthday from space, you were the most famous person on the planet for a week. That video went viral. Millions of hits. You touched people. Got them right here." He thumped his chest.

Now Hersch had to laugh. He'd always been a little playful, and the idea of the video had tickled him as well as being a fitting tribute to his hardworking mom. He could never have predicted that it would be shared so widely. He said as much to Jay, who again cut him off midsentence.

"Don't be so modest. It was a stroke of comic genius. Plus, you have a great singing voice. Then you nearly didn't make it back to your mom or anyone else. You can't make that stuff up."

Hersch tried not to shrink. He wasn't one for praise. He'd been raised in a very loving family, but they weren't the kind of folks who doled out heaps of praise. *Hard work pays off* was his mom's motto, and he owed his career to her. It was one of the many reasons he'd made the birthday video in the first place.

"And the cake?" Jay continued. "How did you even manage that in a microgravity environment? Magic?" He laughed.

Now this Hersch didn't mind talking about. "It wasn't easy, but it sure was fun getting creative with some prepackaged food and Velcro strips to stop the ingredients from floating away while I assembled it. I had a stash of thermostabilized fruitcake and wrapped it in a sheet of almond paste that I'd dyed with pink food dye. That was the icing."

"My favorite bit was when you lit the candle."

"A trusty LED light and a touch of showmanship."

"Well, that you've got in spades. If you feel like quitting the space game, I could represent you."

Hersch chuckled again. "You flatter me."

"Just a genuine fan." Jay looked down at his phone.

"Since I saw you here, I've been reviewing your story, and I'm in awe. You came from pretty humble beginnings, I see."

Hersch nodded. "But my mom never let that stop us from dreaming big."

"That's why she named you Herschel—after the astronomer."

Hersch was impressed and nodded. "You really have done your homework. My mom always said we could go to the moon and back as long as we worked hard. And, well, I took her words literally."

"You always wanted to go to space. It was your big ambition from the age of four."

"Right. Not the only four-year-old who ever wanted to become an astronaut."

And then he began to worry. Jay was shrewd, that much was obvious, and it wouldn't take much more digging to uncover Hersch's fear of the ocean since the crash. If it got out, his entire career would be over. Everything he had worked so hard for all his life would vanish.

But Jay didn't seem to notice that Hersch was feeling increasingly uncomfortable. "And you made that ambition come true. A scholarship to Yale to study medicine and then a PhD in molecular biology. And somehow in your spare time, you completed thousands of hours of jet training. Then the space program."

Hersch didn't know what to say. It was all too much. And then he noticed they were no longer alone. Mila Davenport had reappeared, and was playfully punching Jay's solid-looking bicep. The two of them must have known each other for a long time. At the sight of her, he felt his heartbeat quicken, admiration for her beauty overtaking his mounting sense of panic.

"Leave the man alone, Jay," she said. "You're worse than my brother when it comes to turning everything into a Hollywood story." How had she known Herschel had needed someone to intervene in such a chance encounter?

Jay grinned as if Mila were paying him a compliment. It was clear he had no intention of stopping his rousing recitation of Hersch's life story. In fact, he barely paused for breath as he continued to rattle off the details of Hersch's career until he reached that fateful last mission.

"Of course I followed the story as it unfolded in the news. Those were rough seas your capsule came down in. The splashdown nearly killed you."

Hersch watched, silently horrified as Jay told the story of his life. The familiar panic set in. He could feel Mila's presence, so near him, as she listened to Jay, but he wondered if she could also hear his heart pounding too hard in his chest.

"Jay," Mila interrupted, her tone firmer now, though it was clear Jay was so persistent a meteor wouldn't stop him.

"But you were a hero," he continued. "You made sure your fellow astronauts got out first." Jay's brilliant eyes were sparkling now, and it was clear to Hersch that he thought triumph concluded this tale, not fear.

Jay pinched the air between thumb and index finger, finally pausing his monologue to take a breath. "You were *this* close to death when they managed to rescue you. Look at you. You're a true hero. These are the kinds of stories people love."

Jay stood back as if waiting for applause. Hersch's horror hadn't faded. He couldn't tell Jay that despite all his training, all his hard work, he could barely even look at the ocean.

When Hersch failed to respond, Jay suggested that Archer Davenport would be a perfect fit to play him in the biopic of his life.

"Oh, so this was your grand plan all along," Mila said. "You're always scheming to find the next big movie for your clients, so you figured you'd just create one yourself."

"I know a good story when I see one," Jay argued. "And, Hersch, you could come on board to make sure you're happy with the way it's told. With Arch attached and you as executive producer, we could make a nice little feature film. In fact, Arch is just over there." He indicated a tall man with his arm around a dark-haired woman. They were talking to each other in the way those deeply in love communicated—as if no one else existed, even though they were in the middle of a very busy art fair. But Jay took no notice. He called, "Arch, there's someone I'd like you to meet."

Hersch groaned inwardly. How had he allowed this conversation to continue? But the answer was simple: It had been a monologue, not a conversation.

To Hersch's relief, the movie star didn't hear. This charade had gone on long enough.

"I think he's busy," Hersch said. "Another time." And before Jay could say anything else, Hersch quickly added, "Nice to meet you, but I've got to head out." Flashing Mila a smile, he walked away as quickly as he could.

\* \* \*

Mila's heart felt heavy as she watched him walk away. How had Jay not seen that he was making Herschel Greenfield super uncomfortable relaying his whole life story blow-by-blow? The poor guy was obviously mortified by the attention and had just wanted to walk around the art fair without being reminded of his traumatic accident. She turned to her brother's agent and said with conviction, "Jay, you're an idiot."

Jay looked surprised at her verbal attack. "What are you talking about?"

"Does it ever occur to you that someone might *not* want their life made into a movie?"

He looked at her blankly. "Why wouldn't he? He's a genuine American hero."

It was clear she was going to have to spell things out. "Think about it this way. If you had come to me right after I had to quit surfing and said, 'Hey, let's make a movie about the dramatic end of your career,' I would have punched you. Herschel Greenfield obviously has better self-control than I do, or your nose would be dripping blood right now."

Jay's gray eyes opened a little wider, and she could see it dawn on him that he might have gone in all Hollywood-guns-blazing without taking a moment to read the room.

He wrinkled his nose in thought. "Maybe my timing was off and I overstepped."

Mila crossed her arms. "No maybe about it. If you ever see him again, don't pitch him, okay?"

Her tone was harsher than she'd intended, and Jay's eyebrows shot up.

"Why does this matter so much to you?" he asked, curiosity entering his voice. "You don't even know the man."

Jay was right. Despite one conversation, she didn't, but she wasn't about to tell Jay, of all people, that she'd felt an instant connection when they'd met. She knew all about career-ending trauma and had picked up that she and Hersch had that in common. Instead, she said, "It just does. So drop it." With the final word hers, she turned on her heel and marched away.

She watched Herschel Greenfield for a couple of minutes. He was gazing at paintings, but she could tell he wasn't taking them in. Should she leave him be?

He might be an astronaut and a tad on the nerdy side, but she'd felt an incredible connection to him when she'd first set eyes on him. He wasn't her usual type, with his short brown hair, moustache, and casual clothes that looked ironed. Now that she knew he was an astronaut, it all made sense.

She glanced at the high-end watch that she almost never took off. Time was important to Mila. She wanted to make the most of every minute, whether in her job as a Realtor or snatching a few more minutes to ride the waves on her surfboard.

She had things to do. She needed to get going. With a last glance at Herschel Greenfield, she turned away and headed to her next appointment—showing a house to people who were available only at six p.m. on a Thursday night. She tried to be philosophical. As a salesperson, she had to bend her schedule to accommodate her clients.

She'd slipped her card to Herschel Greenfield earlier. She really hoped he'd call. Even if he wasn't in the market for a house, she still hoped he'd call.

# Chapter Two

The kitchen at the Davenport family home was filled with sound. The family were known for affectionately talking at the same time, exchanging news and gossip, and sharing recipe pointers as they cooked up one of their famous breakfasts. Buster was hanging around the kitchen, hoping good things would fall on the floor, and depending on whether their mother, Betsy, was watching, a surprising number of bits of bacon or ham "accidentally" fell, where he licked them up with gusto.

Only their newest member—Tessa Taylor—remained her usual quiet and composed self.

Mila had put it down to her artistic and caring nature that Tessa was more introverted than the rest of the family. But now she considered it might also be a sign of a woman deeply in love. She seemed to be walking around in a happy, dreamlike bubble. Even now, while squeezing the oranges for fresh OJ, Tessa's designated job for breakfast, she paused momentarily to admire the sparkle of her engagement ring. Arch certainly hadn't held back on the diamond. It was a sumptuous teardrop on a platinum band. Elegant and understated, just like Tessa herself, but Mila knew it had cost more than most people's annual salaries. She wondered if Tessa knew what he'd spent, but quickly figured no, she'd have been mortified. Unlike Arch, who had no qualms about treating himself to the finer things in life, Tessa was modest. She was used to being careful with money. She still thrifted some of her clothes, even though she had no need to.

The family tended to get together for breakfast at least once a month, usually on a weekend, or, like today, when somebody got everybody together. It was Arch who'd organized the Friday morning brunch. Mila set her own schedule, and everyone else had obviously made time. Erin sometimes worked weekends or nights at the *Sea Shell* weekly paper, so could take a morning off if she wanted to. Howie and Finn ran their own construction business. Nick worked when and where he felt like it, though he'd made so much money from his apps he didn't have to work at all. Arch hadn't yet started shooting his next film, *Shock Tactics*, and Damien was taking a break after his last tour. Betsy didn't teach classes on Friday morning.

Seeing the glint of Tessa's ring, Damien said, "I guess your wedding will be a media frenzy. No getting round it."

Damien was the family musician. Rock star, to put it more accurately. He'd found fame early as a guitarist for a successful rock band who'd managed to make the charts with their catchy first hit. It was hard now to imagine Damien happier than he was when on the stage… with countless pretty women chanting his name. He wasn't exactly a bad boy, but he was no saint either. He knew all about the downside of celebrity that went along with the fame and money.

"Arch promised Tessa a small wedding," Erin piped up.

"Never going to happen," Damien insisted.

"We have a plan," Arch said in a shut-up-and-don't-freak-out-my-future bride tone. "That's why I wanted to have breakfast with you all this morning—to figure out the details."

"Close friends and family only," Tessa agreed, pouring the golden orange liquid into a huge ceramic jug and following the rest of the family into the dining room. "Speaking of which," she continued, setting the jug on the table, "there's something I wanted to ask you two."

She looked at Mila and Erin with a happy grin as she took her seat next to Arch. "I was hoping you would be my bridesmaids."

"I'd be honored," Mila said quickly, feeling suddenly choked with emotion. She was no romantic—far from it—but the thought of taking such a special role in Tessa and Arch's wedding touched the most tender part of her.

Erin clapped her hands together, a look of pure joy on her face. "Me too," she said.

The three of them grasped hands across the table.

"Thank you," Tessa said quietly. "You two already feel like sisters to me."

Her mom set down a plate of her famous French toast and beamed. "And I'm so happy to have another daughter join our family."

"Hear, hear," their father, Howie, agreed. He passed a platter of his famous omelet, already cut into neat slices, around the table.

"I was thinking we could ask Margaret Percy to give a reading," Arch suggested, helping himself to two slices.

"What a great idea," Betsy said. "She did introduce the two of you, after all."

Nick reached for toast. "When are you going to ask me to be your best man?" He looked over at Arch. "I'm the oldest—obviously it should be me."

Finn made a rude noise. "Dude. I'm the best looking, so I'm the sensible choice. Think of your wedding photos."

"Low blow," Nick complained. Finn really was the best looking, which he usually tried to hide rather than mentioning it. Nick thought deeply. "Remember that time I covered for you when you missed curfew in ninth grade? You owe me."

The two brothers looked over at Damien, who

hadn't yet argued for why he should be best man. He held up his hands. "Count me out, man. I'm going to be the entertainment."

Finn and Nick sized each other up across the table. "Wrestle you for it," Finn suggested. He was a builder who worked with his hands and was a lot bigger than Nick, who was an app developer. Nick might be a billionaire, but chances weren't good he could best Finn in a wrestling match. He stood. "Let's go."

"Outside," Betsy commanded. "And not until after breakfast."

Mila rolled her eyes. Her brothers were extremely successful in their own right, but when they got together, they behaved like they were still teenagers.

"Thank you, Damien," Tessa said quickly, clearly seeing her moment. "I'd be honored to have you play, and this way, we'll keep it in the family."

"Okay, so best man is between me and Nick," Finn said, putting on a which-way-to-the-beach show of manliness by flexing his biceps and showing his gorgeous profile.

Arch chuckled. "I would never choose between you guys," he said, looking first at one brother, then the other. "Smith Sullivan is going to be my best man. But I'd like you both to be my groomsmen."

Mila watched across the table as her brothers digested the news. "I guess that means I won't have to make a speech," Nick said, shrugging. "Or listen to *you* make one," he added, pointing to Finn.

"It's a good solution," Betsy agreed. "All my hand-some boys, and Smith, who's like another son to me. It's just perfect." Nothing was more important to her mom than family. Betsy was a respected teacher and an incredible mom. Mila had nothing but admiration for her.

Mila wondered about Tessa's family. Her parents had passed away, and none of the Davenports had met Tessa's sister and brother-in-law or their daughter, though Tessa had said quietly that she was inviting her sister to the wedding, and she would be part of the wedding party. Mila couldn't imagine going more than a few days without seeing her sister, but knew Tessa didn't have that closeness with her own.

"Who is going to walk you down the aisle?" As soon as the words flew out of her mouth, Mila realized her mistake.

Tessa cast her eyes down and said she might ask her brother-in-law.

Mila knew she was too forthright, but she couldn't contain herself. "Wait, aren't these the people who, after your husband died and you had no money, supported you only by sending you hand-me-down clothes?"

Tessa nodded. "They were designer clothes. I'm sure my sister meant well."

Mila glanced at Erin. "If you ever lose a husband, I

promise right now to be there for you. We all will. That's what family does." She felt annoyed that a wonderful woman like Tessa would be treated so poorly by her closest family. Mila had once been famous, and she had a feeling she'd come across people like Tessa's sister and her husband. "I'm not trying to be rude, but are your sister and brother-in-law suddenly available for you now that you're marrying a movie star?"

"Mila," Betsy said, shocked, "you *are* being rude. I'm sure Tessa loves her family."

Before Mila could apologize for hurting Tessa's feelings, Tessa said, "No, Mila's right. I went from embarrassing charity case to someone important when I got together with Arch." Mila could see how much it hurt Tessa to admit that. "I barely know my brother-in-law, but I'm sure they love the idea of being in wedding photos with Archer." Then she bit her bottom lip. "I haven't even given them a date because I know they'll tell everyone they know. They won't be able to resist."

"And then our intimate wedding will become a media circus," Arch said, looking grim.

Erin, whose sensitive journalist's eyes never missed a thing, said, "I bet Dad would love to walk you down the aisle."

Howie immediately got to his feet and said it would be his honor, if it would please Tessa. "You're already like another daughter to me." His warm eyes sparkled.

"I would love that," Tessa said, a pretty flush spreading across her cheeks. "But may I think about it?"

Howie said, "Of course, but I'll be happy to step in if needed."

"I still don't get how you're really going to keep this wedding small and paparazzi-free," Erin said. "People here in Carmel are relaxed about Hollywood stars, but the minute someone spots that ring on your finger and alerts the media, it will take on a life of its own. I know firsthand how hungry photographers are for celebrity wedding snaps."

Tessa looked horrified. Mila knew her soon-to-be sister-in-law's worst nightmare was to have a flashy wedding splashed across the tabloids. Maybe she'd yet to admit it to herself, but Tessa was marrying one of the biggest movie stars in the world. They'd been together for months now, and she still wasn't used to seeing her picture in the press. But for Arch, she would withstand anything. That was the nature of true love.

"I have an idea," Betsy said, reaching across the table for a plate of fresh sliced melon. "Do you remember the time Damien hired a lookalike actor as a decoy to divert attention while he enjoyed a quiet holiday before a big concert tour?"

"That guy was so much better looking than you," Mila said with a laugh. "I can't believe it worked so well."

"But it *did* work," Erin added quickly, shooting Tessa a sympathetic look.

"That's right," Damien said quietly. "I had a perfect two weeks surfing in a hidden spot in Australia." He looked puzzled. "Are you suggesting a decoy couple for the wedding?"

"You might end up marrying the wrong Arch," Finn said. "Awkward."

"No, you foolish boy," Betsy said, though she looked fondly at her son. "I'm suggesting a decoy *wedding*. You pretend you're going to do one date, but secretly have a quiet wedding first. Just the way you want it."

Damien nodded. "It's a great idea, Mom. Have a *whole* decoy wedding." He turned to Arch. "You remember Crystal Lopez, my friend from high school? She's a wedding planner now. Get her on board. She can plan something big and fancy and feed stories to the press while you quietly plan the real one somewhere more quiet."

Tessa turned to Arch, her blue eyes sparkling. "I think it's a great idea. Do you?"

Arch took her hand in his. "Let's do it right here, in the backyard. Small and intimate."

"I'd love that so much." She turned to Betsy and Howie. "If that's okay with you both."

Mila grinned. As if that wasn't her parents' dream

scenario—her mom especially.

"I couldn't imagine anything more special," Betsy said.

Arch tucked a strand of Tessa's hair behind her ear and gazed at her lovingly. "If we go ahead with this decoy event, you do know we'll actually have to go through with two weddings? The one we actually want and the one for public consumption? It's the only way I can see this working."

Tessa nodded. "So long as we can have our perfect, real wedding here with the people closest to us, then I won't mind having a second, showy party for your fans that the press can attend." She thought for a moment. "My sister's been sending me these wedding venues— Scottish and Irish castles, Caribbean islands where people get married and spend absolute fortunes." She faltered. "I think in order to keep our real wedding intimate, I'll let my brother-in-law walk me down the aisle of the big, flashy do, and my niece can be a flower girl. That would make them a lot happier than a backyard wedding."

"Brilliant," Mila said, happy that being a bit rude had ended up with such a great result.

Betsy grinned, clearly in seventh heaven. "I love the idea of the decoy wedding not even being in this country. Really throw the paparazzi off the scent by planning something big abroad."

Tessa looked at Arch. "What do you think?"

Before he could reply, Damien said, "I've got a musician friend with a castle in Scotland he rents out for weddings." Damien was fast becoming the family wedding planner.

Mila was about to make a comment about this unlikely role when Erin said dreamily, "Oh, I'd love to go to Scotland. The lochs, the literature. So romantic."

"And some fine Scotch whiskey," Finn added.

"Well, that, and I'd like to see you in a kilt, brother." Damien laughed. Buster barked his agreement.

Howie lifted his glass of orange juice. "My great-great-grandfather was from Scotland. We'd be honoring his memory."

"Well, then, Scotland really is perfect," Tessa said. "It's still connected to your family, but since it'll be so different from what we'll do quietly at home, it could even be fun. A big party for all your fans to sigh over. But by then, we'll already be happily married, at a ceremony that's about us."

"Agreed," said Arch. He sighed with contentment and helped himself to some steaming black coffee. He was happier than Mila could ever have imagined him. She smiled. The love in the air was infectious.

"We should do the real wedding ASAP," Arch said. "Before anything can be leaked to the press."

"Good idea," Tessa said. She gazed at Arch. "I don't see any reason to wait."

"Me either."

"Well, then, that's settled," Betsy said. "While Damien's not on tour and all the family's in town." She went to fetch the calendar from the kitchen wall. Betsy had an online diary, but she still liked to put important dates on the big calendar that hung in the kitchen.

"When are you thinking?" she asked them, looking at the squares, a lot of which were already filled. "Four weeks from now?"

"You'll never keep the secret for four weeks." Damien shook his head.

"I agree," Arch said. "How's two weeks?"

Even Tessa looked surprised at moving with such speed, but then she listed all the ways they could make it work. "The simpler, the better," she said finally. "Yes, I think we can get married in two weeks."

"Dresses off the rack," Mila said, knowing there was no time for anything to be custom made.

"How do we keep your real wedding top secret?" Erin said, thoughtfully tucking into a waffle. "I mean, I know the journalist's drive for a scoop. We'll have to run this like an undercover military operation if we want to keep it out of the media."

"Drive all the attention to the castle wedding by making a deal with the press," Finn said suddenly.

"What are you suggesting?" Arch asked. "A little dance with the devil?"

"Exactly," Finn replied. "*Court* the press, flatter them, invite them in. Contact one of the big glossy mags and give them the rights to the wedding. An exclusive interview and a photoshoot."

"Not a bad idea," Damien said. "At least if you placate the press, you'll have control over the coverage."

Mila looked at Tessa, who had stayed suspiciously quiet during this suggestion. She couldn't imagine Tessa agreeing to splashy photoshoots, posing with her bouquet in an elaborate staged embrace with Arch.

There was a rare lull in the chatter as the rest of the family trained their attention on Tessa. Even though she was the newest, and not yet even an official Davenport, Tessa's quiet calm inspired respect from the others.

Arch took her hand and waited for her verdict.

"I think it's a fantastic idea. We'll donate the fee to a charitable cause. Maybe divide it among charities we both support."

"Perfect," said Arch.

"We can use that lovely caterer who did the Fairbanks wedding. Francesca's. I made sure to get her card," Betsy suggested.

"Francesca books up months in advance," Erin said. "We ran a feature on her once. A high-end chef from Milan who came here, fell in love with Carmel-by-the-Sea, and decided to change careers." Then she glanced around. "For weddings, she takes bookings a year in advance."

Howie said, "I'll do the catering. Hamburgers and

hot dogs on the barbecue. What do you say, kids?"

After shooting his dad an exasperated look, Damien said, "Call Crystal. She probably works with Francesca all the time."

"Does Crystal work miracles?" Finn wanted to know.

"As a matter of fact," Damien replied, "she does. I was on the beach at my place in the Bahamas, just chilling, and she called and asked me to perform at the birthday party of some billionaire's kid. I swear, one minute I was saying no, and the next thing I knew, I was singing 'Happy Birthday' to a bunch of tweens jacked up on sugar."

"Sounds perfect," Howie agreed. "And at least you know you have a backup plan. My barbecue and I aren't booked at all."

Mila fell silent during the rest of breakfast. All this talk of weddings, happy futures… Seeing Arch, maybe the least able to commit of all her siblings, entrust his life to another person? It made her feel suddenly very… single.

Or was this odd feeling connected somehow to Herschel Greenfield? His face, his voice kept floating back to her. The memory of him had hooked inside her, and it wasn't letting go.

"You look miles away, Mila." Her mom's soft voice penetrated her reverie.

"You got me," Mila replied. "I was thinking about

some new clients, a young couple looking for their first home." She avoided her mom's knowing look. Betsy Davenport could see right through to her children's innermost cores. It would be annoying if she weren't so full of love. Mila kept her head down and forked up another piece of omelet. As much as she hated to admit it, Herschel Greenfield had gotten under her skin. Worse, even though she'd given him her card, he'd yet to call.

# Chapter Three

Breakfast was over, the dishes washed and put away, and no one seemed in a hurry to move on. Howie brewed another pot of coffee, and the Davenport family took their usual places in the living room, with its furniture made for comfort rather than elegance. Mila curled up her long legs and sank into her favorite damask armchair. Arch, Tessa, and Finn shared a couch with Buster, who was taking up more than his share of the space.

During a lull in the wedding-planning conversation, Erin, who had her finger on the pulse of local news through her job at the *Sea Shell* newspaper, said, "I heard that Herschel Greenfield is thinking about moving to Carmel-by-the-Sea."

Finn looked impressed. Like the rest of the family, he was used to movie stars moving into the area, but he didn't even recognize most of them, let alone care. Mila saw that a world-famous astronaut got his attention. He said, "Hersch Greenfield? The guy who nearly died during splashdown after all those months in space?

He's a legend."

Erin looked at her brother as though he might be needing help with his homework. "Yes, that Hersch Greenfield."

Mila stayed silent, waiting for the rest of the family's reaction. Arch spoke next. "Jay said he was quite taken with Tessa's paintings." There was so much pride in his tone Mila couldn't help but smile. Tessa's cheeks turned pink. She still wasn't used to receiving compliments about her art, and it was cute to see her blush. Arch continued, "Jay's always hustling. Now he wants to make a biopic of Hersch's life—with me playing the lead role. He's buzzing about the idea. You know how he gets when he thinks he's on to something good."

"You should do it," Finn said.

Arch seemed less convinced. "I've never played someone who's still alive. I don't know how I'd feel about it—it's a lot of responsibility to get their story right. Especially someone as heroic as Herschel Greenfield."

Arch settled back and cradled his coffee cup in both hands. "I suppose it would be good in that I could really study his mannerisms and actually talk to him about his experience. Get some really in-depth research. Dig down to how it really felt to be him in that moment when the waves were crashing and it seemed certain he would drown."

Finn whistled through his teeth. "Man, you're going method."

After getting up long enough to lightly punch his brother on the shoulder, Arch said, "I don't know. Seems like an interesting project. A new direction for my career, maybe."

Mila found that she was shaking her head. She couldn't keep quiet for another second. She couldn't believe Jay was still pushing his own agenda when she'd told him in no uncertain terms that Herschel Greenfield was *obviously* not interested. In fact, he had clearly been mortified by the idea. "Jay was out of line to have even asked you about that. It's like he heard zero of what I said." She couldn't help herself—she was irritated, and it came out in her tone.

Suddenly, she realized everyone was staring at her. Arch in particular looked confused, even a bit upset. "Wait, what happened? When did you talk to Jay?"

She stood under the pretext of getting more coffee, but really, she couldn't sit a minute longer. She'd never been great at sitting still anyway. She had too much energy, and that just intensified when she was annoyed. She moved around, avoiding the gazes of her family. "Herschel was just standing there, minding his own business and admiring Tessa's artwork." She left out the part where he'd been staring at the painting of Mila in the surf and how he hadn't been admiring the picture so much as reliving his terror of the ocean.

"And then Jay stormed over, guns blazing, and launched straight into his pitch. I mean, I get that Jay is successful because he's so pushy, but not everybody wants their life splashed on the big screen. Herschel Greenfield did not look like he wanted anyone to make a movie about his life. He looked like he wanted to move on from a truly terrifying experience."

Mila paused to take a breath.

Arch was still looking puzzled. "But Herschel Greenfield is a hero. He saved the rest of the crew at the risk of his own life. We need more stories like that—of courage and devotion. People love to read about the person who risks everything to save other people. It's in our DNA. Those are the stories we all love to read and watch on screen. He should be proud of what he did."

It was hard to explain to her family that when you'd been through a traumatic experience, you didn't want to relive it over and over. She still had nightmares about her own surfing accident that had wrecked her career all those years ago. The broken back had healed, but the bad memories would never completely fade.

Despite what people might have thought, it hadn't been the fear of losing her career that had been so life-altering. It had been that awful, shattering moment when she'd thought she might not make it out of the ocean alive. Only a few had been through such an experience, and she and Hersch were two of those people. If it made her a little protective of the guy, she was okay with that.

She decided not to defend her position any further. They could think what they wanted.

Arch settled back in his seat and reflexively reached for Tessa's hand. Mila doubted he even realized he had done it. He shrugged, obviously still confused, but willing to let the matter go. "Okay. Well, Jay thinks it's a good idea. From the way he was talking, it was already a done deal, and Herschel Greenfield was on board with a biopic."

Mila couldn't help but roll her eyes. She made a sound of derision. "I'm positive Hersch hated the idea. I couldn't have been clearer with Jay about dropping it already. But he's like a dog with a bone."

Archer shook his head at her like she should know better. "Julius Malone never gives up on anything he wants to do until he's explored every possible avenue. I'm going to take a leap and say that Herschel hasn't heard the last from my agent."

It wasn't Arch's fault that his agent was so cut-throat. Jay was only doing his job by trying to push a project that would be an amazing opportunity for his client. But it didn't stop her blood from boiling.

Erin, who was pretty much famous for being the peacemaker in the family, sensed Mila's feelings and deftly changed the subject as she asked, "So, are we allowed to bring dates to this wedding?"

The distraction worked. Arch turned to his younger sister and said, "Sure. I mean, it's friends and family." Then his expression turned first curious and then mischievous. "Why? Is there something we don't know? Who's the plus-one you want to bring? Have I met him?"

Erin shook her head as if to say she had no one special in mind and then turned to Mila. "Are you going to bring a date?"

For some reason, the image of Hersch appeared in her head. Probably because they'd just been talking about him. How crazy that it had popped into her head so quickly, the idea of her and Herschel on an actual date, let alone in front of her family. But no one needed to know her private fantasies, so she simply replied, "Maybe. Or I might just go solo."

Erin nodded. "I probably will too." She lowered her eyes for a brief moment.

Something in her tone and demeanor suggested she would rather not be alone. It was pretty clear Arch had picked up on that wistful tone, too, because he said, "Hey, Jay will be coming, and he's single. I'm sure he'd be your date."

Mila couldn't believe her brother. Really? Did he not know Erin at all?

"I don't need a pity date, thank you," Erin said. "Anyway, Jay is never single. He's always with some lingerie model."

"I thought you liked him," Arch said.

"I do like him. But I've always thought he's too much in people's faces. I know that's his job, but it sounds like he was pushy with Herschel." She paused. "I know, I'm a journalist, and I'm supposed to be pushy too. But there's a reason I work for the *Sea Shell* and write articles about local dogs and whales and who's having their golden anniversary. I never wanted to be the kind of journalist who pushes hurting people to reveal secrets they'd rather keep to themselves."

Mila smiled and felt vindicated. She loved how, in her own way, Erin had just eviscerated Jay and yet somehow still managed to be nice. She'd never be as diplomatic as her sister—her nature was too fiery—but it was a quality she deeply admired.

Betsy spoke up then. "I'm glad you brought up the idea of people bringing dates, Erin. We should really get an idea of numbers as soon as possible. Arch and Tessa, I'd like you two to sit down and really think about who you want at our friends-and-family gathering. Your father and I will do the same and keep the list as small as we can without offending anybody. That's the hardest part of organizing a wedding, I think."

Howie looked a bit concerned. "But my brothers and all their families are invited, right?"

They had seemingly endless uncles and cousins on their father's side. It was partly why he had such a loving and friendly nature—he was used to being surrounded by people, sharing what he had as well as a joke or two.

His wife said, "We'll talk about that, Howie." Erin definitely got her diplomacy from their mom. It seemed to Mila that if Tessa was not going to invite her own sister and niece to their close family wedding, maybe Howie's brothers and their families could manage with a fancy Scottish wedding in a castle as well. It was hardly the rotten end of the deal. But she knew how close her dad was to his brothers, so maybe they'd figure something out. Betsy and Howie had an amazing ability to make their family home welcoming for as many people as needed to be there.

Damien reminded them that Crystal Lopez could be a real asset. "You know she's completely trustworthy. She could have sold me out a hundred times to the paparazzi and never has, even when she desperately could have used the cash. Why don't you get her on board? She knows her stuff. It would sure take the stress out of organizing everything yourself."

Tessa said, "I'm sure she's excellent at her job, Damien, but I really want to plan my own wedding. At least, just this one for me and Arch and the family. Do you think Crystal would be on board to plan the big, showy wedding in Scotland?"

Damien nodded confidently. "Oh yeah. That's the great thing about Crystal. She can do a small intimate party or a massive glamorous shindig for thousands. I'll send you her number."

Mila was surprised that, in his laid-back way, Damien was pushing Crystal so hard. Maybe there was something he wasn't telling the rest of the family. Despite his rock-star persona, deep down Damien was an ordinary guy, just as thrilled by a solo swim in the ocean as he was by a huge crowd going wild for his riffs.

While Damien was texting Crystal's number to Tessa, Nick said with a broad grin, "So, Damien, you writing a love song for this wedding?"

Finn snorted. Even Mila had to smile. Damien had famously never written a love song in his life. To everyone's surprise, he looked up and seemed to ponder the question. His dark eyes, known to brood, turned reflective, and he swept a hand through his longish hair. He looked over at Tessa and Arch sitting so close together on the couch, hand in hand, the picture of devoted love, and said, "Maybe."

Mila was struck by the impact of Arch and Tessa's love for each other on the family. Their unlikely but wholehearted love had infected the siblings with a sense of romantic possibility. She wondered if this was why she couldn't shake the image of Hersch from her mind.

# Chapter Four

Early Saturday morning found Mila in her favorite place on earth—on top of a wave. She liked to hit the surf early, when it was just her and a handful of other serious surfers. About half a dozen were out this morning, all of whom she knew by name. The sky was gray, but the sea was throwing out some big curlers, and she was in her element. She waved to a guy named Tex who'd caught a wave and was cruising past her in to shore, and then she saw her own wave coming. It was a nice way to end her morning. Her whole body felt pleasantly tired, her muscles worked from a good couple of hours of surfing, and so she figured it was time to ride this one right into the beach.

It was a move made with the ease and precision born of years of practice. She jumped to her feet and felt the water rolling beneath her, the board and wave dance partners. She felt the wind against her face as her hair streamed back, and for the millionth time, she thought, *This is where I belong*. Her mind flashed back to Tessa's painting of her in this very pose… and to

Herschel Greenfield, who'd been staring at the picture when she first saw him.

As she rode in to the beach, she spotted a lone man looking in her direction. He clearly wasn't a surfer. He was sitting on a jut of rock in jeans and a T-shirt—an outfit that left no doubt as to its owner's powerful physique. Despite herself, she was intrigued. In her book, there was nothing sexier than a man who respected his body enough to look after it.

Once she'd reached the beach, she realized the man was Herschel Greenfield.

Her heart began to thump a little faster.

Gathering her composure, she unhooked from her surfboard and slid it beneath her arm. Herschel stood and smiled at her. There were two cups of coffee in his hands. Could it be that he really was waiting for her? The thought gave her a thrill.

He came toward her and said, "I bet you would love coffee about now."

She laughed. "If you'd bought me a bouquet of roses, I couldn't have been happier." Still smiling, she accepted the cup and took a sip. Hot and strong— exactly the way she liked her coffee. And her men. Which was why she couldn't help noticing how Hersch's muscles bulged beneath his modest white T-shirt. Then she looked at the cardboard cup and realized it was from her favorite coffee shop in Carmel. She paused, one hand now resting on her board and the other grasping the coffee. She said, "How on earth did you know my favorite coffee shop and exactly how I like my coffee?"

He looked a little sheepish. "I'm a scientist. I'm excellent at research." At this, she merely raised an eyebrow. "Okay, Jay Malone called me about that movie he wants to make."

She was so surprised her mouth dropped open. "Damn, that guy never gives up, does he?"

Hersch shrugged. He didn't seem too put out. Maybe he was more relaxed about all this than she'd first thought. Or, more likely, he was just a nice guy who wasn't used to shutting people down.

"When I got the call, I figured it was an opportunity to do a little research about you. Jay told me I'd find you here early in the morning every day the surf was good. He said you and your sister have a standing coffee date at Saint Anna's coffee shop, and so I called them. They know your order as well as you do." He raised his coffee cup in a salute. "And here I am."

She couldn't believe he'd gone to all that trouble rather than call her. It was adorable.

She thanked him, and they went to sit on a rocky ledge. She couldn't help but notice that his left thigh was almost touching her right one. As she sipped her coffee, she sighed with pleasure. "I love Saturdays."

He chuckled. "Why Saturdays in particular?"

"First, if it's a bright morning like today and the

surf is rocking, it already puts me in a good mood for the rest of the day. There's nothing like the feeling of you and the waves, working together. No other human beings. Just the elements. And then on Saturday afternoons, I get my social fix when I teach surfing to beginners. It's so much fun. I've got a whole van full of wetsuits and boards, and I teach kids and adults who've never surfed before." She sighed happily. "It's such a privilege to share the sport I love with people who are just starting out."

She turned to watch his reaction, but he merely nodded in a noncommittal way and then sipped his coffee. She wondered why he was here. Was it because he wanted her help buying a house? Trying surfing? Or something more than that…

Her usual self would have just asked outright, blunt and confident—like, why would she care, anyway? But she didn't feel her usual self around Hersch. She felt a weird combination of mellow and electric. If she was honest with herself, it was intoxicating.

She gestured toward the beautiful ocean, which was glistening in the morning sun that was growing stronger now. She couldn't lose her edge completely, so she asked, "Would you like to put on a wetsuit and get out there?"

Beneath his moustache, his mouth tightened. He shook his head briefly. "No, thanks." He paused, and then his mouth softened again. "Thank you for the offer, though."

She nodded in what she hoped was an understanding way. "That wouldn't have anything to do with what happened to you last year, would it?"

He turned to her fully now, and as he twisted, she saw the tightness of his chest and arm muscles through his T-shirt. She was suddenly aware of her own body in the wetsuit, still pleasantly damp and aching from exercise. And maybe something else too. He looked into her eyes, and there was such warmth in that blue-gray color that she was momentarily taken aback.

"I don't know what it is about you," he said, looking suddenly serious, "but unlike your friend Jay, I feel I can trust you."

If he'd done enough research to find out how she liked her coffee, no doubt he knew all about her accident. A simple Google search would take care of that.

"You can," she said, meaning it.

"My not wanting to surf has *everything* to do with what happened last year. I look at the ocean, and I just can't stand it. I feel…" He trailed off.

In the gentlest way she could, she said, "You don't have to explain. There's no pressure. But just so you know, I'm here every Saturday. I'm sure I've got a suit that would fit you." She allowed herself another brief look at his taut body. "If you ever have the urge to try, come to my class. We'll ease you in slowly. I promise that once you're in, you'll learn to love the ocean again."

Hersch didn't look convinced, but he smiled anyway, his teeth brilliant white. He thanked her and then said, "I didn't actually track you down to learn how to surf. I've decided to hire you as my Realtor. Jay says you're one of the best in town. And I prefer to talk face to face, not on the phone." Then he grinned. For a man whose face was normally solemn and slightly nerdy, such a wide smile transformed him into a charming man. Her heartbeat sped up, and, embarrassingly, she was aware of a slight flush coming to her cheeks.

He continued, "I've been searching online for houses, but to be honest, I don't know what I'm doing. I can fix a spaceship in orbit, but finding the right house for me is more complicated."

She laughed. "You came to the right place. I'm excellent at what I do."

"I just need someone to guide me so I don't buy one that's one storm away from the roof blowing off. Or, I don't know, sitting on a swamp or something. I figure that's where you come in. From what Jay says, you know this area better than anyone. You know the neighborhoods. You know the houses. I want to hire you."

Obviously, Mila was more than happy to be Herschel Greenfield's Realtor. She agreed to work with him, secretly a little thrilled to get to spend more time with this sexy, intriguing man. In fact, she couldn't think of the last time she'd met a man who'd intrigued her quite so much. He wasn't the best-looking guy she'd ever met, and certainly his sexy banter left something to be desired, but she felt that they'd connected on a deep level over their shared ocean-related traumas.

"I can do a proper survey for you, obviously, when I'm not wearing a wetsuit and have my computer with me. But give me a quick rundown. What are you looking for?"

"First of all, I want to move quickly. That's a priority. I'm looking for something with space and privacy. At least three bedrooms, a garage, and I'd like a home gym."

It wasn't the huge list of demands she was used to from other high-profile clients, but it wasn't nothing either. "Price range?"

He shrugged. "From looking at properties online, I know I can't afford the waterfront homes the movie stars are buying, not that I'd want them…" Here, he allowed himself a wry smile. "But most of the other homes are within my budget. It's more about finding the right *quiet* spot."

He emphasized the word *quiet*, and her interest grew. Was Hersch trying to hide out here in Carmel? Why the focus on privacy? Sure, he was a public figure, but it wasn't like he was hunted by the press like

Damien or Arch.

"Cool," she replied, mentally flicking through her mental file of all the houses currently for sale. She knew the market inside and out, and it didn't take long before she snapped her fingers and shot Hersch her best winning smile. "I actually know of one that isn't even listed yet. The owner came into the office Friday and had a meeting with me, so it's at the very beginning stages. I think it could be perfect for you. They've already bought their new home, and they also want to move fast. It's not a waterfront home, but you can see the beach and the ocean from the back bedroom windows, and—"

She stopped speaking as Hersch visibly shuddered. She kicked herself. Her excitement had gotten the better of her, and she'd already made a blunder.

He shook his head. "No view of the ocean. I don't want to see the ocean—I don't want to hear it—I don't want to smell it."

She looked at him, understanding. but the fact was, there was no getting away from his bizarre decision. "And you're moving to Carmel-by-the-*Sea*?" She wasn't at all sure she should be wasting her time with a client who wanted to move to a seaside community but not be near the ocean.

She was hoping he might grin again, but Hersch's face remained serious. "I know it probably sounds crazy. But it's near enough to the space program that I can commute fairly easily on the days when they need me onsite. I just feel drawn here somehow. I can't explain it."

"Did you close your eyes and put your finger on the map, and it landed on Carmel?"

Now he did laugh. "Not exactly. I remembered visiting here on vacation and really loving the area." He paused and looked around them at the beach, which had grown busier since they'd sat down. There was a pleasant breeze, and dogs yipped as they happily chased balls and Frisbees across the sand. Mila thought of the family dog, Buster, who loved to roll in the sand, and smiled.

Hersch continued, his voice quieter now, "And maybe my subconscious knows that if I don't at least go somewhere with an ocean nearby, then I'm basically giving up and throwing in the towel on my career."

In that instant, Mila realized just how deeply their common bond ran. It had taken every ounce of the strength she'd had left to get back on that surfboard after her accident, but there hadn't been a single moment where it had crossed her mind that she wouldn't. Mila hadn't been physically able to continue the career she loved so much, but if Hersch could save his, well, then, she'd have to find a way to help him.

She touched his arm. The movement was brief, but it sent a thrum of longing through her fingertips. She said, "I have to tell you, Carmel is a really special place.

Your instincts didn't lie." She thought a little more, trying to engage the practical and professional side of her brain. "You might like Carmel Heights. It's nearby, but set back from the ocean. You'll also get more house and more land for your money because, as you can imagine, most people want proximity to the ocean and the sea views."

Hersch looked pleased. "I think Carmel Heights could be good, from what I've seen online. And yeah, plenty of land would be fantastic. I like my privacy. And did I mention a two-car garage?"

A stray piece of dried seaweed tumbled by on the sand. He *had* mentioned that, and three bedrooms. "So you're looking for a family home," she said. Why had she assumed he was single? Probably from the way he looked at her, but plenty of married guys did that. Still, she was a little disappointed.

Quickly, he said, "Oh, no, I'm single. I just like a lot of space around me. And I want the room for a home office and a home gym. I work out a lot."

She was surprised by the relief she felt. And she could completely understand the need for a home gym. His muscles bulged under his T-shirt, and his arm had felt so solid and so strong when she'd touched it. She found herself wondering what his body looked like beneath his unassuming clothes. Ripped, no doubt, and perfectly toned. He'd be able to pick her up with one hand. And maybe she would let him…

She realized he was staring at her, waiting for her to say something. She swallowed hard. She had to stop imagining him naked and her licking every inch of his body. What was wrong with her?

Getting a grip on herself, she asked, "Pool?" And then immediately regretted it. Of course he didn't want a pool. She was trying so hard to stop thinking about how sexy he was and how she'd like to lean right over now and kiss him that she'd momentarily forgotten the man had issues with water. "Sorry," she said. "Forget I ever said that."

Trying to be as professional as she could, considering that she was still in a wetsuit with salt water caking her blonde hair, she said, "You and I should have a proper meeting and really drill down to what you're looking for, and I'll show you all the available properties. I'm going to make you my top priority."

"I appreciate it." He grinned at her again, and she felt as though she'd won the lottery getting that smile.

And then, unable to stop herself, she said, "You know you're really missing out by not learning to surf. We only begin in the shallowest water. I'll make sure nothing bad happens to you."

He shook his head and, all of a sudden, seemed to withdraw into himself. Politely, he said, "Thank you, but I cannot imagine myself on a surfboard."

His response was stiff and formal, nothing like the ease with which they'd been talking before. She cursed herself. Here she was all mad at Jay for pushing in and overwhelming Hersch, and then she went and did the very same thing. She promised herself she'd keep cool about it and not keep pushing him. But even as she made the promise, she knew it would be hard to keep. She liked things to go her way. If he could just get comfortable on a surfboard in shallow water, he could begin getting over his trauma. She knew that because she'd done it herself.

Right now, however, his whole body was saying, *No, no, and no*. So she swiftly transitioned back to their conversation about real estate and said, "I'll head into the office for a couple of hours before I start teaching this afternoon. I'll see what I can find for you."

"I really appreciate that. That fellow Jay wasn't wrong."

How annoying to owe Jay one. She stood, and Hersch rose at the same time. She lifted her nearly empty paper cup. "Thanks for the coffee. It was perfect." She glanced at her watch. "I'll let you know if I find anything this afternoon."

# Chapter Five

By the time Hersch got back to his hotel room, he was already beating himself up. Why, of all the Realtors in Carmel-by-the-Sea, had he insisted on choosing Mila Davenport? Was it because she was beautiful? Which she undoubtedly was. He'd felt the connection with her before they'd even met in the moment he'd first set eyes on that painting of her fearlessly riding a wave as though she were some kind of water goddess. When he'd turned and found himself facing the woman herself, he'd been as close to speechless as he'd ever been. She was even more beautiful in real life.

Even through the ordeal of having his own life story pitched to him by some hotshot Hollywood agent, he'd felt that she understood and supported him. He felt a connection that was much more intense and deep than a simple physical spark, though of course he'd be kidding himself if he denied that the attraction was there. It was more like an explosion inside him than a spark. Yes, it overrode even that intense attraction—a meeting of two souls that had much to offer each other.

He'd already decided to hire a local real estate professional when she'd given him her card. It struck him as a happy coincidence, a sign maybe, that moving to Carmel was the right thing to do. He'd had his doubts about buying property in this gorgeous but beachy town. But when a Realtor landed at his feet, he'd be a fool not to follow his instincts.

And it wasn't just about Mila's pretty face, rocking-hot body, and that unspoken connection. He was a scientist—he trusted statistics. So when he'd decided to go ahead with purchasing in Carmel, his thorough research told him that Mila Davenport was one of the top salespeople in the area. And when Jay phoned him, he'd confirmed she was one of the best. In fact, Jay had told him he was thinking of buying in Carmel as well, and that Mila was the Realtor he'd choose. So, Hersch had decided to go ahead with the woman he'd wanted to hire when she'd first presented him with her card.

However, he hadn't exactly gone about acting on that decision in the most straightforward way. He hadn't emailed her or phoned her like a normal person would. No, instead he'd gone down to the beach, to the very edge of the water that had nearly sucked him under forever, and watched her ride those waves with the fearlessness and grace he'd admired in her portrait. Watching her in real time, he'd seen something magical about the way she danced on the waves. He'd felt a yearning deep within him. Almost a pull, as though something was encouraging him to wade out into the water just to be with her—even as the very thought of doing that made him break out in a sweat.

The scientist in him tried to investigate his own motives and accept that maybe her being a water goddess was part of her attraction. He had a feeling that there were a lot of people who could find him a house he would want to buy, but not so many who would challenge him in the way she did. Because he had to get over his fear of water, or he was never going on another mission to space. The thought chilled him to his very core. Being an astronaut was his whole life. He couldn't imagine another way of living.

Herschel Greenfield had never faced a challenge he couldn't rise to. He was famous for it. He was single-minded in getting around every obstacle put in his way. And there had been many. How else had he gone from being one of the millions of kids in the world who dreamed of being an astronaut to finding himself one day up in space looking down on that gorgeous, glowing blue and white planet? No matter how big or how small, when he set his mind on a goal, he didn't rest until he'd achieved it. When he'd decided to bake his mom a birthday cake in space and sing her "Happy Birthday," he'd figured out a way to do that, even when it had seemed an impossibility. Was he really going to give up the career he'd spent his life preparing for, the career he loved, because he was scared of water?

Even the thought made him feel ashamed.

He went to the window of his hotel room and looked out to where the ocean teased him, still looking gray and hardly postcard beautiful, but alluring all the same. Each rising wave appeared to him as a challenge. He stood there, looking at the surf that seemed to tease him, and said aloud, "I'm going to give myself this week, and then I'm going to make myself get there."

He wasn't even sure what his words meant. Get there? Get where? Did he think he was going to be swimming in a week? Or would his aim be to put his big toe in the water?

Even the thought had his heart pounding and panic rising in his chest. However, he'd always been a natural athlete, which had helped him pass with flying colors all those excruciating physical tests required of astronauts. It wasn't difficult to *imagine* himself on a surfboard. He was fairly certain he had the stamina and ability and muscle strength to do it. His balance was excellent too. He could even walk a tightrope.

The picture formed in his head, and it stuck there. Mila, as he'd seen her that morning, riding so proudly, standing so gracefully, knees bent, hair streaming back in the wind. And himself, beside her on his own board. Maybe he wouldn't ride with her confidence and style—she was a former professional, after all—but one day he might stand on a surfboard and ride a wave.

No, one day he *would* stand on a surfboard and ride a wave. He had a long way to go to get there, but he would start small. One baby step at a time.

Mila Davenport looked like she ruled the waves. If anyone could help him get back out there, it was she. Besides, if she were next to him, watching his progress, he'd be doubly determined to overcome his fear. He wanted, he realized, to impress her.

But did he still have it in him to impress a woman like Mila? One year had passed since he'd nearly drowned. It didn't seem like so much as a minute had gone by when he pictured the disaster that had nearly cost him and his crew their lives. The whole scene was still vivid, raw in its intensity. He'd lived with this terrible fear for a year. Now it was time to suck it up and move on.

With nothing better to do, he pulled up the online real estate listings for Carmel Heights. Yes, Mila had said she would take a look at what was available, but again his nature as a researcher and a scientist meant that he couldn't hand control over to someone completely. He needed to know as much as he could before going into a new situation. She said she was good, Jay Malone had said she was good, and the reviews on her website were of happy clients who sang her praises, but Hersch knew himself well enough to know he'd be making his own assessment of her skills and ability.

He flipped through the listings, and while he was pleased at the lack of ocean views and the amount of land the properties offered, nothing appealed to him strongly. He was looking for the wow factor, like he did with everything else in his life. He just wasn't the kind of person to accept something ordinary. Unless it was an ocean swim

Clicking off the real estate listings, he checked his email. Amazingly, there was one from Jay Malone. Subject line: *Love to chat more about our movie project.*

How had the agent even found his email address? He opened the email with some trepidation, wondering why the heck a top Hollywood agent had nothing better to do with his time than hassle a burned-out astronaut. Worst of all, the word *no* seemed to mean nothing at all to Jay Malone. Clearly, this was a man who never gave up. And then Hersch smiled to himself wryly. Maybe he of all people could forgive Jay this trait.

The email was simple. A line of pleasantries and then straight to the hard sell. Jay had *loved their meeting* and was *beyond excited to talk more.*

Hersch couldn't imagine anything to be less excited about. Jay signed off with a final, pushy reminder to get back in touch ASAP. He shook his head. It took less than a second to decide to ignore the email. And then suddenly, he couldn't stand his hotel suite another minute.

He needed to get out of his head and move his body.

He put on his running gear. In his book, a good, hard run could fix any kind of mood. As he pulled the navy blue T-shirt over his head, he touched the Saint Christopher's medal that always hung on a gold chain around his neck. It had been passed down from his grandfather. His mother swore the medal had seen her dad safely through World War II, and scientist or not, sometimes Hersch believed it was part of the reason he'd come home safely from space. He never took it off.

It was the time of year when he'd normally be training for an Ironman competition. He loved the challenge, lived for it, really, and it was the most fun way he could think of to stay in top physical shape for his missions. But the Ironman meant completing the swimming section, and how was he going to do that when he couldn't even dip his big toe in the water? It infuriated him that something so simple was holding him back.

He pulled on his shorts and socks and then warmed up with his tried and tested routine of calisthenic stretches before heading out.

He chose a trail far away from the ocean in Garland Ranch Regional Park in Carmel Valley. It was beautiful, green, and lush, with a few lingering wildflowers and a small grove of redwood trees at its heart. He began running and soon felt as though every trail went straight uphill without ever having a corresponding downhill, even though he'd chosen what should have been an easy run by his standards. He was running hard and fast, a sweat quickly forming as he tried to burn off his frustration, feeling the sweat drip down the sides of his face. Even as the breath was dragging into his lungs, he blinked sweat out of his eyes and took a moment to really appreciate the scrubby greenery and natural beauty of his surroundings.

Mila Davenport was right. There was something truly special about Carmel. It was the right place to make his new home.

And that couldn't happen soon enough. He'd been in his hotel for only a few days, but he really needed to get out of there. He could already picture himself in his new house. In spite of the fact that nothing had inspired him in the online listings, he had a feeling that Mila would come up with something. She seemed a lot like him—somebody who really rose to a challenge. Not so long ago, she'd been flying high as one of the top female surfers in the world, when an accident had wrecked her career. The more he'd learned about her, the more he'd found himself completely engaged in her story. He'd kept clicking and reading, clicking and reading, discovering all that he could about her career and the accident that had ended it.

He'd studied the photographs, read the numerous

media articles. His heart had gone out to a young and stunning Mila with the world's biggest grin, blonde hair wet from the ocean and slicked back, and pearly-white teeth on show. She hadn't known then how quickly everything she'd worked for and believed in could be taken away. The life she'd worked for had been over in a matter of moments. Just one bad wave.

They had that in common, too, because if he wasn't very careful, everything he had worked so hard for and believed in was going to be swept away by his fear of the water. It was such a stupid thing, and as his feet pounded solid ground, he felt his frustration rise again to the surface. He ran harder, pushing himself. He was going to have to keep pushing himself, in all manner of uncomfortable ways. He could do this. He knew he could.

Mila still had her sunny smile, but he saw the shadow behind it. The older and probably wiser Mila had learned the hard way that life wasn't fair, that talent, hard work, and luck weren't always enough. Luck could be both good and bad, and there wasn't a damn thing you could do about where it fell.

But at least she'd found a new path for herself. He deeply admired the guts and dedication it must have taken for her to hang up her board professionally and retrain for a completely different career. Not only had she started over, but she'd also worked her way to the top of her second profession. She had gumption in spades, and he liked that. In fact, it was sexy as hell.

He looked up, and suddenly he was able to picture Mila looking down at him from the top of the hill he was climbing. She was giving him that warm, knowing smile she had, daring him, and it made him pick up the pace and pound the ground. Despite the burning sensation in his legs, he smiled back. Mila Davenport had gotten under his skin. If she did find him a house—no, scratch that. *When* she found him a house, he wondered what the appropriate amount of time would be before he could invite his Realtor out for a date.

It had been a long time since any woman had appealed to him the way she did. In the past year, he'd not felt even a flicker of interest about a person of the opposite sex. It was as though every part of him was struggling to come back to life. Even his libido. But since he'd met Mila, he seemed to have switched on again. Switched on to Mila Davenport.

He rounded a bend and realized that his speed had almost doubled. Just the thought of Mila spurred him on. But then doubt began to creep in, swirling its sly way around his guts. Maybe he'd gotten ahead of himself. He only had to think about going on a date with Mila when he began to write the whole story in his mind. He could envision so clearly the romantic restaurants, holding hands, weekend hikes, and then moving to a physical relationship. Their chemistry would be electric. They would become enchanted with each other until, one day, they'd get married. It wasn't hard to picture her looking up at him with confidence as he slipped a ring onto her finger.

It was a tempting fantasy, but he'd seen how hard it was for his friends who had wives and families to leave for space, knowing the dangers they faced. He'd never wanted to leave anyone he loved at home. It was too painful for everyone involved, and he'd witnessed too many times the breakdown of a perfect couple when faced with the immense distance space put between them.

And kids he'd have to leave behind? Well, he didn't think he could do it. He loved his mother dearly, and he'd become pretty famous with her birthday cake in space, but it wasn't like he had a choice in having a mother. Having a wife and kids was a decision—one that should never be taken lightly.

Not that he lived like a monk, of course. He enjoyed the company of women and sex as much as the next red-blooded male, and Mila seemed like a woman who could do casual, which at this point was all he was capable of. Even as he could imagine her accepting his ring, he could also imagine the two of them burning up the sheets. Neither had acknowledged it, but the chemistry was undeniable. He was, after all, a man of science.

By the time Hersch returned to his hotel room, he knew two things—he was going to work really hard to find a house he could be at least reasonably happy in for the next couple of years. And he was definitely going to ask out his Realtor.

Some challenges were meant to be faced, and he was determined to succeed in this one.

# Chapter Six

Mila checked the waterproof watch that tracked her every movement and every appointment. She had a couple of hours before her surf classes began, so she headed into the office, centrally located in town. She was used to cramming one more thing into her daily schedule. In fact, she positively thrived on wringing every possible moment out of each day, so she rushed home, showered, and put on linen trousers and a soft blue sweater. Usually, that's where she would have stopped on a Saturday, but now she blow-dried her hair, swiped some mascara across her lashes, and applied a watermelon balm to her lips. When she went into the office, she was always in her business persona, even if it was only for a couple of hours before she slipped back into her wetsuit and took her place in the ocean once more. There was land Mila and ocean Mila, and she was pretty good at jumping between those two personas. She had the transformation down to a slick ten minutes. Five, if she was really pushed for time.

Even though she was on a tight schedule, she allowed herself to pause as she pulled out of her drive-way to absorb the sense of sanctuary that her little house always gave her. Apart from a pretty wooden archway entwined with fragrant white clematis, it was unremarkable from the outside—just a simple cabin from the late 1930s with a modernized interior. But to her, it was a little piece of paradise

When she'd been riding the high of big-time prize money from surfing, Erin, her very sensible sister, had advised her to be smart and use the money to buy a house. At the time, it hadn't been at the top of Mila's shopping list, but Erin, in her quiet way, had persisted. They'd started looking just for fun, and then one day, this house had come on the market. It was called Mermaid's Hideaway, and even before they'd stepped inside, the two sisters had looked at each other and known—this was The One. If only it were that easy with men.

The cabin was brown with red trim, unassuming and quiet, tucked as it was behind a wooden fence. It boasted a mature garden, as the real estate listing had said, and from the very back of her garden, she could see the ocean. That had been absolutely critical to her when she'd come up with her list of must-haves for her own home. She didn't need to be right on the ocean—she couldn't have afforded waterfront anyway—but she absolutely had to be able to glimpse the water and be close enough to walk to the beach with a surfboard.

The house checked those boxes, or she wouldn't have looked at it.

So she didn't mind that Mermaid's Hideaway wasn't a grand home, with its two bedrooms, one bathroom, and less than a thousand square feet. She wouldn't have wanted the trouble of looking after a bigger home anyway. Life was too short for dusting and vacuuming. It had been built by craftsmen almost a hundred years ago and boasted scarred hardwood floors and rustic wooden walls that she'd never change—they were too charming. The centerpiece of the living room was a big fireplace with a copper hood. The kitchen had a stained-glass window and wooden cupboards that she thought might be original to the house, but a previous owner had done the best kind of renovation by keeping the charm of the old while adding the convenience of the new. Stainless-steel appliances, and top-end ones at that, and a modern stone countertop made her little kitchen a pleasure to cook in. Not that she was the world's greatest cook, but she could throw together a decent meal if she had to. Her mother had made sure of that.

Skylights let in more light, and she'd painted her bedroom the softest possible shade of blue. The ceiling rose up to a peak, and from her bedroom window over the garden, she could glimpse the sea. She liked to think that it was the first thing she saw every morning when she got out of bed and the last thing she saw at night. It left her with an incredible sense of peace.

She sometimes thought that it was buying her own house that had planted the seed of interest in a real estate career. Dan Ferguson had been the listing agent—he owned his own real estate firm—when she'd bought her place. He was a jovial man in his fifties who worked hard but also enjoyed life, and she'd liked him immediately. She'd pestered him with questions, not only first-time-buyer questions, but also hey-I'm-interested-in-real-estate questions, and he'd cheerfully answered them all. So, when she'd finished licking her wounds and accepted that her surfing career was in fact over, she'd gone to Dan and asked him to train her. It hadn't been an instantaneous decision, of course, but she'd gotten there. So far, her career change was working out. Of course, she missed those moments of competition when she crushed it and walked away with a trophy, but she could still surf, and now she could give others the pleasure of learning how, and that was more rewarding than she ever could have imagined. Also, she'd turned out to be pretty good at real estate sales and made a very tidy living.

With a last glance at herself in the rear view mirror and a final check of her watch, she pulled out of her driveway and drove to the real estate office in town.

She greeted the receptionist who manned the phones all weekend, but found that she was the only agent in the office. Her colleagues were either out showing houses or taking a rare Saturday off.

She settled at her desk and fired up her computer. She was pretty good at keeping the list of the current inventory in the area—and even a little beyond it—in her head, but she hoped there was something she'd overlooked, the kind of house that would be perfect for Herschel Greenfield. Concentrating, she sifted through every single listing, carefully combing through the ones in Carmel Heights, but she simply couldn't imagine Herschel in any of them. Funny how she had this clear image of what he needed—even though they'd only just met. It was more than a professional instinct, but something running deeper. Still, she'd have to show him a few options to get the ball rolling, as he wanted to move quickly.

She pulled together the few listings that had most of what he wanted. Finding a house with three bedrooms was easy, and most had a two-car garage, but he wouldn't want a property that lacked the wow factor. No, he'd want a home that had architectural appeal and was well-crafted and built to last.

She was wondering if it would be worth it to paper the area with flyers saying she had a buyer looking for the exact home he wanted. She rarely did that kind of thing, but there were times when it paid off. Herschel was a guy with money in the bank and a short time frame. He could be a gift to the right person who was thinking of selling their home but didn't want the hassle of going through the whole process. She could show up with a buyer and streamline the sale.

She was still tapping her pen on her notepad when Dan Ferguson stormed into her office, looking less than pleased. Dan was one of the top Realtors in the county. He was a guy who spent way too much time either behind his desk or wining and dining his high-profile clients, and he had the portly belly and ruddy complexion to go with his lifestyle. Dan's wife worried about his blood pressure, but as he'd said to Mila, he was a sales guy through and through. If a client phoned in the middle of dinner and wanted to buy a house, he'd leave his steak half chewed. If he had to show houses at six in the morning because somebody had a flight to catch, he'd get up at four thirty. Nine to five just didn't work for him, and consequently his colleagues ended up following suit, trying to keep up with the number of deals he managed to close.

Mila saw through Dan's bluster and knew that deep down he was exhausted, but Dan wasn't open to changing his ways. He was an old dog, and there were no new tricks that could tempt him. As he liked to tell everybody, he'd put three kids through college, and on their twenty-fifth wedding anniversary, he'd bought his wife the engagement ring he would have loved to give her when they first got together. When Mila discovered it cost a quarter of a million dollars, she figured it probably gave Dan a bigger boost than it did his wife.

No way would she want that amount of money sitting on her finger every day as she made coffee or washed the dishes.

Despite his insatiable chase for cash, Mila liked Dan. He'd taken her in when she'd had zero real estate knowledge and guided her through this cutthroat business, sharing his tricks of the trade. After she'd passed her exams, he'd offered her a place in his office and had mentored her generously, and so she knew that beneath that expensive suit was a kind and open heart.

When she saw Dan looking all kinds of wound up, she said, "Dan, calm down. Take a breath. What's going on?" She gestured at a leather seat across from her desk.

But instead of taking a breath, he sucked air like a bull about to bellow. "I had it, Mila. I had it this close." He held his thumb and index finger almost within touching distance and then snapped his fingers. "And suddenly, poof. It was gone." He shook his head as if he were shaking water from his ears.

"What was gone?"

He looked dejected. "My deal. A house has just fallen out of contract. I was so sure it would go through. Now I've got to relist. I cannot tell you how hard I worked on this one—only for it to disappear."

Mila believed he had worked hard on one listing in particular, so she tried not to get too excited. There were loads of houses that Dan was juggling on his books, any one of which could have fallen out of contract. But one of them was a house in Carmel Heights that she'd really liked. She said, "Which listing was it?"

He swiped his iPad on and showed her. Her heart began to pound. It was the very house she'd first thought of when Hersch had been listing his requirements. She'd seen it a while back, before Dan had found a buyer, and remembered wishing she'd had a client for it because she loved the home herself. It wasn't grand, but it had been designed by a renowned local architect. Set away from town with plenty of land, it had five bedrooms instead of three—she was sure Hersch could live with that—and a sizable garage. It was a house full of understated quality.

Her gut said it was perfect for Hersch.

She glanced at her watch. She'd seen him about seventy-five minutes ago, but there was no time to waste. "Dan, I have a new client who might like that house. Could I show it to him today?"

Dan's red cheeks faded to a color that made him look slightly less in danger of his blood reaching boiling point, and his eyes widened. "You serious?"

"I'm serious."

Looking a little unconvinced, he scratched his graying head and said, "My clients really wanted a quick sale. I don't want to waste time."

Mila felt her lips twitch into the beginnings of a smile. "What if I told you that you could give your clients exactly that? My guy is after a quick buy. Please, don't relist it until tomorrow. Can you give me this afternoon?"

Dan still looked skeptical, but Mila could tell he was hoping she held the answers to his bind. He let out a breath and said, "I'm going to go home, open a beer, throw something on the barbecue, and spend an evening with my wife."

She smiled at him. "And can I show my client that house?"

"Knock yourself out, kid. The sellers don't live here, and I've got the key."

With less than half an hour before she had to head back to teach surfing, she called Herschel. She found herself feeling a bit like a teenager again as she waited for him to pick up but tried to shake off the sensation— this call was purely professional. She was about to give up when Hersch finally answered, sounding a little out of breath.

"Are you okay?" she asked.

"Yeah, I was just running." She heard him come to a stop. "What's up?"

Unable to hide her pleasure, she said, "I told you I work fast. I may have pulled off a miracle. I'd like to show you a couple of houses today. Are you available later this evening?"

He chuckled. "I'm living in a hotel room and don't currently know anybody in town. You bet I'm available."

Mila said she'd pick him up at his hotel after her class finished at five thirty. After they hung up, she quickly made appointments to see the other two houses that she didn't think would be right for Hersch but would be good to show him as a prelude to The One. As a seasoned salesperson, she knew darn well that everybody wanted a choice. If she showed him only that one house, even though it might be perfect, he might be convinced there was a better one out there. The trick was to show him two or three that were okay but not great and then a winner, and he'd make a decision that day.

Of course, that only worked if she'd gotten it right, and the house was his perfect match. But she had a good feeling.

She put her real estate persona away with her heels and briefcase, snugged herself back into her wetsuit, and was off.

* * *

By three o'clock, Mila was back on the beach with the newbies. Saturday afternoons were some of the best hours of her week. She'd caught the teaching bug early in her career when she'd helped Damien, Erin, and their cousins—when they'd come into town—to surf when they were younger. She still loved helping children, and every once in a while, when a kid caught that first wave and she saw the pure joy blossom on their face, she wondered whether she was helping to create a champion, somebody who might one day become the surfing superstar she'd once been. And even if that never happened, even if she just gave that child a few blissful hours on the waves, maybe a little more confidence, maybe just some fun and belly laughs, then it was all worth it.

A preteen named Tabitha, who had been dropping by for a few weeks now, managed a short run. She had the biggest grin on her freckled face. When she jumped off her board, Mila paddled over to her, and the two of them high-fived.

The two hours flew by, and then she was packing up. Already, her thoughts were moving ahead to showing Herschel the recently available house. It was something special—she just knew it.

The students had all dispersed and she was hanging up the last wetsuit when somebody called her name. She turned to find Arch standing there in a ball cap and sunglasses, about as much of a disguise as he bothered with when he was in Carmel.

She was always pleased to see her big brother and gave him a hug, but when she drew back, he removed his sunglasses, and she saw his expression was serious.

"What's going on?" she asked. "Has something

happened?"

"I'm worried about Tessa."

Alarm sluiced through her. She adored her soon-to-be sister-in-law and already felt protective of her, as if they had actually grown up together. "What is it?" she asked. "Is she sick?"

Arch quickly reassured her that Tessa was fine. Then he slumped against the van. "The thing is, she's insisting on getting her wedding dress from a thrift store."

Mila burst into laughter. Surely Arch wasn't actually upset about something so trivial? But she could see he was serious, so instead of teasing him as she was dying to do, she stopped laughing and hid her amusement. "Arch, that's just who Tessa is. That's what you love about her. She takes real pride in finding treasures at thrift stores. You know that."

"Yeah, I know that. And I don't want to sound like a complete jerk, but I'm Archer Davenport. Can you imagine the field day they'd have online if my bride turned up to her wedding in a used dress? They'd talk trash about Tessa. I mean, what if the original bride spotted it? She'd make a killing in the tabloids, and I'd be the butt of every joke told by late-night talk-show hosts."

Mila swallowed down the urge to make a few jokes of her own. She got it, even though she personally quite liked the idea of a thrifted wedding dress. It wasn't like it was going to get a lot of use, so why not buy one that had already walked down the aisle? However, she could see Arch's point that Tessa and he might be ridiculed online and in the press, and that would put a shadow on their happy day.

"Why not look at it this way?" she said thoughtfully. "Maybe if a picture of an A-list celebrity's bride in a thrift-store dress did go viral, then more brides would get secondhand dresses and help save the planet, one wedding dress at a time."

Arch raised his eyebrows. Clearly, he didn't want a speech about the three Rs—reduce, reuse, and recycle—so she said, "I'll talk to her and see what I can do."

"Thank you," he said. "I need to divert a disaster."

At that, Mila huffed out a sigh. "Do I have to remind you that Tessa is stubborn and opinionated? A little bit like somebody else I know? A big reason she is so special to you is because she isn't like every other woman who might want you to buy her a bespoke wedding dress in Paris from Dior. Isn't that a good thing?"

Arch seemed to soften and pulled his sister in for a one-armed hug. "I'm marrying Tessa because not only is she not like any other woman I've ever met, but she's exactly right for me. So yeah, I'll take stubborn and opinionated, and I'll deal with it if she wants to get half her wardrobe at thrift stores. You're right. It's part of what I love about her. But, just for this one shindig, could you talk to her about getting something nice from a designer? It would mean a lot to me. It would mean a lot to Jay. It would mean a lot to my career."

Mila relented. "Okay, I'm on it. The Davenport women are meeting with Tessa tomorrow to do some wedding planning. I'll talk to her then." She checked her watch. Argh, she wasn't going to have time to shower before meeting Hersch. "But right now I have to run."

"Hot date?" he asked with typical big-brother curiosity.

She grinned at him. "Not exactly. I'm hoping to sell a house to an astronaut."

"Not a sentence you hear every day," Arch said, shaking his head. Then he looked at her. "I'm assuming you mean Herschel Greenfield. You sure it's not a date? Jay told me there was some serious chemistry between you two."

She fired up at that. "Jay Malone was doing his best to bully Herschel Greenfield into making this biopic about his life—starring *you*, I might add." She jabbed a finger into his chest. "I don't think it was chemistry that he picked up on so much as a united front against his terrible movie idea."

Arch threw his hands up in surrender. "Hey, I didn't mean anything by it. And I'm sorry to hear you still think that about this project. I think it sounds interesting. A story that could really inspire people."

"It would be a fantastic movie, and I'm sure that with your name attached, it would be greenlit. But if Herschel Greenfield doesn't want to see his most painful moments on the big screen, shouldn't we respect that?"

Archer pushed away from the side of Mila's van. "Well, you and I might, but Jay Malone? He's another story."

# Chapter Seven

Once more, Mila found herself running home to make the quick transformation from surfing Mila to successful Realtor Mila. Still irritated she wasn't going to have time to shower, she washed her face, slipped back into the linen trousers and sweater she'd worn earlier, tucked her salty hair into a messy bun, and put on some expensive moisturizer to condition her skin.

As she slicked a little gloss over her lips, she thought about what Arch had said. She was surprised that Jay Malone had mentioned to Archer the chemistry between her and Herschel. She'd never thought of Jay as that observant, especially not when he was in the middle of pitching a project. She'd done her best to knock that idea into the long grass, but he'd noticed more than she'd have liked a nosy agent to see.

She had absolutely felt that chemistry too. And, as she jumped back into her car and headed to the hotel to pick up her newest client, she was all too aware of the little spurt of excitement in her belly at the prospect of seeing the most attractive man she'd met in a long time. Some clients were better than others, but she rarely felt this excited about taking one to look at a few houses.

Since Mila was a woman who was always aware of time, she noted with approval that Herschel was waiting outside his hotel when she pulled up. He got points for that. He also got points for the cute chinos that bore the crease of an iron and a crisp short-sleeved blue shirt that showed off his seriously impressive arm muscles. He'd made an effort, and it wasn't going unnoticed. He smelled good, too, she noted as he got into the passenger seat, and he had a leather folder and pen with him. He was taking this seriously, which she appreciated.

"Hello," he said as he shut the door and carefully clicked his seat belt.

"It's good to see you again," she replied, trying to hide as best as she could just how good it felt. "I've got three homes I want to show you today." Promising herself to remain professional, she gave him her standard spiel about how today was really just about getting a feel for his likes and dislikes and giving him an idea of the market. She never liked people to think she could find them a house in one day, even though she sometimes could. He nodded and smiled at her, and she felt her stomach flip again. He really was dreamy.

★ ★ ★

Herschel settled into his seat as soon as he confirmed that Mila was an excellent driver. He didn't make a habit of being driven by other people, and it felt strange to hand control over to someone else. However, the perks of being a passenger meant he could watch her profile as she drove. Mila had an elegant face, a determined jaw. He liked how natural she looked, skin glowing and lips shining, and he could smell the ocean in her hair. That salty scent should have repelled him, but oddly, he found it attractive.

Her vehicle was some kind of SUV that had room for surfboards or clients, depending on which activity she was doing that day. It was neat and clean, but he noticed a tiny trickle of sand on the floor of the driver's side that revealed the other part of her personality. He'd seen her in her wetsuit, and he'd seen her dressed for an art show, and now he saw her in her business garb. She looked cool and professional. Her hands were strong and capable on the wheel, and the watch on her wrist was both expensive and the kind that divers wore when plunging to some ridiculous depth in the ocean.

She said, "I think all three of these homes give you most, if not all, of what you're looking for. But houses are like people, in my opinion. You have to meet them and get to know them, and they either work for you, or they don't." She smiled at him. "Sometimes you have to date a lot of people before you find your match."

His heart beat a little quicker. Was she flirting with him? His eyes were steady on hers as he said, "And sometimes it's love at first sight."

He didn't even know what had made him say that, but her reaction was immediate. Her green eyes opened slightly wider, and maybe her breath caught, and then she laughed, but that one moment hold told him everything. She *was* flirting with him. She felt the connection as strongly as he did. He wondered for a second if she had entertained the fantasy of them married, the way he had. He'd have to make it very clear that marriage was *not* in the cards for him. Every time he headed off on a mission, he was well aware he might not come back. He wouldn't put the people he loved at risk like that. Long ago, he'd decided it was a sacrifice he was willing to make for his career.

A few minutes later, they pulled up to the first house on her list. Hersch tried to not feel disappointed. He recognized it from his earlier online search and had decided it was pretty run of the mill. He'd been hoping Mila would perform some kind of real estate magic. But he decided to keep an open mind. If she thought there was something worth seeing here, well, then, he trusted her judgment.

Mila parked, and they stepped out of the car. She told him that the owners were on vacation for a couple of weeks, and so it had been easy to get an appointment on Saturday at dinnertime. She consulted her notes. "The house has been on the market for a couple of months, so I think they'd be flexible on the price. I'm not sure what they're looking for as a closing date, but we'd push for an early one. Often, if you present sellers with a really attractive offer, they'll be more flexible about things like closing dates."

He nodded, barely taking in the words when his thoughts were wholly occupied with how incredibly sexy she looked while she delivered crisp business news. As she turned the key in the lock and then guided him around, he saw that the house was pretty much what he'd seen online. The photos hadn't lied: three bedrooms, a two-car garage, a perfectly serviceable kitchen, and a pretty big yard. It was a solid, if unremarkable, family home. He didn't hate it, but he didn't love it.

After dutifully walking through every room, she asked, "What do you think?"

He told her the truth. "I don't hate it. But it's not love."

She nodded at him and smiled, and he could tell she appreciated his honesty. "Well, at least you don't hate it," she said. "I'll consider that a plus. Let's go see the next one."

The second house was only about five minutes away and pretty similar. It had been built in the late eighties, and had panoramic views of the mountains and a slightly different layout. The décor was more rustic, but it was also a solid family home. There was even a basketball hoop outside.

As they walked out into the sunshine, Mila said brightly, "You could keep in shape playing basketball. I bet my brothers would come up and shoot some hoops with you."

Hersch laughed. "I guess that's a selling feature." He thought Mila's suggestion was pretty darn cute, and he suddenly had a warm and cozy vision of meeting her family. But as soon as the image arrived, he shook it away, aware he was entering dangerous fantasy territory. Besides, if a basketball hoop was the biggest selling feature the place had, what did that say about it?

Mila didn't look the least bit disheartened by his noncommittal comment. If anything, he detected a barely suppressed excitement. She said, "There's one more I'd like to show you. It's just come back on the market, and I'm curious to see what you think."

"Great," he said, relieved she might have something up her sleeve after all.

# Chapter Eight

When Mila's car pulled into the long drive, Hersch felt his interest perk up. He had not seen this house online. In fact, the first thing he saw wasn't the house, but the trees, which were old and beautiful, and then the way the house almost followed the lie of the land. The house was gray, and he could see that even though it was in the trees, it was full of windows. It was beautiful.

He didn't say anything as she let him in the front door, and he walked through as the house itself invited him in. Through some instinct, he followed his feet as they led him right into the living room and its wall of windows looking out into a forested backyard. It took his breath away.

Mila appeared by his side. "No ocean in sight," she said. "Bonus."

"I love the trees."

He turned and noted the elegant tile fireplace, the sophisticated furnishings and fittings, the muted colors that allowed the space to flow. He admired the doors that opened onto a huge veranda that ran the whole length of the house. It was as much an outdoor house as an indoor one.

As they surveyed the rest of the property, he liked that Mila let him lead the way. He headed through a dining area into the kitchen, which was modeled in a classic style. He was pleased that it wasn't modern and fancy. He disliked the trend for stainless steel and gadgets he'd never use—utilitarianism belonged in a spacecraft, not in a home in the trees. No, this was a kitchen where he pictured himself cooking—and enjoying it for once. Outside was a big seating area that had a fireplace for cooler nights and a lower deck that featured an outdoor Jacuzzi perfect for soaking in after an intense workout.

The kitchen led back to a hallway and a grand staircase. She pointed out a powder room on the main floor, and he nodded before they headed upstairs. The primary bedroom was a thing of beauty, with French doors that opened onto a large balcony overlooking the long stretch of acreage.

"Incredibly private," Mila said, sounding pretty pleased with herself.

He had to agree. No other buildings in sight. Just pure nature. A table and chairs on the balcony looked perfect for enjoying his morning coffee, and he imagined starting each day out there, greeted by the sunrise over the hills.

Returning to the bedroom, he was pleased with the tastefully decorated ensuite bathroom and walk-in closet. The closet was divided into his and hers, but neither of them said a word about that. A gas fireplace rounded out the features. He nodded thoughtfully and headed back out to the hallway. There were three more bedrooms and a three-car garage. He tried to control his excitement. Mila had delivered everything he wanted and more. The house was definitely at the top end of his budget. But it was perfect. It held the magic he'd been after.

When they'd finished touring the house, she led him back to that wonderful kitchen and asked, "What do you think?"

Herschel was normally a man who tried to keep his enthusiasm in check and to think about things from all sides. But this time? He couldn't help himself. He felt himself grinning. "I love it."

She beamed at him. She'd stayed pretty profession-al throughout the tour, highlighting features and explaining square footage, but now she let out her own enthusiasm. "I just knew you would. I had an instinct. But here's the thing. It sold, but the deal fell apart just this afternoon. You're the first person to see it, and if you want it, I think you need to put in an offer today. Like, literally right after we walk out of here."

He was surprised by the need for speed, but it didn't deter him. He would have said yes on the spot, but because he didn't want to be a pushover, he said, "Let's walk around the outside."

She took the lead again as they strolled in the warm evening light. She pointed out that the grounds were low maintenance, and because there were so many trees, he'd have his privacy from every aspect. "Of course," she said, "the house does need a little updating. The kitchen's got room for an expansion maybe, and some of the colors on the walls could do with a refresh."

He nodded. He'd noted all of that too. But the construction was top quality, and the house didn't look like any other he'd seen on the market. It was unique. And somehow it felt right to him. It felt like… his.

Mila consulted her notes again. "The sellers are an older couple who are downsizing and want the move to be easy. Basically, they want you to take everything—furniture, linens, dishes in the cupboards, everything."

For the first time, she looked a little uncertain. It was true that maybe this would be off-putting for many people who wanted to put their own stamp on their new home, but he didn't have time for home decoration, so he said what he was thinking. "That's a selling feature for me. It would save me a lot of time and a lot of shopping. I'm not a big one for shopping, as you might imagine."

She smiled and commented on what a neat fit it

made, and then together they went back inside for a second walk-through. This time, Hersch did more thorough checks of the building. Now that he was seriously going to buy it, he should take a little more time. Mila was the perfect companion. She didn't keep butting into his perusal by pointing out the house's good points. She was letting him find them for himself. The room that he imagined might be a gym would need added lighting, but it had big windows, and doors that could be opened on a sunny day. He could see himself working out in here.

Now that he was thinking about taking on everything from the linens to the dishes, he took the trouble to open some of the kitchen cupboards and peruse the china. It wasn't entirely to his taste, but it was fine. Upstairs, they made a cursory tour of the guest rooms and then spent a little more time in the primary bedroom. He watched her turn a slow circle and then felt a sudden surge of lust. Mila, him, a big bed. A man couldn't help but have ideas.

She seemed to be thinking on a different track, however. "I think you could update these linens and curtains and maybe change the paint. I'd get rid of that painting of the peacock, myself. Make the space your own."

*Make it your own.* For a minute, all thoughts of buying a house flew out of his mind, and he had a vision of himself and Mila tangled up in the sheets right there on that bed. Damn it, he needed to do a better job of controlling his attraction to her. She was showing him a house, not asking him to throw her on the bed and ravish her! But the image took over his mind, and he found himself beginning to sweat... just as if they were actually entwined beneath those sheets.

To calm down, he walked over to the window and forced himself to look out. "This is a great view." Which he must have already said about three times.

Mila walked into the huge ensuite and called back, "I'd buy the house just for this tub. It's got a skylight, so you could soak your sore muscles after working out and look up at the stars." He followed her in, and she turned to grin at him. "Maybe you'll see your friends up in space."

He didn't bother to tell her that there was no way he could see anybody in space from here. He assumed she'd been joking anyway. But now he couldn't stop thinking about Mila in that tub... barely covered by a cloud of bubbles. As the fantasy grew, he was dimly aware of Mila commenting on the quality of the fixtures. She didn't mention that the tub was big enough for two, but his mind was already there, and now he could see her stretched out, naked, as he leaned over to take her soapy breasts into his hands. They were standing so close that he could smell the ocean in her hair again and could almost count the freckles across her cheekbones and the bridge of her nose. It was becoming harder by the second for him not to kiss her.

After a lifetime of not making impulsive decisions, he made one. "I'll take it. I'll pay the asking price, and I have the money ready. How soon can we close?"

She looked as though she might hug him—even took a tiny step closer. He held his breath. Was she about to embrace him? But no. She stopped and flashed him that megawatt smile again. "You, Herschel Greenfield, might just be the perfect client. And my gut says that if we sign the agreements and transfer the money, you're in as soon as you'd like to be. Since the sellers don't have to move everything out, it couldn't be easier." She turned and pivoted a little coquettishly. "I'm positive that in less than a week, you could be sleeping in that bed." Then she paused. "Though I have to warn you, sometimes deals do go sideways. But let's hope for the best and not borrow trouble."

So Mila Davenport was a realist. And honest. He liked that a lot. But he needed to get out of this bedroom before he could act on any of his raging fantasies. But as they returned to the living room, he couldn't help but picture her on the floor in front of that fireplace, reflected flames licking her naked body. Who was he kidding? This woman had gotten under his skin.

He said, "Let's go make an offer."

# Chapter Nine

Mila was on cloud nine. She loved it when her instincts about people and houses were right. She was definitely a bit of a matchmaker in that sense. She'd scored Herschel the perfect match on her first try. Those first two houses had been a warmup, and she had a feeling Hersch knew that too.

They drove back to her office, chatting happily as if they'd known each other for a long time, not a couple of days. Mila felt herself relax, even though the deal was one of the quickest and most exciting she'd ever made.

She settled Hersch at the conference table in the office and then excused herself to phone Dan Ferguson and tell him the good news. He picked up right away. Dan always did. He might say he was going to take a night off work and spend the evening with his wife and a cold beer, but she knew as well as he did that if there was a deal on the table, he'd be back here like a shot.

When he answered, he didn't beat around the bush. "Mila. Your client like the house?"

"Dan, put that beer away and crack open the champagne. He's making an offer tonight. Full price, cash. His only hard line is a quick closing. He'd move in tomorrow if he could."

Dan chuckled. "Mila, honey, it was a great day when I decided to teach you everything I know. Sometimes I think that the student has surpassed the master."

"Never. But I did learn from the best."

Dan said, "It's late back East, where the owners live, but we'll submit the offer anyway. We should have this all wrapped up by tomorrow."

She went back into the office and gave Herschel the good news. She said, "If all goes well, you'll be sleeping in that primary bedroom in a matter of days." Why did she keep mentioning the bedroom? What was wrong with her? No sooner did she picture that beautiful bedroom with the balcony and the view and the fireplace than she imagined the two of them curled up in that bed, slowly peeling each other's clothes away. She had to stop herself. Right now!

While she got the paperwork together, she said, "Is this the first house you've ever bought?"

Hersch lifted his gaze from the survey that had already been done on the property. He was definitely reading every word—something very few of her clients ever did.

"I already have a house in Mountain View near

work," he said. "This would be a second home. But it's a lot nicer than my first home. I could picture living here full-time one day."

She liked that answer. "Carmel is amazing. I couldn't imagine living anywhere else. I'm sure you'll feel the same way too, once you get settled. Just one night in that cozy bed and you won't want to leave." As soon as the words left Mila's mouth, she felt like clapping a hand over her lips. She had mentioned the bed *again*.

Herschel paused just long enough for her to think that maybe she wasn't the only one so focused on the bed. She felt such a strong longing to be in his arms that it frightened her.

She wrote up the offer, and he signed it.

She went through the motions of sending the offer, her head still foggy with desire. It was those darned rippling arm muscles and his calm, thorough way of being. The combination created a dizzying desire for him to not only throw her across that bed, but also take her in his arms and tell her everything was always going to be okay. As long as they had each other.

She shook her head. This was crazy. She barely knew the guy, and here she was dreaming about their great romance.

With the email sent, she reflexively checked her watch: nearly eight p.m. On a Saturday. She looked up at Herschel. "All done," she said. "Hopefully, we'll make a deal tomorrow."

He smiled. "You've certainty delivered everything I hoped for."

She held her breath. Was he also hoping to share his Saturday night?

He said, "Well…"

She waited, but nothing followed. She was sure he'd been on the verge of asking her out. But he didn't, damn it. She contemplated inviting him back to her cottage. This wasn't the Middle Ages. She could ask a man out without waiting for him to do it. But she sternly reminded herself of her rule about mixing business and pleasure. It was rarely a good idea, and they still needed to sign off on the deal. So she said, "Well… I'll let you know as soon as I hear anything. Shall I drop you back at your hotel?"

He nodded briefly, and she couldn't help but feel rejected. It was stupid, but she'd been so sure the chemistry wasn't one-sided. Why was he holding back? As they got into her SUV, she clung to the idea that he might invite her in for a nightcap at the hotel bar. The place he'd chosen was known for its dirty martinis. Maybe she could mention that…

She drove through the warm evening, enjoying the atmosphere of downtown Carmel as it floated through their open windows. It was peaceful. Carmel was a small town after all, but it still held the promise of a fun Saturday night, with the wine bars humming and the restaurants full of customers. As she thought of dinner, her stomach rumbled, and she realized she hadn't eaten a thing since before surfing. She would love a good steak with a glass of full-bodied red wine. Surely Herschel was also hungry? He must need a lot of protein to maintain those impressive muscles.

She tried to steer her thoughts away from a candle-lit date, and pulled into his hotel parking area. She switched off the engine and turned to face him only to find he had been staring at her profile. She felt electric with his gaze trained on her face. She opened her mouth to mention the martinis, but then closed it again. Instead, she asked, "How is this place? It has a good reputation."

"It's excellent. Quiet, private, very comfortable."

She nodded. Would he invite her in? The notion seemed to hover there for a second, but then he said, "Thank you for everything. I'll be giving you a great review."

Then he leaned forward and gave her a kind of awkward hug. Forcing her voice to stay neutral, she said, "I'll talk to you tomorrow."

\* \* \*

Hersch walked into his hotel room, kicking himself. There had been a moment when it had been obvious he could have kissed her. Why hadn't he taken the opportunity? He'd been unsure about whether the feeling was mutual, but then, she kept mentioning the bed. She was feeling that attraction, too, whether it was conscious or not, but instead of seizing the opportunity to kiss the most beautiful woman he'd ever met, he'd frozen.

Of course, he had his reasons. The house deal had yet to become official, and he'd made a vow to stay unattached so as not to harm someone he loved. And yet, hadn't he also figured Mila might be okay with things being casual? That she wouldn't think that his asking her out meant he was proposing? Instead, he'd made a fast exit, and now, instead of being accompanied by the most exciting woman he'd met in a long time, he'd be eating alone in the hotel restaurant.

Again.

To distract himself, he allowed thoughts of his new home to take over. He didn't want to jinx himself by being too confident that it was his, but he had a very good feeling this was going to work out. He couldn't wait to check out of his room and move his one suitcase over to that incredible house. Somehow he just knew that place was meant to be his. If another buyer turned up, he'd just outbid them. That's what people did in real estate. He didn't want to pay more money than he had to, but he knew deep inside that he belonged there. The knowledge surprised him with its suddenness and its intensity.

A lot like the way he felt about Mila.

And there he went again—what had it been, thirty seconds before she popped back into his brain?

*Why hadn't he kissed her?*

But no, he wasn't that guy, the single man who took advantage of a female Realtor when she was taking him on a business call. A gentleman did not act like that, and his mom had definitely raised him to be a gentleman.

Thinking of his mom, he picked up the phone. He'd told her he was looking at houses down this way, but she didn't realize how serious he was about the move. He hit the number on speed dial, and she picked up right away, though she sounded a little breathless.

For a second, he was worried. "Mom? Are you out jogging?"

Her warm laugh sounded in his ear, as rich and full as if she were standing at his side. He could almost smell her perfume—white roses—and instantly wanted to tell her about Mila. He shook his head. He needed to snap out of this.

"At this time of night?" His mom laughed again. "No. I just got in. I was at the movies with June." June was one of her best friends, and the two widows often went out for a meal or a movie together. He was glad his mom had someone like June around when he was out of state or on a mission. The two gossiped like schoolgirls.

He said, "I've got some news."

"Is it the kind of news where I should be sitting down?" she asked, suddenly sounding less lighthearted. They had a deal—before he told her about any of his missions, he made sure she was sitting down and had a glass of water beside her. Eleanor Greenfield could not be more proud of her son, but she also worried during every single second he was on a mission.

To save her any anxiety, he said, "I think I just bought a house in Carmel."

"You did?" Her voice rose with amazement. "But that's so quick. You barely got there. I thought you were just scouting the place."

He settled on the plaid couch in the suite's main room, but then got up to shut the curtains to block the view of the ocean. Seated again, he told his mother about the house. As he listed all the things he liked about it, he grew even more enthusiastic. At the end of the recital, he said, "You'll have to come and see it, Mom. It's gorgeous. With a big guest room for you."

"Oh, honey, I can't wait." Then, being Mom, she said, "Are you going to know any people there, though? You have so many friends and colleagues in Mountain View. I thought you were happy there. Won't you be starting all over in Carmel?"

Mila flashed back into his brain—her talent and her beauty and her brilliance—and he blurted, "I met a woman."

His mom laughed with delight. "The kind of woman you might actually introduce to your mother?"

It had long been his mom's complaint that he didn't bring girlfriends home to meet her. But no matter how much he liked his girlfriends, he couldn't let himself get carried away and let any of them become more deeply involved in his life. Not when he spent months away for training or up to a year in space. He sat back and tried to picture Mila and his mom having lunch or tea together... and he realized he liked the picture.

"I think you'd like her. She was a top-level pro surfer and then had an accident that ruined her career. She still teaches surfing for fun, and she looks pretty good out there on the waves, but she's a real estate agent now."

There was a moment's silence while his mom seemed to process her son actually volunteering information about a woman he liked. "Wait," she said. "Is she the one who sold you the house? You've fallen for your Realtor?"

He heard the smile in her voice, and he couldn't help but smile too. "I met her before she became my Realtor... but then she found this perfect house for me. She knew exactly what I needed. She's smart, sassy, knows what she wants. I definitely think you'd like her."

"I think I would too. Maybe it's time you gave romance a real try."

Part of him yearned to follow his mother's advice, but that constant, gnawing fear of leaving loved ones behind was too strong. "You know how I feel, Mom. Maybe when I retire."

"*Maybe* is a long time for a woman to wait for grandchildren."

This was where the conversation had to stop. Swiftly redirecting, Hersch said, "I'll let you know the minute I hear the offer has gone through. You'll come. We'll have a housewarming."

"Sounds great," she said. "I love you, Hersch."

"Love you too, Mom."

He hung up. And wondered what he was going to do for the rest of the evening. He couldn't stop thinking about Mila. If he'd asked her to dinner, would she have agreed? He kicked himself again. He could have said he wanted to celebrate the good news of making an offer on the house. Which would have been true. Sort of.

He decided on a long, cold shower. But that didn't really work, as it reminded him of all the time Mila spent in cold water. And then he began to imagine her in the shower... washing that long, beautiful hair. Feeling hot, he shook the image away.

Was his mother right? He'd never yet been tempted to break his rule of no wife and family, no big romantic commitments. But he had to admit that if there was a woman who could make him rethink his decision, it was Mila.

# Chapter Ten

Mila was a natural early riser, and she saw no reason to sleep in, even if it was a Sunday. The Davenport women were meeting at her parents' house this morning to talk wedding planning. She loved her family more than anything, but before she could cope with the thought of bridesmaids' dresses and what kind of cake they should serve and—most important of all—what Tessa was going to wear, she really needed to get out on her board. Nothing beat that first rush of the wind on her face as she started her day.

After a quick coffee and a little oatmeal and agave syrup for fuel, Mila suited up, grabbed her board, and walked the short distance to the beach. The waves weren't huge this morning, but there were still a couple of diehards patiently waiting, and she jumped on her board to join them. She paddled out to a likely spot. While they waited, she chatted with Tina, another woman who was often out early, and Stefano, a young waiter in town who spent every minute he could out on the water. Conversation ended the second any of them saw a likely swell approaching, and after a couple of hours, she'd caught enough respectable waves that she felt ready to face the wedding-palooza. By ten a.m., she was dressed in jeans and a comfy white cotton shirt, ready to help plan a wedding.

She picked up muffins from Saint Anna's, their favorite café in town that always stocked the best baked goods, and then drove to her parents' place. She'd been checking her phone more than usual, waiting for confirmation of Hersch's house deal. She was itching to ring him and share the good news. It was afternoon back East. She'd imagined she would have heard something by now. As she closed her car door and headed up the steps to her childhood home, she checked her messages and email one more time, hoping she'd have news. Nothing. She was about to walk in when she figured it was worth giving Dan a call to see if he'd heard anything. As always, he picked up on the second ring and told her he'd been trying to reach the couple selling the house, but he hadn't been able to get through to them yet.

He could obviously sense the urgency in her voice, because he said, "Don't worry, Mila. They're getting on in years and probably don't check their email the second they get out of bed like we do. As soon as I talk to them, I'll let you know."

She hated waiting, but Dan knew his clients. No doubt they were talking over the offer, or maybe—

almost impossible to believe—he was right, and they were the sort of people who didn't check their email on a Sunday morning.

Calling out a hello, she found she was the last to arrive. Erin, Tessa, and her mom were sitting around the kitchen table with a pot of coffee and some croissants Erin had obviously brought, along with a delicious-looking frittata that was undoubtedly one of Tessa's homemade and nutritious recipes. Although Arch was firmly on the mend after breaking his leg during a movie stunt, she hadn't given up on steering his diet toward healthier options.

Mila hugged everyone and took a seat at the table. Tessa looked excited and also a little overwhelmed. She wore a white cotton shirt with cherries embroidered on the hem, and the pink of the fruit matched the flush in her cheeks. In front of her was a fat file folder, which sort of surprised Mila, as she had expected Tessa would want everything simple and streamlined—especially if she was insisting on a thrifted dress.

She said to the bride, "How are you holding up so far? You still planning to marry my brother?"

Tessa glowed with happiness as she replied without a second's pause, "I still can't believe I got so lucky. Sometimes I just stop what I'm doing and stare at my ring, or Archer walks in and I have to pinch myself to make sure I'm not dreaming or sitting in a darkened theater watching him do what he does best."

Mila had to stop herself from rolling her eyes. She adored Tessa, but that was a bit much for a girl to hear about her brother. Archer might be a famous actor, but he was also her super annoying sibling. Several wise-cracks sprang to mind, but before she could utter one of them, Betsy said, "You're looking pleased with yourself this morning, Mila."

For a split second, Mila was tempted to tell the truth of what was on her mind. She was crushing on a man, and hard. But even though these women were closer to her than anyone else on earth, they'd ask questions, and since nothing had happened yet, she'd just feel like a fool. For now, she would keep this crush to herself. She arranged her muffins on a plate and announced she had a feeling she was going to make a big sale this weekend.

Her mom was looking at her as though she knew full well there was more to her good mood than a house sale. Nothing got past Betsy Davenport, especial-ly when it came to her children. After all, Mila sold houses all the time—phenomenal houses, at that—but rarely did they make her feel effervescent on the inside like she did now. But her mom also knew when to push the matter and when to stand back. As soon as Mila smiled enigmatically and then looked as if she had nothing more to add, Betsy jumped up, smoothed her chic blue shirtdress, and fetched a plate of fruit from the fridge. With that, they had the perfect blend of healthy and decadent breakfast offerings.

While Mila poured herself a mug of fresh coffee, Erin turned to Tessa and tapped the folder. "I love how organized you are. What's in here?"

Tessa shook her head, and her dark hair fell across her forehead. "I don't feel organized at all. I don't know where to start when it comes to a glitzy wedding. Jay says we should announce our engagement publicly soon, so I really want to have the bare bones of my big, fancy, fake wedding already figured out. Arch suggested I read some bridal magazines, and I've been tearing pages out of them and jotting down ideas, but none of it really feels like me. I talked to Crystal Lopez, Damien's friend, and he was right about her. She got Francesca to agree to cater our family wedding even though it's less than two weeks away. Plus, she's talking to another planner in Edinburgh who can help us there. She seemed to think there was no wedding problem she couldn't solve, but she also encouraged me to bring some ideas to the table. So this file is half my real wedding—the family-only one—and half some pretty big ideas for the Scottish wedding. I thought I could start this morning by running some of them by you."

"Excellent," Mila said. "I've never been to Scotland, and I'm kind of looking forward to the rugged terrain and the men with gorgeous Scottish accents wearing kilts that show off their fine legs." She paused and happily bit into a blueberry muffin. It was soft and sweet. A little mischievously, she added, "Have you talked Arch into wearing a kilt?"

Tessa laughed, and Mila was glad. She didn't like seeing her soon-to-be sister-in-law so worried about something she didn't even want in the first place.

Tessa said, "The first thing he made me promise when we agreed on a wedding in Scotland was that he didn't have to wear a kilt."

Betsy made a clucking sound and said, "Howie will be disappointed. He hasn't been able to find a Davenport tartan, but I'm pretty sure he's hoping to find he's part of a clan and wear a kilt. I hope that's okay, especially if he walks you down the aisle."

Tessa said simply, "Howie can wear whatever he wants to my wedding. I'm just so happy he's going to be there."

Her response was one of the many reasons Mila loved Tessa as much as if they'd spent a lifetime as sisters.

Tessa went on, "I'm so happy all of you have welcomed me into your family the way you have. It means the world to me." She could hardly finish the words as she choked up with tears. And then, of course, Erin and Betsy started blinking furiously. Mila had never been quick to cry, but she couldn't help but feel overcome by Tessa's sincerity. It was so refreshing to meet someone so openhearted.

Naturally, Betsy pulled herself together first and put her hand over Tessa's. The two women's diamond rings sparkled in the morning light. "I couldn't have chosen a better bride for Archer," she said warmly, releasing her hand after a hearty squeeze to tuck a strand of her honey-colored hair behind her ear. "You make him so happy."

Mila could take only so much emotion at ten in the morning, so, remembering her promise to her brother, she said, "Before this turns into a full-on sobfest, what are you planning to wear?"

Tessa wiped the corners of her eyes and then sat up straight as though ready to face opposition. She looked almost guilty. "I really want to get my dress at a thrift store. I just can't bear the thought of spending an awful lot of money on a dress I'll only wear once." Before anyone else could speak, she said, "I know Archer has a lot of money. It's not really about that. It's about who I am and the values I live by. Of course, I do understand I'm going to be a celebrity's wife, and I'll try never to embarrass him, but it's my wedding too. At least with the family, I want to be myself."

Mila had thought her brother was being a big drama queen when he'd told her she had to talk Tessa out of wearing a thrift-store dress, but Tessa was serious. Mila could totally get behind the whole notion of thrifting, but she did think Archer had a point about the media frenzy that would ensue if it got out that his bride was wearing a secondhand dress to marry him.

Erin, who was munching on a slice of cantaloupe, looked puzzled. "If it was me, I'd make him take me to Paris and get a designer bridal gown from Dior. Or London for an Alexander McQueen number. I mean, it's your *wedding*. Why not have a little fun with it? You only get to do this once."

"Hopefully," Mila joked, not being able to help herself.

But when Tessa looked truly sad, Mila realized she and Erin had accidentally ventured into sensitive territory.

Tessa said quietly, "But it's not my first wedding. The first time I got married, I had the big poufy dress, and I let myself be talked into something that wasn't me. I don't want to do that again. With Archer, I'm truly myself, and I need to start that very important first day of our marriage showing the world who I really am."

It was hard to argue with that. Mila wouldn't compromise herself for any man either. She glanced at her mom, and saw an expression on Betsy's face that made her think Arch had also confided in his mother his fears about this thrift-store dress.

Betsy sliced the frittata. "I have an idea. Instead of wearing a thrift-store gown, what about a family one?"

Once again, Tessa's blue eyes turned sad. "I'd have loved that, but my mother didn't keep her gown. My sister's much smaller than I am…" She trailed off and then quietly added, "Besides, I can't imagine wearing her dress."

In the most casual way possible, Betsy said, "I was thinking about my wedding dress. I've kept it all these years because it was so beautiful, and I've had a very happy marriage. Would you like to see it? I think you're about the same size I was when I got married."

Who was she kidding? Her mom was trim and worked out almost daily and was probably the exact same size she'd been in the eighties. Dad always told Mom, and anyone else who was around, that she looked as beautiful now as she had on their wedding day, and he really wasn't exaggerating.

As she watched Tessa absorb this offer, Mila was impressed at her mother's tact and smarts. Trust Betsy to find the perfect solution. She could also see that Tessa was quite thrilled by the idea, but she immediately looked at the two sisters.

"What about Mila and Erin? Surely one of you should wear your mother's gown."

They glanced at each other and shook their heads. "It's a great dress, but I don't want it," Mila said.

Erin agreed. "It's just not my style. But even though it's from the eighties, it's classic. It could look really good on you, Tessa."

Mila looked at her mom. "You would never let us play dress-up in that gown, no matter how much we begged. I guess now I know why. Because it was meant to be worn again in a real wedding."

Betsy put down the muffin she hadn't even taken a bite of and said, "Why don't you take a look at it, Tessa? Absolutely no obligation, of course, but it would be an alternative to thrifting. You'd be wearing a dress that's been worn before, which suits your ethics, and if anyone asks, you can tell the truth—that it was my wedding dress, and it has sentimental value to the family. That gives it a whole different kind of cachet. At least, I think so."

Tessa nodded, looking both scared and excited.

Betsy excused herself to fetch the gown, and Mila took the opportunity to say in a low voice, "If you don't like it, use the word *butter* in a sentence, and I'll say I don't like it on you." Tessa would struggle to turn down Betsy's offer even if the dress looked terrible on her.

"Oh, good idea," Erin agreed. "One mention of butter, and I'll back Mila up. You don't have to wear it if you don't love it."

The three of them fell quiet then and tucked into breakfast. It was pretty obvious each of them was waiting to see what Tessa would think of the dress. And if she liked it, would it fit?

A few minutes later, Betsy returned with the dress bag that Mila remembered always seeing in the back of her closet. Before Betsy even unzipped it, she said to

Tessa, "No pressure. I mean it. If you don't like it, that's fine. It's just one option, okay?"

Tessa nodded and gazed, almost transfixed, as Betsy unzipped the bag. Mila got up and pulled the bag away so that her mom could reveal the dress in all its glory. It really was a beautiful gown, simple and elegant. Betsy had been smart enough to stay away from the huge shoulder pads and flounces of the eighties and had chosen something that was timeless. The dress was ivory silk with tiny silk-covered buttons down the back, a drop waist, and a fairly full skirt.

As she looked at it, Tessa's eyes filled with tears. "It's so beautiful, Betsy. Exactly what I would have chosen. I can't believe it."

Betsy looked almost as pleased as Tessa, and even Mila felt a catch of emotion in the back of her throat.

"It looks to be exactly your size," Erin said in a half whisper, almost in awe of how perfect the dress might look.

"Go into the bedroom and try it on," Betsy encouraged her.

Tessa rose and almost reverently took the dress on its padded hanger and made her way upstairs to Betsy and Howie's bedroom.

While she was gone, Erin said, "She really loved it. I just hope it does actually fit."

Mila, always focused on the practical, said, "If it doesn't, we'll have it altered. No problem." She turned to her mom. "Offering your dress was a stroke of genius. It could solve everybody's problem. Archer won't be humiliated by somebody online claiming that his bride is wearing her castoff dress, and Tessa still gets to wear a gown that has had a previous life. But the beauty of it is she knows who wore it and how happy you are with Dad. That dress must have some really good mojo."

Glowing, Betsy nodded. "I like to think so."

When Tessa descended the stairs and walked into the room, the three women gasped in unison. The dress was The One. No two ways about it. Tessa looked beautiful in it, and she was so thrilled. There was a pink tinge to her cheeks, and her eyes shone. By some lucky chance, she'd worn low-heeled cream pumps with her jeans, and while they didn't exactly match the dress, they showed that even the length was perfect.

Tessa twirled slowly in a circle, then looked around at the three women. "What do you think?" she asked in a timid but hopeful tone. She lifted up her hair. "I couldn't get all the buttons done up myself, but I'm sure it fits."

Erin leaped up from the table and stood behind Tessa to help.

The word *butter* did not come up.

Somehow, they all knew Betsy had to be the first one to speak, and after a second, she finally did, in a voice full of emotion. "It looks completely different on you than it did on me. And I think you look beautiful."

Now that she'd weighed in, both Erin and Mila spoke at the same time.

"It's gorgeous," Erin said.

"It's absolutely you," Mila agreed. She felt truly happy for Tessa and for Archer—and also for her mom, who was so happy to see her dress being worn again by someone she loved.

The three of them went with Tessa to Betsy's bedroom, where there was a big full-length mirror. While Tessa turned this way and that, they all agreed that the dress needed no alterations. She could have pinned a veil on her head, shown up at church, and been married that very day.

As Tessa turned in front of the mirror, she said, "It's the most beautiful thing I've ever worn. I wish my mother were here to see it." As she teared up, they all shared a group hug.

Mila breathed in the familiar scent of her mom's perfume, and Erin's apple blossom shampoo. As she pulled away, Mila looked again at the dress, and then, with a small gasp, she noticed what looked like a water stain on the hem. With some trepidation, she pointed it out, and Betsy looked horrified.

Her mom knelt and inspected the stain more closely and then looked up at Tessa. "I'm so sorry. I should have stored it better."

Tessa followed their gazes, looking a little upset herself. "I really want to wear your dress. I can't even imagine myself wearing anything else now. How bad is the stain? Can't we get it out somehow? I'm sure if we looked on the internet, there must be lots of tips and hints."

Mila couldn't think of anything worse than trying a bunch of homemade remedies. She said, "I'll take it to my dry cleaner. They're really good. If anyone can lift that stain, they can."

Tessa argued that she should do it, but Mila immediately reminded her that she was keeping the wedding a secret until they announced the big, fancy shindig in Scotland. The last thing they needed was for her to get busted taking a wedding dress to a dry cleaner.

Tessa put her hand over her mouth. "You're right. I keep forgetting that I'm going to be noticed because I'm Archer's fiancée."

"You'll get used to the media glare," Mila assured her. She'd once been in the media's crosshairs often. She didn't miss it, but she'd also learned to live with the scrutiny of her private life when she'd been semi-famous for pro surfing.

They left Tessa to dress and returned to the kitchen. Mila could see her mom was still agitated about the stain, so she gave her another hug and whispered in her ear, "I'm gonna bring that dress back to Tessa in better condition than when you bought it."

Betsy drew back and gave her daughter the widest smile. "I've always loved your natural confidence, Mila," she said. "No matter what life throws at you, you meet it head on. It's a joy to see."

Mila smiled back, her heart full. There was nothing nicer than a compliment from her mom.

Tessa returned, carefully laying the dress in its protective bag over the back of a chair, and then sat down.

"Well," she said, looking around the table, "now that the hardest part is done, let's talk about this fancy Scottish castle party." With a giggle, she opened her folder and began to walk them through elaborate plans for bagpipes and vintage champagne glasses.

Suddenly, a dreadful thought occurred to Mila. "You aren't expecting us bridesmaids to wear thrift-store gowns, are you?" She hoped she didn't sound as horrified as she felt.

Now even mild-mannered Erin looked concerned. She obviously hadn't considered that a bride who was willing to wear a secondhand gown might expect her attendants to do the same. But Tessa giggled again and said, "I wish you could see your faces right now. And no. I thought we might go shopping together and find dresses you both like. Can we go this week?"

Mila relaxed. That seemed reasonable. "Sure. Let's plan a shopping trip."

Erin agreed.

"Are you feeling nervous about the big wedding?"

Mila asked. "There will be a lot of people there and probably fans lining up around the perimeter, which means a lot of security… Plus, the paparazzi and media will be flying overhead in helicopters. And don't get me started on the drones. I hope you don't mind me saying this, but you seem way more relaxed than I thought you'd be."

Tessa seemed unfazed. "Now that I know I'll have my perfect small family wedding in the world's most gorgeous secondhand dress, I'm happy. Besides, Arch will be by my side for the splashy event, so I know I'll be just fine."

As the conversation turned to the smaller, family wedding, Betsy took over with some ideas about catering, as she'd lived in Carmel for so long and had thrown many parties. "Howie and I thought we might tell the caterers we're having a party for our wedding anniversary. That way, no one will suspect a thing."

"Oh, that's a wonderful idea," Tessa agreed, sounding enthusiastic.

There were a few big questions remaining, like who would conduct the ceremony, but Tessa said Archer had some ideas about that and, with a coy smile, she refused to reveal any more.

Fueled with some more coffee, they had fun looking through the file. But Mila couldn't keep her mind focused on wedding planning. Every so often, she surreptitiously checked her phone to see if there was any news on Hersch's house.

Nothing got past her mom. "Waiting for news on this big deal?" There was a twinkle in her eye, but Mila avoided her gaze.

"Nothing yet," she replied, and then, seeing how much time had passed already, got to her feet. "I'll get this dress to the dry cleaner tomorrow when they open. Once you and Arch announce your engagement, people will start snooping around." And with that, she hugged three of her favorite people in the world good-bye and headed for her SUV.

It was four o'clock in New York. How long did it take to see a great deal when it was staring you in the face?

# Chapter Eleven

Hersch was working out in the hotel gym, thinking about how much he couldn't wait to have his own place. He might not be as famous as Archer Davenport, but since he'd sung "Happy Birthday" to his mom from space, he'd become memorable, as Jay Malone had pointed out. Repeatedly.

He could tell by their furtive glances that people in the gym recognized him.

Unfortunately, it wasn't the first time that morning. A glass wall separated the gym from a studio that had so far been empty, but today a yoga class was in there. One woman had noticed him and done a double take and then nudged her friend with her elbow, and the next thing he knew, an entire yoga class of women doing downward dog was checking him out while he pedaled up a mountain on the stationary bike. It was not the kind of attention he relished, especially not when he was dripping with sweat.

He was trying to ignore the stares when his phone rang. He'd kept his phone with him all day, hoping to hear from Mila, and had stopped himself several times from texting her to see if she had any news. Obviously, she would call him when she did. He had to relax.

But now his stomach jumped when he saw Mila's name on his phone. He wiped sweat off his face and then answered.

Without even bothering with a hello, she said in an excited voice, "Great news! You got the house!"

He could barely get out the words. "That's fantastic."

"It sounds like you're running."

"Worse," he panted. "I'm cycling up a mountain in Chamonix."

She burst out laughing. "What?"

"Well, it's a virtual background. I'm in the gym at my hotel, but at the moment Chamonix looks a lot better."

She said, "Sooner than you can believe, you're going to be cycling in your own home gym. As soon as the money clears, the house is yours. And the really good news is all the checks have already been done by the last buyers—the survey and all those more laborious tasks—so you can rest easy and be in that house in a matter of days."

He loved how excited she was, and somehow that made him even more happy than he was already at such great news.

"I can't thank you enough, Mila," he said, meaning

it so sincerely he wished he could say it a thousand times over.

He could almost feel her bright smile as she said, "You better put the champagne on ice."

His workout was definitely over for the day, so he hauled himself off the bike and wiped it down, all the while talking to Mila. He said, "Champagne can wait. I promised my mom that calling her would be the first thing I'd do when I found out."

"That's nice," she said, sounding very supportive. "That was the first thing I did when I bought my home. My mom was so proud of me, and I couldn't wait to tell her."

"I imagine your mom is proud of you for lots of reasons," he said quietly.

There was a pause, and he could tell that Mila was touched. "I'm just really lucky to have such a great mom. She's always there for me, especially when things are tough."

Hersch felt his heart swell in recognition. "The same for me." He was going to continue when Mila swiftly turned the conversation back to the house.

"I'll send through a few emails as soon I get into the office."

"You're in the office on a Sunday?"

"Only for my most important clients," Mila said.

Though he knew she was joking, Hersch couldn't help hoping he was important to Mila Davenport. He ended the call with more words of thanks, and she told him it was her pleasure. And then he couldn't get the idea of Mila and pleasure out of his mind… What would it feel like to be the one who could actually give Mila pleasure? It would be as good as seeing Earth from space for the first time. Mind-blowing, just mind-blowing.

As soon as he was back in his suite and showered, he called his mom.

With a sigh of contentment, she said, "That's just wonderful, honey. You know, I've been a bit worried about you. I thought you've been kind of down lately, but now you seem different. Is it just the house?"

He knew she was fishing for more details about Mila. Part of him wished he'd never told her about his crush, but the truth was he suspected Mila was a big part of how upbeat he was feeling these days. He said, "I'm excited about the house and to start spending more time in Carmel-by-the-Sea, but if I'm honest, it's also down to this woman I've met."

"The Realtor?"

"The Realtor."

"Can you tell me more about her? She must really be something special—I can hear it in the way you speak."

Hersch sat back in the plump hotel chair. How to describe Mila? She was one of kind. "Well, for a start, she's beautiful. Truly striking. Tall, blonde, muscular.

But it's much more than that. She doesn't seem to be afraid of anything. She's just got this way about her that makes me feel like anything's possible too."

His mother made a puzzled sound. "But you've always been like that yourself, honey. You've always believed you could do anything you put your mind to. And you did."

Hersch swallowed, and suddenly all his excitement vanished. Mila had guessed something he'd kept to himself. No one in the world knew about his fear of the water, not even his mother, and he wasn't going to burden her with his irrational fear now. He said, "Maybe I've changed a little. Got a little older, a little wiser."

She let out a sigh. "Oh, my darling boy. When I nearly lost you, I thought my world had ended. I've forgotten to really think about what it's been like for you."

There was a moment of complete silence where they didn't need to say a word, each processing, each thinking about the other. But if there was one thing his mother's confession confirmed, it was that no matter how much he cared for a woman, he couldn't put her in a position where he'd leave her to go on a mission from which he might never return.

After a moment, his mom said, "I can't wait to see your house. As soon as it's ready, let me know, and I'll fly down."

He loved that about his mom. She was sixty-one going on thirty-five, full of energy and always making plans for the future. Before they ended the call, she said, "And when I come, make sure I get to meet Mila."

# Chapter Twelve

Mila took the stained wedding gown with her to the office on Monday. It was a busy day, but the hours she'd put in on Sunday afternoon meant everything was going smoothly on the closing and the deed transfer. With a cup of hot black coffee by her side, she'd worked steadily, not only on Hersch's house, but also on a couple of other deals she had cooking. She was trying to help a nice young couple buy their first home so they could start a family, and another couple were thinking about selling their exciting treetop two-bedroom but hadn't decided yet. She was itching to list such an unusual house. She checked in with both couples, and then at lunchtime, decided she'd better get Tessa's wedding dress to the dry cleaner.

It was a gorgeous day, and she relished the fresh, salty air and that buzzy feeling she always got at the start of a new week—like anything was possible. Her office was just a few minutes from Ocean Avenue, where so many of Carmel's restaurants and high-end boutiques lined the streets and where her trusted dry cleaner had been operating for twenty years. She loved living here, even after all the travel she'd done when pro surfing. No other place in the world gave her the tingly feeling Carmel did. It was home.

She passed Saint Anna's, where she resisted popping in for another coffee, or a pastry—treats were mostly relegated to the weekends and Tuesday coffee dates with Erin and Tessa. In the window, she saw a young family she'd worked with to secure them a new home last year. The smiles on their faces when they spotted her were so wide and sincere, she waved back enthusiastically. It was the part of her job she relished the most—helping people find their dream homes. Yes, the thrill of closing a big-dollar deal was a high of its own, but serving the community and getting to meet so many new people week in and week out gave her the kind of job satisfaction she knew she needed since her surfing career had ended.

Then she noticed her former clients raising confused eyebrows. She looked down. Of course. She was carrying a wedding dress—they could see it through the clear plastic zipper bag. She tried to gesture that the dress didn't belong to her, but since this was impossible to do one-handed, she just shrugged and waved goodbye. She wasn't planning to get tied down anytime soon—even if her mind was full of a certain man right now.

She hiked up the bag and was about to push open

the door to the dry cleaner when she literally bumped into Herschel Greenfield. Apart from the immediate electric thrill she felt from coming into contact with his body, she was also a little spooked. Had she just summoned his presence by thinking about him so much? It was like the universe was having fun with her. When she recovered her composure and focused, she was pleased to see his face had lit up.

She grinned and suddenly had no idea what to say to the man she'd been talking to in her head all day long.

"Hey there," he said. "Where are you going in such a hurry?"

Had she been walking quickly? Probably. She was always conscious of time. "I'm just taking a wedding dress to be cleaned."

"Oh," he said, and then the light in his eyes faded. "You're married?" He sounded extremely disappointed as his eyes darted to her left hand.

She laughed. "Oh, hell no. Marriage is not for me. I can't imagine being stuck with one man all my—" She abruptly stopped. What was wrong with her? Again, she'd blurted something completely inappropriate. She was mortified.

Hersch must have thought it was inappropriate, too, because his expression became confused and then hurt—as though he was taking her words straight to his heart. She stared at him, puzzled by the strong reaction. But then she realized something else. Even as she spoke, she'd wondered whether it might not be true anymore, because there was a very secret part of her that had started thinking of Herschel Greenfield as The One.

To her embarrassment, she blushed. Mila Davenport never blushed, not even when her bikini top rode up while surfing, not when she misremembered the square footage of a house, not even when her career had been upended. Desperate to move the conversation to a different track, she said, "Are you going to the dry cleaner too?" It wasn't the most scintillating question, but at least it was neutral ground.

Hersch shook his head. "I'm heading to the paint and bedding stores. I have no idea what I'm doing. I just feel like I should start getting ready for when I get the keys to that house." He gave a kind of helpless shrug, which was so charming that she regained her confidence and grinned.

Plus, she'd now had time to take in the athletic, casual clothing that showed off his incredible physique, even if nothing actually matched. If ever there was a man who needed the help of a woman with a good sense of design and color, it was Herschel Greenfield. She said, "Do you want some help? I'm a pretty decent amateur decorator."

He looked so relieved she nearly laughed. "I cannot tell you how much I would appreciate some help," he said. "I can service the oxygen generator in a space shuttle, and I can conduct experiments on flammability with a clear mind after a hundred days in microgravity, but pick a shade of paint for the bedroom? Find a bedspread that'll match? I haven't a clue."

Mila grinned again. There was something adorable about someone so smart he was kind of nerdy and didn't know how to navigate a paint store. In order to spare him from an entire house decorated in beige, she said, "Just let me drop this dress at the dry cleaner. I'll be right out, and then we can go together."

She went in, and Martin, the owner, assured her that no one would ever know there'd been water damage once he'd worked his magic on the dress. He enthusiastically explained his special technique. She didn't quite follow it, but understood that a solution could gently pull the stain off the ivory satin without any damage. That was all she needed to know. She took the receipt and headed back out to where Herschel stood on the sidewalk. It felt good to see him waiting for her, and she was already looking forward to helping him run errands.

He said, "Who's getting married?"

"Just a friend of mine," she said, trying not to feel guilty. It wasn't a lie. Tessa *was* a friend of hers. But even though she was sure she could trust Herschel, it was better not to mention that her famous brother was about to tie the knot before it was officially announced.

The paint store was a five-minute walk, and they spent the time in easy conversation, just like when she'd taken him to see the houses. It was striking how easy he was to talk to, how relaxed she felt in his company. After all, there weren't many people in the world for whom she would extend her lunch break. Hersch might be the very first outside of her immediate family.

Once inside the paint store, however, Hersch's mood immediately seemed to dip. He stood among all the thousands of paint swatches and color-pathway books and looked at her with something like desperation. "I don't even know which color to choose." He held up a book and grimaced. "How is ochre different than tan? What *is* ochre, anyway?"

She had to laugh. "Don't worry," she said, "I'm going to help you. We can narrow this down."

He glanced around to where a woman and her decorator were comparing shades of green and two couples were poring over swatches. "It's been so long since I decorated my other house that I barely remember how." He sighed. "I don't mean to sound old-fashioned, but most men who buy houses have wives to help them. I never did."

Hersch might be a little stuck in the 1950s, but he was also so lost it was cute. She took the whole book of various shades of tan out of his hands and put it back. "The first thing you need to understand is that before you make a decision, you take swatches home and look at them against the walls in your house. The light changes all the time. What you might think is ever-green in the morning looks more like pine at night. You won't be able to change everything all at once if you move in right away, so I think we should start with your bedroom. Most of the other rooms seemed okay for now, but you really want the primary bedroom to feel like it's yours right away."

Mila blinked. She'd mentioned his bedroom *again*. But if Hersch noticed, he didn't show it. Instead, he said, "How can I take any swatches there if I don't have the keys yet?"

"Let me see what I can do." She quickly texted Dan and asked if it would be okay for her client to take another look at the house he was buying. As she'd suspected, he replied right away that it was no prob-lem.

She told Hersch the good news, and his eyes filled with light again. "What are your favorite colors?" she asked.

He pulled a dorky face. "I don't know. Blue?"

She shook her head. Such an obvious answer for a man.

Still, she could do something with that. She grabbed a few cards that offered a main shade and then complementary colors for trim and accessories, making sure there was always at least a little blue. But he was really starting from scratch.

"I'm tempted to start with the bedding and decorate around that," she said.

He seemed quite open to all her suggestions, so they walked to a luxury bedding store she really liked. Even better, the owner turned part of her showroom over to creating entire bedrooms for inspiration, which Mila thought might make it easier for Hersch to envision what his room would look like.

But as they walked through the store together, most of the bedroom setups looked either too feminine to Mila's eye or too traditional. She could see that Hersch wasn't very interested in any of them. He headed over to a rack of interior-design magazines and began to flip through. She watched his expression from across the room, noting what a handsome figure he cut against gold-flecked wallpaper. He paused, sensing her eyes on him, and then came over to her with the open magazine.

"I like this one," he said.

The photograph featured a modern-looking bed with a bedspread so dark a blue it was almost black, with white sheets and pillows with the same dark navy stripe combined with pillows in solid navy. The wall behind it was a smudgy gray. It was understated and sophisticated. She said, "What do you like about it?"

He thought for a second. "I like the depth of the color. It's almost as if you could fall into it and float.

Plus, it looks like a black-and-white photograph. I've got some gorgeous photographs taken from space. They'd look really good against those walls."

She nodded, pleased. She loved how he'd chosen something that would be so simple to make work. In less than half an hour, they were walking out with all the bedding he would need, plus ideas for complementary draperies or blinds. They'd have to measure first, and anyway Herschel wasn't sure he even wanted curtains, as there was so much privacy.

They headed back to the paint store and picked an entirely different palette of soft gray possibilities, which would make his framed photographs really pop.

She said, "I think you might need to get a couple of new pieces of furniture for that bedroom too. The current owners' stuff is just too traditional."

He heaved a sigh of relief. "I'm so glad you said that. I am happy to take it all, just so long as I don't have to keep it all. I was thinking of donating some of the better pieces to a charity."

She leaned in close and whispered, "I'll never tell them if you don't." Since she didn't think they would ever come back to the Carmel area, as they had decided to settle in New York near their children and grandchildren, she figured she and Hersch were on pretty safe ground.

When they walked out of the shop, he said, as though admitting a great secret, "I have to tell you, I don't mind keeping that bed. It looks perfectly service-able, but I would like to have a new mattress."

For a moment, Mila let her mind go to the dirty places it wanted to. She pictured Hersch, naked, waiting for her on that bed, and the image drove her wild. She redirected her enthusiasm and agreed. "If I were buying somebody else's bed, I'd want a new mattress too."

She could see he was looking at her with a kind of questioning gaze. She let herself hope that he was also imagining them together on that bed... But then she realized what he was really asking.

She laughed softly at herself and shook her head. "Yes, okay, I'll go mattress shopping with you."

She checked her watch, mindful that her to-do list was never done. However, Hersch was a great client. She was happy that she'd worked so hard earlier in the day, and of course her cell phone was always on. She could allow herself a bit of freedom. She was with a client, after all...

The moment they walked into the mattress store, she could tell he was somewhat overwhelmed by the rows and rows of options. Before a salesperson could even approach them, she said, "You have to lie on the mattresses and pretend you're sleeping, or you won't be able to make a good choice. A mattress is a very personal thing."

He looked embarrassed. "Just lie down in the middle of the store? Do I take my shoes off?"

"I don't think so. I think these are specially made for people to try out."

He looked a little skeptical, but she could see he was willing to follow her advice. A salesperson spotted them and came over. The young man, dressed in a smart blue suit, introduced himself as Ted and asked what they were looking for. She realized he was assuming they were a couple.

Hersch cleared his throat and said, "A bed. For a primary bedroom."

In a deep, reassuring voice, Ted said, "If you're going to be purchasing your main bed, then may I suggest one of these three?"

Since she was a salesperson herself, Mila immediately respected his approach. A good salesperson knew instinctively to narrow down the choices to something that Hersch could handle. She could see Hersch's shoulders droop with relief that he had to think about only three beds. Of course, they were high-end beds, but she suspected that was the kind of thing Hersch was looking for anyway.

Her personal opinion about beds was that since you spent a lot of time on them, you should buy the best you could afford. She didn't have to voice that, because she strongly suspected Ted would have the same opinion and would give Hersch the guidance he needed.

Another couple called Ted away, and he recommended that they try the three mattresses and see what they thought. He promised to come back over and check in with them. Mila was happy they would be able to do this bit of shopping without Ted watching them. It wasn't exactly relaxing to lie down in front of a complete stranger, and to test a bed properly, you needed to try to imagine it was in your own room already.

She said as much to Hersch, who obediently got on the first bed and then looked up at her. "Aren't you going to join me? I feel like an idiot lying here by myself."

She didn't have to be asked twice. She'd been thinking about this since she'd first seen him. Although it wasn't as private a space as in her fantasies, she settled beside him. He smelled wonderful—like fresh air and healthy male. She fixed her gaze on the ceiling in case he saw the desire in her eyes. In the most neutral tone she could muster, she said, "You should move around a bit. See how it feels against your body."

He rolled so he was on his side, staring at her, and then she did the same. As soon as she looked into his eyes, she knew that he mirrored her desire and couldn't hide it any more than she could. They didn't speak. The sensual sparks were doing all the talking for them. What's more, those sparks were so hot she thought the mattress might catch fire.

Finally, he said, "This one feels good."

She nodded. "You need to compare it with the others to be sure."

But clearly neither of them wanted to move. A few more seconds of staring into Hersch's soulful eyes passed before Mila made herself roll over and swing her feet to the floor. "Let's try the next one."

As they settled on another luxurious mattress, Mila's heart began to race. She wanted to rip off Hersch's clothes and run her hands over his impressive body. But they were in public. It was a special kind of scintillating torture.

Again, they shifted their bodies to face each other. Again, she knew they were both imagining what it would feel like if they were under some covers rather than on top of a bare mattress in a store. Again, it took them an age to move on to the third mattress.

When they'd tested them all, Hersch got to his feet and extended a hand. She accepted it, a thrill coursing through her body as she felt his firm grip help her up. He was so darned strong.

"It was the first mattress for me," he said, and she noted his voice had turned a little husky.

Oddly, it was the same mattress Mila would have chosen, so she was able to give her unqualified approval.

He bought the mattress and arranged to have it delivered, and then as they left the store, he turned to her with a slightly sheepish look. "I know you've done so much for me already, Mila, but is there any way I could convince you to come to the house to take a look at the swatches there? All your advice and guidance so far has been so valuable."

If such a thing were possible, her heart simultaneously soared and sank. She was thrilled that Hersch wanted to spend more time together, even if it was over paint swatches. But she was also mentally going over her to-do list.

He could see her hesitation. "I'm sorry. I've taken up too much of your time already. Forgive me for asking."

But, she decided, there wasn't anything that couldn't wait, and if anyone needed her, she had her phone with her. So she said in her flirtiest tone, "How about I do it just because I think you're cute?"

He opened and then closed his mouth before his cheeks flushed. Clearly, her teasing flustered him. She had to admit she quite liked that she could make this big, muscly astronaut blush.

# Chapter Thirteen

For a guy who hated shopping, Hersch had never enjoyed a shopping trip more. Mila was so fun to be with, made everything seem easy, and had a very discerning eye. Or at least it seemed so to a man who had no eye at all for color or fashion or design.

As she unlocked the door to the new property, he recalled that moment when they'd bumped into each other while she was holding a wedding dress and he'd thought she was married. His relief at learning she was single had flooded his veins and filled him with hope that something could happen between them. At the same time, she'd so instantly laughed off the very idea of marriage and said it wasn't for her. This should have been music to his ears, because that was his position too, but while he hadn't even kissed her yet, she was all he could think about. There was a secret part of himself that had begun thinking of her as The One.

What a strange reversal that he, who had always been the commitment-phobe, was now faced with somebody at least as bad as he was. The universe had a fine sense of humor.

With an accepted offer in place and hopefully only days before he moved in, Hersch considered himself to be entering his own house. It was a great feeling to look around the gorgeous space and know he'd be living there soon. He noticed little touches he hadn't seen before—the nice recessed lighting and the way the late afternoon sun lit up the trees at the back of the property. He loved that he didn't have to do anything but bring his toothbrush and a few clothes, and he'd be home. Naturally, he'd ship over some of his possessions from his other house. Mostly, he liked the idea of some of his photographs upstairs in that big bedroom. He didn't care at all about views of the ocean, but he always wanted a view of the sky. There was a skylight in his bedroom as well as in the bathroom, and even though there was some fancy roller blind thing on each that worked by remote control, he didn't think he'd ever use it. He liked the idea of going to bed at night looking up at the stars, and waking up in the morning with the day breaking overhead.

They unloaded the duvet and pillows and things they'd bought earlier that afternoon, and then Mila practically ran up the stairs ahead of him. He loved her enthusiasm.

"I don't know who likes this house more—me or you," he joked.

She turned to him, and he was struck by her silhouette in his bedroom doorway, tall and strong and incredibly sexy.

"I just like that I found it for you," she replied with a smile.

He wanted to race over and pull her into his arms, but before he could act on that impulse, she turned and disappeared into the room.

When he walked in, trying to calm his unsteady breath, she was attempting to spread the enormous duvet on the bed.

"Let me take the other side," he said, picking up the heavy fabric. Without words, they maneuvered around the bed, smoothing down the duvet in its new sheets, slipping the cases on the brand-new pillows, and resting them against the headboard.

"The color looks great," she said. "And when you paint the walls that smudgy gray, it'll look even better."

"It's already beginning to feel like this place is really mine." Saying the words aloud brought a new sense of satisfaction and pleasure. Suddenly, he had an idea. "I'm going to pull out the carpet and have wood floors laid, stained a very dark color."

"I think that's a great idea," she said enthusiastically. "It'll look sleek, modern, and go really well with your framed photos. And you said you have no design talent."

He laughed and put a hand to his chest in defense.

"It was in the picture I liked. It had dark wood floors."

"Well, it's a good idea." She went back to the bed and began to rearrange the pillows. "There," she said, stepping back and admiring her handiwork. "It looks perfect."

"Very inviting," he agreed, wondering how long he could stand not taking her in his arms and kissing her deeply, over and over again.

And then Mila appeared to take him at his word. She slipped off her shoes and pretty much jumped onto the bed. He couldn't stop himself. He kicked off his own shoes and lay beside her.

They stared up at the skylight for a moment, and then he said, "This is the worst mattress in the world. It was more comfortable to sleep in a pod in space."

She turned to him and nodded. It was adorable.

"I'm so glad we went to the mattress store today. It would be criminal for you to have to sleep on this." She looked up at him from under her lashes and said, "I, for one, wouldn't want to be rolling around on this bed. I like your new mattress a lot better."

His let out his breath slowly. The tension between them was undeniable. And it was delicious. As their eyes connected, he felt so strongly the urge to lean forward and kiss her he had to clench his hand into a fist to stop himself. Again, he had to remind himself she was a professional. She was technically working right now, not inviting him to kiss her. Even though she was a really hot woman lying on his bed, he had to act honorably.

So, instead of ravishing her, he lamely said, "I think my telescope would look really good in that corner."

She followed his gaze and murmured her agreement. Was she disappointed that he wasn't reaching for her?

After a few moments, she rolled off the bed and said, "Let's take a look at these swatches against the walls."

The switch was so quick it took him a moment to catch up. "Sure," he said, sounding as puzzled as he felt.

She was already rummaging around in her bag and pulling out paint swatches. He couldn't believe how many colors could be called *gray*.

He didn't pay much attention as she talked through the swatches, holding them this way and that against the light. He told her he trusted her judgment, deferring to her excellent taste and decisive manner. Since the magazine photo he'd liked had conveniently listed all the paint colors used, they'd picked the same swatches. Now that they were here, Mila suggested that they go a little bit either way on the color spectrum, or whatever she called it, to make the most of the way the light hit the walls. Just like Ted at the mattress store, she narrowed it down to three, all of which he liked.

She said, "The best thing to do is buy little sample cans and paint squares on the wall so you can decide which one's best. Look at it in the morning and in the afternoon and in the evening."

That sounded sensible to him, so he agreed and said he'd go and buy the paint.

After a pause, she said, "Normally, I never do this, but if we get my dad or Finn to buy the paint, they'd get a discount. They're in the business."

He perked right up at that. "They're not in the business of painting walls, are they?"

She shook her head. However, she told him that they had lists of tradespeople they used. She'd ask her dad who was the best and get Hersch a couple of numbers. He smiled. Was there anything Mila Davenport couldn't organize?

"Your family are a pretty talented bunch."

She paused to think about it. "I guess we've all got our thing. If you want a hit song written, go to my brother Damien. We all know that Archer is only too ready to play your fine self in the biopic that Jay Malone is dying to make." She pretended she didn't see his shudder of revulsion. "And my dad and Finn can build you a great house, renovate the one you have, or build you a movie studio in your basement. Nick can develop an app for you. Actually, chances are you already use one of his. Erin will probably interview you when you move in."

"It's like a one-stop shop at the Davenport house."

She chuckled. "You'd be surprised. And if you need any tutoring in the classics, my mom's an expert."

"Duly noted."

She grinned, and he could see how full of love she was for her family.

Soon, they left the house. As a mark of confidence in his ownership, he left the new bedclothes behind.

# Chapter Fourteen

Mila was spending a rare night at home. She threw in some laundry, cooked herself a healthy meal, and then pulled out her phone to text Archer. He was waiting to hear if she'd been successful in convincing Tessa not to shop for her wedding dress at a thrift store. She wasn't certain if it would be breaking the mustn't-see-the-bride-or-her-dress-before-the-wedding rule if she let Archer know that Tessa would be wearing their mother's bridal gown. No doubt he'd never even noticed it before and had no clue what it looked like. She and Erin had admired it so often they could have drawn it from memory. They'd spent hours begging their mother to let them play dress-up in it and become the perfect princess or bride. However, their mother had been adamant it was not for play, and now Mila understood why. She just hoped the dry cleaner would be able to remove that stain. Tessa would be radiant in that gown.

There was a funny feeling in Mila's chest, almost as though something had stabbed her. Was it jealousy?

But no, she'd never want to wear that dress if she got married. Besides, she couldn't imagine tying herself down to one man. She'd always been the love-'em-and-leave-'em type. Maybe the whole wedding fever thing was getting to her. Everyone was so excited, it was hard not to get caught up in the romance of it all. Or maybe it was just that she found Herschel Greenfield so intriguing that he made her question her own ingrained life choices.

Shaking her head at her foolishness, she texted her brother.

*You don't need to worry. Tessa's going to wear the perfect wedding dress, and it won't be coming from a thrift store. It's Mom's. Surf tomorrow?*

She ended the message with the surfing emoji and a big picture of the sunshine.

She didn't always feel like surfing with her siblings—the ocean was her thing, her special place—but sometimes it could be a fun way of spending family time, and she had a feeling that Archer might need to get out and get some exercise. His leg had healed beautifully from the break, but she knew from experience that catching some waves and working on his balance would be really good for his PT. It wasn't fair only to rely on Tessa for his rehab—she now had two weddings to plan.

Thinking about surfing brought her mind back to

Herschel. She couldn't imagine being so afraid of the ocean that you would insist your house not have a view of the water. She so wanted to help him with this fear, but in this case, she couldn't even lead the astronaut to water, let alone make him surf.

Shaking her head, she put her clothes in the dryer and then sat in an armchair with her laptop balanced on the armrest. She toyed with the idea of catching up on some more email, but instead found herself heading straight to YouTube. Her fingers typed his name, and within seconds, she pulled up the video of Herschel singing "Happy Birthday" to his mom in space. She felt herself grin as he explained it was his mom's sixtieth birthday, and then he pulled out the guitar he'd taken up with him before revealing the cake he'd somehow managed to bake. It was decorated with LED lights for candles.

She remembered seeing bits of the video on the news and had been charmed, like the rest of the world. Her gaze darted to the bottom of the screen, and she saw that the video had millions of views. It was strange. Now that she knew him in real life, she knew Herschel was a private kind of guy. He wanted a house with lots of land so he could roam freely, away from any neighbors. He wanted privacy and quiet and to be close to nature. Yet here he was, making a happy spectacle of himself in space just for the love of his mom. She had to admire how he set aside his more introverted self to do something special for the number one woman in his life. She grinned again as the song ended and had to admit that she wanted that man. Badly.

As tended to happen with YouTube, another, related video began to load. This one was a news story loaded with the horrific details of how Hersch had nearly died. She drew away from the screen, afraid to watch though he'd made it out alive. As the story unfolded, she found her eyes filling with tears. It was almost unbearable to listen as the news reporters so calmly disclosed the rescue efforts. The malfunctioning capsule floundered in the stormy ocean, and one by one the astronauts were rescued. Just as it was Herschel's turn—the last man out—a ferocious wave knocked the doomed capsule sideways.

She shook her head at the screen. He must have been so scared.

One of the commentators, a former astronaut, explained how astronauts' muscles tended to atrophy while they were in space, and no matter how strong a swimmer Herschel Greenfield was, it would be all too easy to drown after months in microgravity. While the world held its collective breath, amazingly, miraculously, he was picked up. The footage was pretty rough, but she saw the brave way he lifted his hand in a wave as he was hauled up onto the rescue boat.

She wiped a tear off her cheek. How thoughtless

she'd been to push him to get back in the water—to offer surf lessons so many times. She vowed to stay away from the subject and respect what the man had been through.

Even as she had the thought, though, she knew deep down that he needed to find his way back—at least to be able to get his feet in the water, maybe swim a little bit.

The next video was a montage of his exploits as an Ironman competitor. She felt her jaw drop at how easy he made it look, though she knew it was physically grueling. Her jaw stayed dropped as she checked out his hot body. That man knew a thing or two about how to build muscle. The montage ended with his last competition, two years ago. He'd been a pretty high-level Ironman competitor, but he hadn't competed since that last space mission.

She could help him. She only hoped he would give her a chance.

* * *

Herschel had gone for a long run, come back, and done a good stint on the exercise bike. He'd even, God help him, looked at some home decorating shows on HGTV and then shaken his head at the preposterous designs some people liked. He just couldn't get excited about home décor without Mila Davenport around. And he couldn't get her out of his head.

Finally, he got into bed with his laptop. Pretending he was just going to check the news headlines, Hersch found himself on Google, doing a search on Mila Davenport. Obviously, he already knew a little about her—she'd been a champion surfer and on the cover of a sports magazine—but there were lots of old videos of her on YouTube. He was drawn to them and clicked on one where she'd just won a big competition in Australia. He lost his breath at her amazing feats on the water, but also by how beautiful she was in interviews afterward. She was so natural, so glorious and free. *Fearless* was the word that kept coming to his mind. She gave a big but humble smile as she received her medal and some pretty hefty prize money.

He watched another video, utterly entranced by the way she moved in harmony with the ocean. He even forgot for a moment how much he hated the damn water.

From the moment he'd met her, he'd found Mila gorgeous and sexy, but oddly, he found her more appealing now than he would have found her younger self. This more mature version was intriguing to him, and the fact that she'd gone through something difficult and triumphed only intensified her allure in his eyes. Yes, she'd been a goddess riding those waves, and maybe her smile wasn't quite as carefree, and she didn't look out at the world with the certainty she once had, but he thought her twisted path made her more interesting and probably more compassionate.

Sexy thoughts clouded his mind as she told an interviewer about her amazing ride, until his attention was suddenly brought back to the screen as right on camera, a guy, obviously another surfer, confidently strode toward Mila and gave her a huge kiss. He was over-muscled in a really show-offy way, and if that blond, streaky hair was natural, Herschel would shave off his own moustache and eat it.

In fact, Hersch felt his right hand clench into a fist. He wanted to punch the guy's lights out. He watched, glued to the scene and unable to look away, like it was a car crash. The surfer dude made sure that the minute he'd finished that inappropriate on-camera kiss, he kept the attention on himself by slinging an arm around Mila and turning to face the interviewer. He was stealing Mila's thunder, and Hersch hated it. What a jerk. No one should ever eclipse Mila like that.

Finally, he flipped to the next YouTube video, and there he encountered the story about her injury. He couldn't help but watch the ride. It looked terrifying—the massive wave curling over her, the way she stood on the board as though she owned the waves, ruled the ocean. The sky behind her was a perfect blue, the sun a blazing orb that made a dazzling spectacle of her long blonde hair. Her body was so confident, so strong, and yet lithe and supple. Her strength was incredible. And then, seemingly out of nowhere, the wave turned on her, huge and roaring, curling in a way that made him sick to his stomach, and she succumbed to its power and size. He felt physically ill watching her body swallowed whole by that wave, her board tossed into the air above her and then disappearing too. He was glued to the screen, watching in what felt like slow motion for her body to reappear, but it never did. The announcer, who had been going on about her perfect form and the great ride and relaying some of her stats, gasped, and then his voice changed as he relayed the fall. The camera moved away from the ocean and followed a medical team as they rushed from the beach to her aid. They, too, seemed so small and helpless against the backdrop of another huge wave that loomed in the background.

Hersch held his breath. Although he knew that she'd come through this accident and was alive and well, he couldn't help but fear for her safety. From what he could understand, the wave had taken her off course and slammed her onto a reef on her back, and she was left floundering, unable to swim back to shore.

Nausea struck Hersch so suddenly he put his head between his knees. His body began to shake as the memory of being swept out into the ocean took over. He practiced the deep-breathing techniques the medics had taught him. In through the nose, out through the mouth.

When he looked back at the screen, Mila was being

carried down the beach on a stretcher, a lock of her wet, blonde hair trailing behind. He reached out his hand and touched the screen, not even realizing at first that he was doing it.

* * *

By Thursday, Hersch's house deal was good to go. The money had transferred, and Hersch was due at her office any minute to pick up the keys. She was amazed at how her heart fluttered a little bit every time somebody new walked into the office. Was it him? And then she'd see it wasn't, and her heart would sink. She'd get her head back into work only for the door to open again... and more disappointment.

Honestly, she felt like a teenager. She couldn't remember the last time she'd felt like this about a guy. What was wrong with her? Clearly, she needed some sex. Maybe that was all she needed—for her and Hersch to burn up the sheets a little bit and get this out of her system. She couldn't stay this distracted. If things went on like this, she was going to make a mistake at work. It was like she had no control over her body anymore. She tingled just at the thought of him. Yep, she was woman enough to admit she had it bad.

When he finally did arrive, around midmorning, she could see through the glass wall of her office that he'd been out hiking or running or had come from the gym, because he had ruddy cheeks and extra-bright eyes and was wearing workout gear. She loved that in an office full of Hugo Boss and Armani suits, he showed up in a pair of bright red shorts that showed off excellent legs, running shoes, and a NASA T-shirt. He looked athletic and dorky, and she loved it.

She was finishing up a call, so she waved him into her office. He hesitated at the door as she said her good-byes and entered only after she smiled and beckoned him in again. Up close, he looked so healthy and sturdy that she couldn't help but compare the image to the man she'd watched on YouTube last night, who'd been swept into the ocean and nearly hadn't made it back.

She was suddenly flooded with relief to see him so vital. Almost unable to help herself, she got up from her desk and, without any further consideration, threw her arms around him. That sexy smell of him filled her nose, and she inhaled deeply.

Almost breathless, she whispered into his ear, "I'm so glad you're still alive."

He returned the hug, giving her a slightly awkward pat on the back, and then they pulled away.

She could see that he was taken aback by the hug and her overfamiliar greeting. Mentally, she kicked herself. How had her emotions gotten the better of her? She was used to being poised, to maintaining control of herself.

To try to regain some composure, she pretended

she was greeting him for the first time. "This is all such great news. I've never had a house sell so fast. The sellers—"

"Wait," he interrupted. "Why did you say what you said when I walked in? I mean, I'm glad I'm still alive, too, but it's not the normal way you greet everyone you sell a house to, is it?"

She wished she hadn't said anything. It had been the impulse of a moment. What on earth was wrong with her? She shook her head, but she had to be honest. "I went online and watched the video of you singing 'Happy Birthday' to your mom in space. I remember seeing it at the time, but I'd forgotten how adorable it was. And then, you know how YouTube delivers you the next video on a topic you're interested in? It was, well, the rescue operation." She couldn't go on, because she would tear up if she said any more about what she'd seen and how she felt.

He had a strange look on his face, and she thought maybe she'd upset him just by mentioning that terrible incident, but when he glanced up and caught her gaze, she saw a rueful twinkle. In a quiet, almost reverent voice, he said, "I watched you too. Old videos of you surfing. And then the same thing happened to me. I saw your accident." He blinked a few times and then swallowed hard. He held her gaze and said, "I'm so glad you're still alive too."

Mila's heart thudded, and her throat choked with

emotion. Those awful moments flashed into her brain, and she could almost feel the searing pain as she hit that reef in Australia.

They gazed at each other, bodies just inches apart. She wanted so badly to reach up and touch him. To whisper, *Everything is okay, everything is okay.* It was a tenderness she wasn't accustomed to, and again she was taken by surprise.

She would cry if she didn't shift the energy right away—and if there was one thing Mila didn't do, it was cry over the past. In a lighthearted way, she said, "What? That was just a normal day out in the surf. People break bones all the time, and they come back, and they heal, and they move on." She took a deep breath, and she could see that he wanted to say more, but she couldn't handle the emotion right now. "Listen, given that we've just done the quickest deal ever in real estate history, and you're getting the keys only a few days after seeing the house, I'm taking you out to celebrate."

He looked almost taken aback, and then he grinned. It completely transformed his face, and she felt herself melt a little as he said, "I was actually going to ask *you* out to dinner to celebrate. How's tomorrow night?"

She laughed, delighted that he was obviously interested in continuing to spend time together. "Great minds," she said. "We can fight over the check at the end. Sound good?"

"Sounds great," he said, "but I'm going to win that fight. My mom did not raise me to let a lady pick up the check—especially when she's found and delivered my dream home."

She laughed and was thankful that not only did she have a date of sorts, but the awkwardness between them had fully disappeared.

"And more good news," he said, glancing at his watch. "If I call before noon, I can get my bed delivered today."

At the mention of the word *bed*, she suddenly felt like a blushing virgin as the image of the two of them tangled up in his brand-new sheets engulfed her with such a powerful burst of lust that she had to take a breath. She glanced up at him to find such an intensity in his gaze that she knew he was feeling it too.

But first things first. All business now, she said, "Let's get these papers signed, and then I can give you the keys."

"I am very much looking forward to that."

"And," she continued, "since this is my hometown, and you're new to the area, I'll book us a restaurant. Seven sound okay?"

Again, he looked a little surprised that she'd taken the lead, but then he said, "Perfect." He looked down at himself as if he'd just remembered he'd come to her office still in his workout gear. "I've got lots to do until I see you tomorrow."

# Chapter Fifteen

Maybe she had been a tiny bit worried that Herschel would show up for dinner in clueless, badly chosen clothing, but she was pleased to find, when she picked him up outside his hotel the next evening, that he was wearing a stylish pair of designer blue jeans and the nicest shirt she'd yet seen him in. It wasn't that she was shallow—although a man who took pride in his appearance was a turn-on—but she'd spent more time that she'd admit picking out her outfit for the evening and didn't want to feel foolish. It wasn't like this was even a real date—just a dinner to celebrate the house deal, which was more than the usual glass of champagne with clients, but not enough to make her think Herschel was going to make a move.

Slipping into the passenger seat, he said, "You look beautiful." He said it not the way a practiced womanizer tells every woman she's beautiful, but like a man who was genuinely taking in and appreciating what he saw. Somehow that made her feel way more beautiful than usual. Because, although she'd been blessed with her mom's good genes, a man hadn't made her feel special in a very long time.

She thanked him and then looked down at herself. She wasn't sure how smartly dressed Hersch would be, so she'd chosen a very simple coral cotton dress from the dozens she'd tried on. Now she realized she'd made the perfect choice. It was cut beautifully, with a scoop neck, and it clung in all the right places. She'd added minimal gold jewelry, gone light on her makeup so that it left her bronzed and glowy, and let her long blonde hair flow free.

"We're heading to Bentley's," she said. Because she knew the owners, she told him, she'd made sure to reserve her favorite table—in a corner with a view of the ocean. It wasn't until she saw his reaction that she realized her mistake. She paused and then said, "I didn't even consider you might not want to have an ocean view. I'm so sorry. They just have wonderful food, and I figured—"

But he cut her off. "That's okay. I'll just be looking at you anyway."

If there had been any doubt in her mind whether this might actually be a date, then some of that was squashed by that cute, flirty comment. Again, she felt a sweet stab of lust. Because he didn't pay idle compliments. He always told the truth. It was charming and refreshing.

She relaxed and drove the familiar streets, enjoying

the soft evening light and pointing out a few of her favorite cafés and bars, already hoping Hersch might want to extend the evening with a nightcap after dinner.

When they entered the restaurant, they were hit with the warm, buzzy atmosphere she loved so much about the place. The lights were low, and the room glowed. She turned to see his reaction. He looked around and then said, "This place is packed. How did you get a reservation on such short notice? And, I'm guessing, one of the best tables in the house?"

She was pleased he'd noticed that this place was in demand, but shrugged as though it were nothing. "First of all, I've lived here all my life. Between me, my mom and dad, and my brothers and sisters, there's pretty much nobody we don't know or at least know of. And then, in the business I'm in, you get 'em coming in and you get 'em going out. I sold a house to the owners' son and his wife. It was a difficult deal, and I saved it for them. So yeah, I can always get a table here."

He looked impressed. "I can see you're a good woman to know."

There was a kind of flirty undertone, and she responded in kind. "You'd better believe it."

Apart from making sure to get her favorite table, she'd also made a few requests ahead of time. After they'd been seated at the most intimate, candlelit table, two flutes of champagne appeared in front of them. He raised one eyebrow at her, and she lifted her glass to tap his. "Congratulations on your new home, Hersch."

Before he sipped, he said, "I couldn't have done it without you."

This was, of course, true, and she was glad he'd noticed. She'd even surprised herself with how fast she'd acted on the house and then wrapped up this deal. Was it just good fortune, or had she worked even harder for this hottie of a client? They sipped the champagne, and she sighed with pleasure. She loved a glass of vintage champagne.

Hersch appeared to feel the same as he took another sip and then asked with a twinkle in his eye, "Have you ordered my whole dinner? Or should I look at the menu?"

She laughed and set down her glass. "I organized the table and the champagne. You're on your own for everything else."

He settled back with the menu, which tended to feature a lot of fresh fish and locally grown produce. She quickly decided on the ahi tuna steak with local vegetables. She took a moment to study him. Even just choosing from a menu, his face had a serious look, as though the most trivial decision deserved the most careful consideration. As someone who could be a little impulsive, she found that trait quite charming. When he moved, the candlelight caught a glint of gold around his neck, and she felt herself enjoying every small detail of the evening already.

As soon as he closed his menu with an air of decision, she leaned forward to study the gold chain he wore. "That looks like some sort of charm. What is it?"

Reflexively, Hersch touched the chain and looked thoughtful. "My Saint Christopher's medal. It belonged to my grandfather, who fought in World War II. He was British and flew for the RAF. His name was Herschel too. The Saint Christopher's was handed down to me mostly, I think, because I also got his name. He was shot down, but he survived, believing that Saint Christopher had protected him on his journey. I'm not sure if the medal saved him or not, but I've always liked the story. Maybe it's superstitious... No, it's definitely superstitious, and I laugh at myself regularly, as a man who believes so strongly in science, but I never take it off." He paused and looked pensive. "Maybe when I nearly died out there, my grandfather was watching out for me. I don't know, but I don't plan to take it off any time soon."

"I get that," Mila said. "Why mess with fate?" And then she added, "Plus, it suits you."

He smiled and touched the chain again.

The waiter came over then and recommended the crab cakes as an appetizer, as well as the fresh oysters.

She raised her brows at Hersch, who said, "Why don't we have both and share?"

She loved this idea and ordered her main meal. She waited, intrigued, to see what kind of appetite Hersch had and was impressed when he chose the steak and lobster. When the waiter inquired about wine, Hersch looked to Mila and said, "I don't tend to drink much, out of habit from my training, but I'd join you in a bottle if you'd like?"

Mila smiled. He had such a charming way of saying things. She said, "They have really good wines by the glass. I don't need a whole bottle either."

So they each chose a glass of good wine. She went for white and he for red. Both were California wines from the best wineries.

With everything ordered, Mila sat back in her chair and really relaxed. She looked at the hot man opposite her and decided she wanted to know everything about him. "So," she said, setting down her champagne flute, "I don't meet many astronauts, like pretty much every other person on the planet. What's it like?"

He chuckled. "The question I get asked most often? 'How do you go to the bathroom in space?'"

She said, "I'm going to guess you talk to a lot of school kids."

He nodded. "Yes, ma'am. Public outreach is just part of the job."

"Well, don't worry. I'm not going to ask about your bathroom habits. What I really want to know is what it *feels* like to be out there. It's so hard for me to imagine."

As she had known he would, he paused as though he was really considering her question so he could give the best answer he could. But he didn't look away, holding Mila's gaze as she anticipated his answer. "My last mission was to the International Space Station. When you live there, there's a small community, and even though it's miles away from Earth in a zero-gravity environment, it becomes very routine. Honestly, you'd be surprised at how mundane the days are. Full of cleaning and checks and documenting the most minute details. And exercise, of course. We spend two hours every morning exercising to keep our bodies regulated and to ward off as much muscle atrophy as we can. Time in space weakens and ages us."

She stared at him, not quite believing that his strong, muscular body could ever weaken. But after watching his crash and hearing the commentator mention his muscle atrophy while swimming, she decided to stay clear of the subject for fear of upsetting him. Instead, she said, "First of all, whatever you do in space is not boring, because it's *space*. And second, take me back to zero gravity. I mean, do you have to, like, strap yourself down to get any work done?"

He shook his head. "It's not that bad. I strap in to sleep in a sleeping bag that attaches to the wall."

She was puzzled. "How do you lie down in space?"

He laughed a little. "You don't. Because there's no

gravity, you don't know whether you're up or down or sideways, and the funny thing is that it doesn't matter to your body. I tend to go vertical just because, and you don't need a pillow, because your head's not going to flop, so you kind of sleep upright, I guess."

She shook her own head in response. "Now I'm super glad we got you that luxurious new mattress. You deserve it."

He grinned, and then the fresh oysters appeared.

As they ate, he said, "I may not want to go into the ocean, but I do love the food that comes out of it."

"And what were you working on up there?"

"A lot of what we do is scientific research. I was a medical doctor first and originally thought I'd practice as a doctor all my life, but I'd always had this fascination with space. Well, when your name is Herschel, and you're named after an astronomer, you get an interest in the stars and the sky along with it—at least, I did. When I was a kid, I loved hearing all the stories about my grandfather in the war, flying fighter planes, and then my dad was a commercial pilot. He passed away five years ago. Cancer. So I guess flying seemed like something I should do." He paused. "I just went a little higher than they did." He chuckled. "I do like to take things to the next level sometimes."

Mila wondered if he'd be willing to take things between them to the next level. She finished her flute of champagne and then said, "It sounds like flying is in your blood."

He nodded. "I think so. I already had my pilot's license, and when they recruit astronauts, they look for people with STEM degrees—that's science, technology, engineering, and medicine. I had the medicine, but I also had a PhD in molecular biology."

She was blown away by how modest this man was. "Wait—so you're Dr. Herschel Greenfield."

He nodded again, looking almost bashful. "Both MD and PhD. That is correct."

"Wow. I can't even imagine what kind of competition there is to get into the astronaut program."

"Oh, it's fierce. You have to have the right background in education. They really like some flying experience, which is why a lot of jet fighter pilots have become astronauts in the past. They used to come more from the military. and now it tends to be quite a few from the scientific and medical communities. But yeah, something like less than one percent of the applicants—and we're talking solid, capable applicants—even get into the training program. And that is rigorous. You also have to have the fitness and the right kind of personality to live in a small space for a long time. We are thoroughly screened."

She was fascinated and just loved how animated he got when he talked about his favorite subject. It was like she was finally getting to see the real man.

He glanced out at the sky, where the night had

crept in and the stars were coming out, and wistfully said, "Do you know what the word *astronaut* means?"

"No," she murmured, intrigued.

He turned his gaze back to hers. "Star sailor. Isn't that beautiful? I like to think the Herschel I'm named for, that astronomer who added so much to our initial body of knowledge about space, would be thrilled to think of a much later Herschel actually sailing around in the stars. I know I'm a man of science, but I have to tell you, being out there is magical. Earth—its beauty echoes through the dark. It's blue because so much of earth is covered by water and from space it seems almost fragile. I wish I had the words to really describe it to you. It's the most humbling experience you could ever imagine. You just stand there, gaping, realizing what a tiny cog in the universe you are, but also how lucky you are to be a part of something so amazing. "

She felt a whisper down the back of her neck like the lightest brush of fingertips. He was so sexy and so darned thoughtful. It was almost too much to handle. She felt herself tipping from wanting him into *desperately* wanting him. Like right now, on this very table.

Trying to get her focus back on what he was saying and not the undercurrent of attraction, she asked, "It sounds incredible. And you describe it beautifully. What kind of research did you do at the space station?"

"I was part of a team working on Alzheimer's research."

"Really?"

He nodded. "To make it simple, it's much easier to look at the mechanics of the disease when gravity isn't getting in your way. A lot of the best research now is being done in space."

"I had no idea. That's so cool." She glanced at him as their plates were taken away. "So, you're super smart, super fit, and you're working to eradicate one of the worst diseases on the planet."

He paused and looked at her. "Well, I wouldn't have put it that way myself, but some of that is true, yes."

The waiter brought their wine, and they clinked glasses again. "A second cheers to the woman who rustled up my dream home like it was a quick omelet." He smiled. "So I already know from working with you that you're an excellent Realtor, with an engaging personality and a head for business. With the help of YouTube, I've also learned you're an accomplished athlete, and the other term I would use for you is *fearless*."

She chuckled, delighted at how neatly he'd summed her up, and even if it was a slightly flattering picture, it was also accurate.

Then he grew serious. "But I bet it wasn't easy making the transition from surfing champ to Realtor."

She shook her head and for a moment lowered her gaze to her wine. Then she looked up and said honestly, "No, it wasn't. But it's worked out okay."

It wasn't like Mila to go into her sad story, and as though he silently understood that about her, he redirected the conversation and asked, "How did you get started surfing? I mean, how does somebody even get to that level at the young age you were when you were competing?"

This was much easier to talk about. She remembered being young and full of an ambition that at times had been overwhelming. "My dad put me on a surfboard when I was about two years old."

"Two?" he asked, clearly stunned. "You're joking."

She laughed. "No. I had my own little life jacket, and he put me on the front of his board, and we'd ride in together on the waves. It's a pretty common way to teach really little kids."

"It might seem common to you, but it sounds remarkable to me."

She shook her head. "It's what happens when you grow up by the ocean. By the time I was three, I was on my own tiny board. But he was always out there with me, making sure I was safe and didn't end up in any riptides. He loves to tell the story of me coming onto the beach and saying, 'More, more,' and he'd take me out into the surf again, and I'd say, 'More, more.' Of all the kids, he said I was his water baby. I don't know—I got hooked. I love the water. I love being on it and in it and on top of it. I love to be in wave patterns, figuring out where that perfect sweet spot is. I took dance when I was younger, not because I wanted to be a ballerina, but because I needed better control of my muscles and better balance for surfing."

He said, "That's funny. When I watched those videos of you, even when I watched you the other day coming in to the beach or out there surfing, I thought to myself, 'My goodness, she's dancing with the waves.'"

She laughed out loud, delighted with him. "That's how it feels when I'm out there. But the sea is an unpredictable partner, and sometimes it trips you up."

"Right."

There was a short pause. "But you were right about having to be fearless. I guess I had natural talent, just something I was born with and that my dad nurtured, and then combine that with years of training, and you're almost there. But if I hadn't been fearless? Well, I never would have entered the world of championship surfing."

There was another pause while the waiter delivered their meals. As he set down their plates, she felt that Herschel was as eager to keep the conversation going as she was. She picked up her fork and then set it down again. "It was fun while it lasted. Now that you've seen the video, you know all about the accident that broke my back and ended my career."

"I saw what happened, yes. But I don't know how

it made you feel. Not just physically, but emotionally."

She swallowed. "At first, they weren't sure I'd ever walk again." She paused, allowing herself only a few seconds to look back at those dark, dark days. "But somehow I knew I would. Even as I was lying in bed in the hospital in agony, I knew deep down I'd surf again. Maybe not at the pro level, but I would figure it out. There are people out there who surf on one leg, and I worked as hard as anybody's ever worked in rehab, and I got there. I walked again.

"Luckily, I had my own house here in Carmel and the greatest family ever. Everybody pulled together to help me and cheer me up when I was feeling down, and they made sure I had everything I needed and got to all my appointments. So I became stronger and stronger, and I got my confidence back. One day, I told the doctor I was ready to try surfing, and she said, 'No, you're not.' But I knew my body, and I knew I could do it. Besides, I was almost at the breaking point of frustration."

She paused and ate a mouthful of succulent fish, toying with what she was going to say next. "I've never even told my family this, but one day I just snuck out and went to a beach in Monterey where nobody knew me."

"Were you at all nervous?"

"More than you can imagine."

He shook his head. "Oh, I can imagine."

"But when I saw the ocean up close again, I realized just how much I had missed her. It wasn't painful at all. It was like seeing an old friend again after coming home from a long trip. And without thinking about it, I got out there, and I surfed. It wasn't pretty, it didn't last long, and my back hurt like hell afterward, but I did it. From that point on, I got my life back."

He looked fascinated, riveted almost. "Good for you," he said. "I'm still struggling with that."

She put her hand on his. It felt like the most natural thing in the world. "You'll get there."

He turned his hand and clasped hers. There was strength and steadiness in that grip. He said, "Yes, I will." And then, as if embarrassed by his admission, he withdrew his hand and began to eat.

She followed his lead, but then decided not to let the subject drop. "You know, honestly, when the doctors told me I'd never surf again professionally, I thought my world had ended. It took a long time for me to get over that and see a way forward without surf competitions being my whole life anymore."

He put down his fork and then leaned closer to her across the table. "I always thought I was okay with dying. Obviously, space missions are as safe as they can be, but I do a dangerous job. But when I got sucked down into the ocean, it was like the sea was deliberately trying to kill me, and I was helpless." He swallowed. "Maybe that was the worst—being so helpless. Even after I was rescued, that's what the nightmares were about—the ocean sucking me under." He closed his eyes for a moment and then opened them. They were full of emotion. "I've never admitted these things to anyone else."

She said, "Only you know about that illicit surfing trip. I've never told a single soul."

"I'm honored by your confidence, and I'll keep it to myself."

"And I'll keep yours." After a pause, she said, "Maybe you don't have to go in the water quite yet. Maybe you can give yourself some more breathing room."

He suddenly looked very firm. "If I don't get back in the water—and soon—I'll never trust myself to go back into space. And no one else will trust me either."

As if exhausted by their confessions, they both began to eat heartily, enjoying the candlelight and the atmosphere of the restaurant with its tables of chattering friends and couples.

She said, "Enough sad stories. How did it feel walking into the house as the homeowner for the first time?"

His smile was huge. "It felt great. I love everything about that house. And thank you for sending over your dad's number. We've already been in touch. He said he'd hook me up with some painters."

She nodded. "I knew he would. My dad's the best."

"I hope I get to meet him. He sounds like a really great guy."

It suddenly crossed her mind to invite him to her brother's wedding. But she stopped herself. It was ten days away, and she didn't really know Herschel well enough yet, and she wasn't at all sure she wanted to bring him to such an important family event. Even the fact that she'd thought of asking him made her pause. If she brought a guest to her brother's wedding, her family would immediately think she had a new partner. No. She wasn't going there. Instead, she said, "I'm going to take you on my secret special tour of all the highlights of Carmel-by-the-Sea. I think you'll love it."

"I can't imagine a better tour guide. Thank you."

After they both ordered coffee and declined dessert, Hersch pulled out his wallet, and she could see he was looking for a waiter. She said, "The other thing I did in advance? Pay the check. Welcome to Carmel, from me and Ferguson Realty. It's on the company tonight."

He put his wallet away but raised his eyebrows. Although he thanked her, she realized that Hersch was disappointed. Had she messed up by putting the dinner on the company card? It wasn't unusual to wine and dine an extra-special client rather than send a gift basket. But from his expression, he'd thought their meal was more special than that... and it was. She could kick herself.

She lingered at the table, waiting to see if he might

lean over and kiss her, but no, all the intimacy of the evening had disappeared. She ached with disappointment.

"If you really do feel that you'd like to get back in the water soon, come to my beginners drop-in surfing class tomorrow."

"Maybe," he said, looking unsure, and then he stood to pull out her chair.

The more she got to know Herschel, the more she wanted him. She just hoped she hadn't messed things up by being her usual assertive self. She couldn't bear the thought that Hersch might walk away from this night thinking she was just his real estate professional.

# Chapter Sixteen

Mila had hoped that Herschel would turn up at her Saturday afternoon surf lesson, but she wasn't very surprised when he didn't.

Her students had already gone home, and she was slow to pack up, each wetsuit feeling heavier than usual. She'd never been like this with any other man, and it was dawning on her that maybe it was because no other man had so quickly meant this much to her.

She was so lost in thought that it took her several moments to realize that someone was calling her name.

When she turned, there was Hersch, a sheepish expression on his face. The relief was almost overwhelming.

"I missed the class, I know," he said, gesturing toward the beach. "I thought I could do this, but then... Well, I kept finding reasons not to... and I was moving my things over to the new house. And then, well, I had a stern word with myself, and here I am. But I can see it's too late."

Mila was so happy to see him that she blurted, "No, we can still do this. We'll start slow, okay? We'll just get you into a wetsuit, and you can remember what it feels like to be in the ocean. Then you take the wetsuit off. That's it."

It hadn't escaped her notice that Hersch had been admiring her body in her own wetsuit. She tried to keep her cool and focus on what a big deal this was for him to show up.

"Okay," he said.

She got him a wetsuit and said, "I'm sorry they're all wet from the lesson. It's much harder to get them on."

Hersch took the suit from her. "I'm used to wetsuits from my Ironman training."

He began to unbutton his shirt. Hersch was even more buff than she had imagined. His skin was tanned and smooth, the muscles perfectly formed, and he was toned—so, so toned—she almost couldn't believe it. It was like the man was carved from marble. When he unzipped his jeans to reveal his swim shorts, her breath quickened, and she wasn't sure she could control herself. She longed to reach out and touch him.

But as she caught his gaze, she saw the fear in his eyes, and she vowed to keep her lust in check and give Hersch the support he needed to get back in the water. Even if it was exquisitely painful not to lean over and lick those muscles.

He pulled on the wetsuit, and she asked, "How does it feel to be back in a wetsuit?"

She could see Hersch was trying to steady his thoughts, and then he nodded. "It's okay. It doesn't feel as bad as I thought." There was a pause, and he added quietly, "Maybe because you're here with me."

She let herself beam. "I can't take the credit. This is all your courage. And it's a great first step back to the water." She allowed herself to touch him lightly on the shoulder.

After a tantalizing moment, Hersch said, "I didn't mention this last night, but in one of your surfing videos, I saw you'd just won a championship, in Australia."

She nodded. It had been a proud moment in her career. "Surfest in Newcastle."

Now he looked a little perturbed. "I was watching it, and you were being interviewed and holding up your trophy, and then some guy muscled his way in and kissed you."

She felt the glory of that recalled moment immediately start to fade. "That was Travis." She'd have left it at that, but he glanced up at her.

"Travis?"

This was not something she was prepared to talk about with Hersch. Or anyone ever. She sighed. She'd already told him secrets she'd never told anybody else. But maybe another glimpse of her past wouldn't be so bad, especially after Hersch had been so honest with her.

"Travis was my boyfriend at the time. He was another surfer, so he got it, he got the lifestyle. But if I'm honest, he was never going to make it all the way. He looked for shortcuts. He just wasn't good enough. At the time, it didn't occur to me that our being a couple made him look good and feel important in the surf world. I think he really thought I could help him in his career. And he liked being in the limelight. A lot. Even if that meant stealing mine. I was probably a fool to let him, but I was young, and we were living the same crazy schedules, and maybe I turned a blind eye to his less desirable qualities."

She turned away to look out at the ocean, gazing not at the water but at the past. She'd been so hurt by Travis dumping her when she'd been at her lowest, she had vowed never to trust a man again. Since Travis, she'd had a series of flings. Fun and exciting but nothing serious. But now she realized it was more than just her vow to herself—she was actually afraid to trust a man again.

When she looked back, Hersch had folded his arms across his chest, and his usual serious expression had soured into a fierce grimace. "I wanted to punch that guy's lights out when I saw him kissing you in that video. Now I want to track him down and knock his teeth out."

Mila was surprised—in a good way. Hersch always seemed so mild-mannered. She loved this powerful, angry energy bubbling up from somewhere deep inside. It was sexy. She was also, frankly, pretty flattered that he'd been that jealous of Travis.

She said, "I've worked really hard to fall in love with my new life and let the old one go. I guess one of the blessings of what happened to me is seeing Travis for who he was. Being half of the golden couple of surfing suited him really well, but being the partner of an injured woman whose career was over? Not so much."

She shook her head. "When we found out I might never walk again, Travis said he needed some space, like he was the injured one." Somehow, the old rejection was no longer so painful when she told Hersch, "He's still taking that space. I haven't heard from him since."

Hersch let out an agitated breath. "Then that guy is an idiot. Because I can't imagine ever letting a woman like you go."

Mila stepped closer, wanting to feel Hersch's arms around her. But something made her stop. The pain of Travis's betrayal felt raw again, and she had already made a fool of herself at dinner last night, ruining the moment. If Hersch wanted something more between them, then he'd have to make the move. Quietly, she said, "Now let's get you out of that suit."

To her surprise, Hersch shook his head. "I'm in the damned suit. If I don't go in the water now, I never will."

Mila let out her breath. She could see how Hersch was struggling to overcome his demons. His bravery was so admirable—and sexy—and again she had the thought that this man was so different and so much more special than any she'd encountered before. Her barriers weren't strong enough to stop the intensity of her feelings for him. "Are you sure?"

He nodded. "I'm sure."

\* \* \*

Hersch walked across the sand so slowly it was like time itself was slowing down. It was the last Saturday in May and a sunny one at that, so the beach was alive with kids building sandcastles, dogs running and playing, couples walking hand in hand, a group of teenagers horsing around. A few swimmers bobbed in the water, but they wore regular swimsuits. He was the only person in a wetsuit, as the waves weren't big enough today to lure surfers. He didn't care. Mila was right. Just putting on the wetsuit had reminded him of Ironman training, of long swims in cold water. The least he could do now that he'd wiggled into it was put his toes in the water. His feet were bare, and he felt the sand soft beneath his feet.

He had spent all night and day thinking about Mila

and wondering why he hadn't just followed his instincts and kissed her at dinner. They'd both shared so much of themselves with each other, the moment was there. Then, when she'd revealed the check had been paid for by her company, he'd lost his nerve. She'd still been acting the part of his Realtor, even though the deal had gone through. And in that moment of hesitation, all the reasons why he'd remained single had come back to him.

And yet, it was like he had a fever, and he was burning for Mila Davenport. So after a long time deliberating, moving a few things over to the new place, organizing things the way he liked them, getting his new bed set up, and booking painters, he had finally taken the plunge and come down to the beach. Yes, it was after the lesson she had offered him, but he was here all the same. And now, with Mila's help, he was back in a wetsuit for the very first time since his accident. There was no way he could have made it this far without her.

Suddenly, he felt Mila take his hand. Her skin was smooth and soft, and her fingers felt like they'd been made to twine with his.

"You've got this," she said and squeezed his hand. "I'm already impressed that you showed up. You walked over the sand. You don't have to go any farther."

"I can go farther." His tone was more gruff than

he'd intended.

"Okay, then—just walk in up to your ankles. That's all you have to do."

He nodded grimly and didn't let go of her hand as they walked to the edge of the water. She must be able to feel how tense he had grown, but she didn't say anything. In fact, she might even be holding her breath, waiting for him to move. It was a good thing she'd been a pro surfer and was used to holding her breath, because for a long, long time, he remained standing at the edge of the surf without the water reaching him.

They kept holding hands as the waves advanced with the incoming tide, and the frothy edge of a wave tickled his toes. He fought the urge to turn and run, fought the panic rising in his chest. *You can do this,* he said to himself. *You can do this.*

A toddler screamed with delight, and gulls wheeled overhead, echoing the sound.

She remained quiet and then took the tiniest step forward, ever so gently showing him the way. Would he follow her? She looked back, that very question in her eyes. Yes, damn it, he would.

His leg could have weighed ten thousand pounds, it was so hard to move it forward even an inch. But he did it. And then he got the other one to meet it. Sweat broke out on his brow.

She said, "You're doing great," in a soothing voice that told him she understood. If Mila could get back to surfing after breaking her back, he could take another step forward. It took everything in him, but he did it, and then a wave broke over his foot.

A whoosh of breath rushed from her mouth as she cried out with joy. "You did it!"

He was stunned. "I can't believe I'm in the ocean again."

She gave him the biggest smile he'd ever seen. "I never had a doubt."

With her encouragement ringing in his ears, he took another step and another, until he inhaled sharply. The water was up to his ankles. He'd done it!

It was humiliating to find that he was trembling. But then Mila threw her arms around him. "I am so proud of you," she murmured into his ear.

Now he was shaking in a whole new way. Her body fit perfectly against his, their damp wetsuits feeling like skin on skin. It was exquisite. He wanted to stay locked in that moment forever, but he couldn't quite let go of the fact he was standing in water again. The fear kept crawling back like a nasty parasite, eating away at his courage.

He murmured, "I can't do any more." It hurt to admit it, but he had to be honest with her.

She pulled away, beaming. "You did great. There's no need to go in any farther. This was a big step."

He took a step back then, a giant one, away from the water. Then he looked down at himself. "I feel kind of stupid now, wearing a wetsuit to put my toes in the water."

She took the same step back until they were level again, and then she leaned in. Their gazes locked, and with the most tender touch he'd ever experienced, she gently pressed her lips to his.

He felt the quiver in Mila's body as she kissed him. In that moment, a phrase went through his head. *She's everything.*

He didn't even know where that came from. But in that moment, she *was* everything. She was a water goddess, and he was a man of the stars and planets. He felt almost as though Earth and sky were merging. He deepened the kiss and felt her lick into him. He was rock hard in a second and felt a need for her that was almost painful. She made a sound in her throat, a low hum. He pulled her closer and she clung tighter.

The kiss could have lasted seconds or hours. He wouldn't have been able to say. And then slowly, she pulled away, her lips pink and swollen.

# Chapter Seventeen

For a moment, Mila let herself stare into Hersch's warm gray eyes. They were filled with lust, as she knew her own must be. She sighed. "I never thought I'd kiss a man with a moustache."

He grinned down at her. "If I shave it off, can we do it again?"

"I need to kiss you again to make up my mind."

Hersch placed his big, strong hands in the curves above her hipbones and pulled her back into him. He kissed her so deeply, so passionately, it was like she'd never been kissed before. His moustache was soft and nicer than she could have imagined. *So this is what it really feels like,* she thought, and yielded to his embrace.

This kiss was even better than the first, slower and more searching, as though he was ready to find ways to bring her pleasure.

At last, they pulled apart, and she said, "You just made my head spin."

Instead of smiling as she'd hoped, he looked deadly serious. "Mila Davenport, my head has been spinning since the minute I met you." Then he did smile. "So what's the verdict on the moustache?"

"Keep it," she said.

And then suddenly, it hit her. It was as if she'd been in a foggy haze where she'd forgotten she shouldn't kiss him. And now, all she wanted to do was get out of there and process what had just happened. Except here they were, in wetsuits that they'd have to get out of… and get half naked in the process. She shook her head. How had she gotten herself into this predicament?

Hersch must have been able to sense the change in her and didn't want to push things, because he said, "Let's get these wet things off." He looked down at the wetsuit.

She nodded, and they walked back to their clothes silently, both lost in thought.

She turned her back to him to get dressed, and he did the same. But once he was fully clothed again, she could tell he wanted to talk. "Mila—"

But she shook her head, her damp hair swinging across her face. She couldn't let him say whatever it was he was about to say, not without her having some time to think first.

"I'm proud of what you accomplished today, Hersch. It's incredible. Really." She stopped there, deliberately not mentioning the last ten minutes of the hottest kiss of her life. "I'm so sorry, but I need to be somewhere else in a few minutes."

She was meeting Erin and Tessa to go dress shopping, and she still had to pack up the van. She wasn't sorry to have to leave. She had a lot to think about.

He nodded. "Thank you for being there with me on my first steps to getting back my own fearlessness." He paused. "And I want you to know, those were the two best kisses of my life."

He turned then to let her go, and it was as if her whole world flipped upside down. He had done what she wanted, but now she couldn't help but stare at the back of his sexy silhouette as he walked away. It took everything she had not to call him back.

But she resisted.

In times of crisis, she had three ways of working things out in her head. One, talk to her mom. Two, talk to Erin. And three, go surfing. She didn't feel like talking to anyone. Instead, she felt achingly alone, there on the beach, in the afterburn of those kisses. She knew that what had just happened went far beyond a kiss. And it was blowing up her world in a way that rattled her to the core.

As she packed up the van, returned it, and then went home to change for her shopping trip, Mila was pulsing with need and desire and want. She could still taste Herschel—his lips, the brushy feel of his moustache, which she'd thought she'd hate but had actually kind of liked. She could feel his body against hers, and one very prominent part of his body had made it very clear that he was seriously interested in her.

She changed into a dress that was easy to pull on and off, and heels, so shopping for a dress suitable to wear as Tessa's bridesmaid would be easy. The three women had great fun checking out the boutiques in town, refusing Tessa's suggestion that they at least take a peek in the thrift stores. They agreed on a sea shade of turquoise, and then Tessa insisted that Erin and Mila choose different dresses in the same color palette. "I don't want you to feel like you're matching dolls," she explained.

This was great news, as Mila and Erin were different in size, shape, and complexion. Mila found a great dress at her favorite boutique, and a couple of stores later, Erin found a dress cut more to her style in a nearly identical color. They both fell in love with silver heels at the shoe store, and they were done.

It was a laughing group who went out for a drink to celebrate. Then Erin had to go, as she had an event to cover for the *Sea Shell*. Tessa was meeting Arch, and so Mila found herself alone on a Saturday night. She hadn't wanted to talk about Hersch with Erin and Tessa, but her mind had been distracted.

Now she walked around her house in a daze. She put away her new purchases and ate some dinner. She lifted some weights and did some squats until her body was pretty much screaming at her. TV couldn't hold her attention. Same with a book Erin had pressed on her. Finally, she checked her watch. It wasn't that late. She texted Erin.

*You still awake?*

The answer came back almost immediately. *Just reading a novel. What's up?*

She called her sister and said, "Picture this. Me, looking very fine if I do say so myself, with a gorgeous man who I've been eyeing up and down."

"Herschel Greenfield," Erin said, as though it was obvious. Her sister saw way too much.

"Right. And I can tell he's totally into me, and I'm totally into him. We had dinner to celebrate the deal on his house going through."

"Aha," Erin said, sounding triumphant. "Not the traditional gift basket, then?"

Mila rolled her eyes. "Anyway. We go for a beautiful, romantic dinner. His idea, I might add. But instead of ending the evening with a kiss, he just switches off when I say the check is on the company, and then we part ways."

Erin sighed. "That's pretty similar to how this chapter of my novel ended. They missed the moment."

"Yeah, but my life isn't a romance novel, Erin, and I'm used to dinner ending in something a little more... hot. And satisfying. It was like I didn't even get past the prologue."

She'd expected shock and horror from her sister that her hot date hadn't ended in a kiss. What she hadn't expected was a loud peal of laughter. She laughed so hard and so long that Mila nearly hung up.

"What is so amusing?"

Erin had to gasp, and then Mila could hear her taking a sip of water. She could picture her sister, red in the face, tears running down her cheeks. So not the reaction she'd been going for.

"I'm sorry. It's just so funny. I cannot believe a man actually didn't take the first opportunity to jump you. Has that ever happened in your whole life?"

She was pretty sure it hadn't. "Beside the point. Because we *did* kiss. Just a few hours ago."

"Why didn't you say? I thought you were acting strange when we were shopping."

"I didn't want to talk boy trouble when Tessa's all loved up."

"So. You kissed."

"Yeah."

She decided to leave out the details about Hersch and the water. He had trusted her with his deepest fear, and Erin didn't need to know what they'd been doing when the kiss happened.

One of the things she liked about Erin, and probably the reason she'd called her, was that she didn't rush into speech. She took a moment to think things through. Funny. Hersch did that too.

Finally, Erin said, "How was the kiss?"

"Imagine fireworks, the greatest surf ride of your

life, and the best chocolate in the world, all wrapped into one."

"That good," Erin breathed.

"Better. And yet, I walked away. He was going to take it further, and I just couldn't go there. I had to meet you two, but I didn't even suggest we get together tonight. I felt thrown off course."

Erin paused again. "It's okay not to leap into something with someone new. Sometimes you need a little time to adjust to how someone makes you feel. It can be overwhelming."

This was why she'd called Erin. Already, she was feeling calmer. "Yeah, exactly. I needed to take a minute to think about it. But now I can't stop thinking about him."

Erin said, "You know, that's good. I like that you're not rushing into something. You know what you hardly ever get to experience in your love life?"

There wasn't much. "What?"

"Anticipation."

"Overrated."

"I don't think so. I think there's something truly romantic in thinking about a person and wondering if he's thinking about you and imagining when you'll see him again and what you'll be wearing, and what he'll say and what you'll say—"

"I'm not a character in your romance novel, Erin."

Her sister refused to be distracted. "Maybe you

should give taking things slowly a try. You might really like it."

She let out a huff of breath. "I can't stop thinking about him," she admitted. "It's driving me crazy."

"Do you want to sleep over?"

She thought about it for a second. They did that sometimes. They'd sleep at one or the other's house and talk into the night and share breakfast in the morning before going about their respective days. But she could tell Erin was already settled down for the night. "That's okay. I think you helped."

Mila ended the call, feeling relieved. Erin always helped her to make sense of things. But as she turned off the lamps in her home and made her way to bed, all she could think about was Hersch's new mattress.

She could have helped him christen it tonight.

# Chapter Eighteen

Hersch pounded down Scenic Drive, multimillion-dollar houses on his left and the ocean tormenting him on the right. He rounded the point, where beautiful sand stretched beneath him, and kids were playing, and people were picnicking, and a lifeguard tower was set up so lifeguards could keep an eye on the swimmers. It would be so easy to jog down those steps, run along the beach, and cool off in the water. Or it would have been so easy two years ago. Despite yesterday's progress, he still didn't feel confident about the water without Mila by his side. As hot as he was, he faced forward so that his view was asphalt rather than rolling ocean waves and the caramel-colored beach.

As he ran, Herschel couldn't stop thinking about Mila. She had kissed him. So passionately it had almost knocked him over. Then she'd had to leave to go *shopping*? He'd barely slept all night thinking about her soft lips and her sexy body, and the way she made him feel like he could do anything. Anything! He had let himself succumb to her completely.

What had he been thinking? The truth was, he wasn't a spontaneous man. He liked to think things through, and he'd always taken life seriously.

But maybe it was time to stop. He still held to his belief that he could never leave a woman he loved and a potential family behind while he did a dangerous job with no guarantee of a return. And if anyone ever needed proof of that, it was a guy who'd come within a hair's breadth of drowning on his return from a mission.

However, Mila was both spontaneous and had been very clear that she wasn't looking for marriage or commitments or ties. And maybe that made everything okay. Maybe if she could hold that attitude and get through her life perfectly well, he could too. Maybe he shouldn't give up on her.

He knew one thing. He couldn't keep going night after night dreaming of her beside him, especially now that he knew she was open to the idea of the two of them becoming intimate.

He ran faster than he should have, for longer than he'd intended, but at least he'd come to a decision.

He would have kept going if his phone hadn't rung. He slowed to a halt, hoping it was Mila. But his screen showed a number he didn't recognize.

"Herschel Greenfield," he said.

"Herschel, it's Jay Malone. The agent. What are you up to right now?"

Hersch grimaced. Hadn't he made it very clear several times already that he wasn't interested in having a movie made about his life?

"I'm out running," Herschel replied.

"Ah, keeping fit. I like it," Jay said. "Well, I hope you don't mind me calling you out of the blue, but I'm at Archer Davenport's place, and we wondered if you'd like to come over and discuss the movie."

*What movie?* "That's kind of you, but I don't think there's really anything to discuss."

Jay laughed. "Once you get talking with Archer and see for yourself what a fantastic actor he is, I think you might change your mind."

Hersch paused. Since Jay had murmured the word *Davenport*, his heartbeat had quickened again as if he were still running. He hated to admit it, but he was curious to meet one of Mila's siblings. Was he curious enough to humor a meeting about a biopic?

Before he could speak, Jay said, "I know you have your reservations, but if you could just spare an hour, or even thirty minutes, we'll supply the coffee, and all you have to do is listen."

Hersch made a noncommittal sound.

"Look," Jay continued, because the man was nothing if not persistent, "at least come and tell the hottest actor working in Hollywood, and one of the best looking, why you don't want him to play you in the movie of your life."

Hersch laughed then. "Since I'm pretty much neighbors with Archer now that I've moved to town, I guess I could come over for some neighborly coffee."

Jay let out a triumphant sound. He said he'd text the address, and Hersch hung up, wondering what on earth he'd gotten himself into. As he headed back to his new home, he wondered if there was also maybe a tiny bit of himself that was flattered that anyone would want to make a movie about him.

* * *

A shower and a change of clothes later, Hersch followed his phone's directions to Archer Davenport's place on Scenic Drive, where he'd been running earlier. He briefly wondered if they'd seen him and that was why Jay had made the call, but he shook away the idea—surely not even Jay Malone was that conniving.

As he walked up to the door, he was impressed by the beauty of Archer's home. He'd expected something spectacular—Archer was an A-list celebrity—but this place was a modern masterpiece of glass and sharp angles. Its crisp white paint job sparkled in the sun.

The dark gray front door was built to be intimidating, with a series of security cameras around the buzzer, but Hersch was used to high-level security. He rang the bell.

To his surprise, Archer himself opened the door. "Come right in," he said. "So glad you could join us.

I'm Arch."

Hersch knew that Archer had recently broken his leg, but the only clue was that he walked with a slight limp. He'd clearly made a great recovery. Archer flashed him a true Hollywood-heartthrob smile and ushered him in.

He showed Hersch through to an enormous living room with floor-to-ceiling windows that showcased the ocean view. Jay Malone, sitting on a cream leather couch, jumped to his feet and came straight over to shake Hersch's hand like they had already made a deal. Hersch was thankful to have something to focus on besides the view. Jay was wearing a sharp navy suit. Did the man ever give himself a minute off?

Archer told Hersch to make himself comfortable. "I'm so happy to have a real-life hero in my living room," he said. "It's an honor."

Hersch tried not to cringe. He was anything but a hero, but these two men kept insisting otherwise. Rather than taking a seat right away, Hersch turned his back on the windows to look at the art. Archer was obviously a collector. He was drawn to a group of paintings that were different, softer and more expressive than some of the others. "Are these Tessa Taylor's paintings? I saw an exhibition of her work. They're beautiful."

Archer looked like Hersch had just paid him the greatest compliment in the world. "Yes, wow. I can't believe you recognize her style. I'm always telling Tessa she's one of a kind, but she doesn't believe me. She'll be thrilled when I tell her that Herschel Greenfield spotted her work and liked it." Then, almost as though he were giving away state secrets, he said, "We're engaged."

"Congratulations."

"Just announced it to the press last night," Jay said in his forceful way.

"Tessa's very talented," Hersch said. He looked carefully at Archer's face, realizing as he did that he was seeking traces of Mila there. What had that taken—two minutes before he was thinking about Mila again?

Jay guided Hersch to a chair, and Arch poured him a cup of coffee.

"I was reading online that your movie with Smith Sullivan is coming out soon. Congratulations."

Arch smiled, but it was a modest smile. "Ah, thanks. We're pretty excited about it. The movie had a great screenwriter and director, and the crew were just amazing. They made it easy for me. Plus, I was working with my best bud, which helps."

"I'm sure that your breaking your leg on set will help with ticket sales," Jay interjected. To Hersch, he said, "The man never broke character, so they kept filming."

Hersch was amazed that Archer was so down-to-earth. He'd been expecting to meet a flashy, self-involved guy, but Archer just seemed like a regular Joe who happened to be good-looking. "I hear Mila sold you a house," Arch said. "She's a great Realtor, but she'll have you out surfing if you give her half a chance. We all surf. You'll have to come out with us sometime."

Hersch felt himself relax and realized he'd very much been on his guard until now. "I'd like that a lot," he said. Which was true even if it was unlikely. "I've been missing doing a range of outdoor activities. I used to compete in Ironman, but I sat the last one out."

Jay clapped his hands and said, "Arch has done an Ironman. Just one, though—not fifteen."

Hersch shuddered a little at the research Jay had obviously been doing. But luckily Archer stepped in and said, "It's hard work and a lot of commitment. I'm not sure I'll ever do another one."

Archer had a warmth and sincerity about him that immediately put Hersch at ease. "I'm not sure I'll ever do another one either," he admitted. "Now I run to keep in shape."

"I run too. Clears the mind."

"Yes," said Jay, "that would be a great way for you guys to get to know one another better. You see, Herschel, for this movie, we want to go deep into character. We want it to be an authentic character study. From your modest beginnings, through to your training for the space program, a successful mission that leads to near tragedy. And you, making sure everyone else got out safely. It's going to be comprehensive and gut-wrenching, and I just know it's going to inspire millions." Jay sat back, looking pretty pleased with himself.

Hersch was about to protest when he heard a woman's voice call Archer's name—a familiar voice—and in walked Mila, holding what looked like the dress bag she'd been carrying the other day. His stomach flipped. Every time he saw her, she took his breath away. She was wearing worn jeans and a loose sweater, and her long hair was wound into a bun at the nape of her neck. She knew how to be a goddess on sea and land both, and it never failed to amaze him. What was she doing here?

Mila obviously hadn't expected to see him either. A split second of confusion, and then her eyes lit up. She was as pleased to see him as he was her. He wanted to leap up from his seat and kiss her senseless and take her far from here to somewhere private. Like his bed. From the way her eyes opened wide and her cheeks flushed as she took in the scene, he was almost certain she was experiencing the same fantasy.

Archer said to Mila, "Can't a man have some privacy in his own home? You ever heard of knocking? I gave you all the key code for emergencies, not so you could waltz in here like you're about to sell the place."

Mila quickly recovered her composure. "Is this a secret boys' club meeting? Shall I go and leave you to your treehouse?"

Arch laughed. "What are you doing here, anyway? And what is that?"

"I came to drop something off for Tessa," Mila explained. "And no, don't ask me any more. It's none of your business."

Hersch smiled a small smile, enjoying their sibling squabble.

"Come on, you two," Jay said fondly, clearly having been a witness to their banter many times before. "We're having an informal meeting. No biggie." He looked at Mila and then Hersch and back again.

Hersch suddenly felt exposed. Could Jay tell that he had a crush on Mila as big as the moon?

Jay said, "What would you think about your brother playing Herschel in a biopic?"

Mila turned on him. "If you bullied him into this, Jay, I swear I'll—"

"We're just talking," Hersch interrupted.

Archer jumped in and said, "Yeah, we're talking about guy stuff here. Why don't you go upstairs and do whatever secret girl thing you and Tessa have planned?"

Mila rolled her eyes. "First, we both know I could take you down in under five seconds. And second, I'm pretty sure 'guy stuff' isn't dressing up and pretending to be someone else. So, yeah, I'd *definitely* rather go upstairs."

She turned to Hersch. "Good to see you." To Jay, she said, "Wish I could say the same," with a teasing smile, and disappeared upstairs.

A few minutes later, Hersch heard her come down, and then the front door clicked shut. Jay and Archer had long gone back to talking about the movie, but all Hersch could think about was Mila. Their surprise encounter made him think that maybe she wanted him as badly as he did her. Hersch wasn't the kind of guy to sit around and do nothing. He was going to win over Mila Davenport, even if she would give him only one night. Casual sex had never been his thing, but at thirty-five years old, maybe it was time to try something new. Having made that decision, he felt better than he had in days.

Because once he'd made a decision, he tended to act on it right away.

# Chapter Nineteen

"Mila Davenport." Mila answered the call in her business voice, even though she knew it was Hersch calling. Her true feelings for him had been written all over her face when she'd bumped into him at Arch's, and now she felt a little embarrassed, as though she needed to claw back some mystique. Especially since she was the one who'd kissed him in the first place.

"Mila, it's Hersch," he said, obviously not understanding that she had put him in business mode.

"You sound out of breath. Is everything okay?"

"I was setting up my home gym."

Mila licked her bottom lip, wishing he hadn't told her that. Now all she could do was picture him in tight workout gear improving that already perfect physique. She closed her eyes and opened them again. *Pull it together, girl.* "Isn't moving enough of a workout?"

He chuckled. "I seem to have more energy in Carmel than I do anywhere else."

He let the statement linger, and she wondered if she might be the reason for that. Over the past week, she'd surfed for longer and lifted heavier weights, trying to burn off some of her sexual buzz. Although she had her reasons, she'd continued to regret running away from him on the beach. Surely she could allow herself just one night of hot sex?

Even now, she was still fantasizing about him all sweaty and hot when she realized she hadn't replied. "I know you might not want to hear it, but honestly, it's that Carmel ocean air that gives people a new lease on life."

He said softly, "That and other things."

Were those *other things* thinking about a night of furiously hot sex? "What can I do for you?"

"I'm inviting you to my housewarming party."

She couldn't have been more surprised and laughed out loud. "You're having a housewarming party? You've barely moved in."

"I know. It's tomorrow night."

"Great." She imagined a cocktail party with little squares of cheese and glasses of uninteresting wine. She'd been to enough of them in Carmel. And then she remembered he was completely new in town. "Who else is coming?"

His voice went low and a little bit sexy. "The guest list is *very* small."

Her blood began to pound at the blatant invitation beneath the words. "How small?"

"You. And me, obviously, as the host."

She'd planned to catch up on paperwork tomorrow night, but he didn't need to know that. A housewarming party for two? Oh, she could find time for that. "I happen to be available tomorrow night. And I would love to come to your housewarming party."

"Great!" He sounded as excited as she felt at the prospect of the two of them alone together in his new house.

"Come around seven. I'll see you then."

* * *

Mila was surprised at the buzz of excitement she felt as she thought about the housewarming party with Herschel. If she had her way, that house would be *very* warm by the time she was finished with him. She got through her work with her usual dynamic enthusiasm, but if she was honest with herself, there was always a low-level hum inside her as the hours passed until she would see him again.

By the following evening, Mila's excitement was off the charts. As she prepared for her date, she opened her bathroom cabinet. Erin had teased her that going into her bathroom was like walking into a high-end spa. As someone who had spent the better part of her life in sunshine and salt water, she'd learned early on the importance of good skin care. Between the various sunscreen products and moisturizing lotions and botanical scrubs, she could easily run her own spa. But her skin-care routine had paid off. She liked to think that if they happened to touch her naked body, no one would know how much of her time she spent in sun and salt water.

She showered and primped and then chose a body cream that was a little floral and a little spicy. As she rubbed the cream into her skin, she could feel how sensitive she was, with a heat coming off her that surprised even her. She'd always had a strong sexual appetite, but somehow, with Herschel, she felt connected on a deeper level. It was exciting but also mildly terrifying, if she was honest with herself—and she always tried to be honest with herself.

Was it possible that after being a commitment-phobe from the moment Travis had dumped her, she was finally changing? Could she really be thinking of Herschel Greenfield as a forever guy? The thought was both unsettling and kind of exciting. He might not be the most spontaneous guy she'd ever met, but she also knew with a deep, deep certainty that Herschel Greenfield would not drop a woman because she'd sustained a career-ending injury. If she believed anything about Herschel, it was that he would stick by a person when they needed him. She understood now as she never had when she was younger how important that was.

Maybe the Davenport kids had all been spoiled by watching their parents' relationship, and maybe after Travis, she'd never thought she could find a relationship like theirs, so she hadn't even bothered to try. But now, with Hersch, maybe it was possible.

There was so much love and commitment in the air with Arch and Tessa that couples and weddings were constantly shoved in her face. That had to be messing with her too. Her celebrity brother, who'd probably bedded more hot starlets than was good for him, had fallen hard for a woman who was genuine and decent and good. If Archer Davenport could find true love, why shouldn't Mila Davenport?

As she slipped into underwear that was more about showing off her assets than anything else, she hoped she wouldn't be disappointed. The only trouble she could imagine with Herschel was that Mr. I'm Not Very Spontaneous might think anything beyond missionary position was too wild for him. And that would never do for her. She mustn't set her expectations too high. That wouldn't be fair. No doubt Herschel had been cramming for exams and worrying about quantum physics while she'd been living life to the fullest. Maybe he treated a woman's body the way he treated some complicated machine in space. If so, she'd still enjoy him as much as she could, but thank goodness she'd been clear that she wasn't likely to stick.

With those completely confused and contradictory feelings, she chose a dress so easy to remove that nobody would need a degree in quantum physics to figure out that loosening the two ties at her shoulders would allow the whole thing to slip to the floor.

Then she picked up the housewarming gift she'd bought today on impulse. She'd gone to the gallery displaying Tessa's paintings and, knowing how much Hersch liked Tessa's work, had bought a piece that would look great in his new house. Tessa had been painting a lot of seascapes recently, but she'd also spent some time in the woods around Carmel and had done a series of trees. This one was of a grove of the cypresses that only grew locally. The trees were whimsical and draped over each other like tired dancers.

She loved the picture and hoped Hersch would too. She'd deliberately bought the piece from the gallery, even though she could have gotten something direct from the artist at a discount, because she wanted Tessa's paintings to move so that the gallery would keep stocking her. She could afford to support her future sister-in-law and really wanted to do so.

She drove up to Hersch's new place and parked, but it took a few moments of breathing deeply to calm her racing heart before she got out. This jittery, nervous Mila was definitely not like the confident Mila who embraced her sexuality and enjoyed men on her terms for as long as she wanted and then said good-bye with no regrets. No. She felt quite different. There was a second when she wondered if she should drive home and text him that she'd suddenly come down with some illness.

But that would be crazy.

After another deep breath, she got out of the car. She picked up the painting that the gallery had gift-wrapped and made sure the card was securely taped to the front. As she walked to the door, she noticed a large cardboard box sitting beside the garage. It had held the mattress they'd bought together, and another shiver went through her. One more deep breath was necessary before she could ring the doorbell.

He opened it so promptly he could have been hovering, waiting for her to arrive. That helped calm her and remind her of who was in charge here.

"Hi there," he said.

"Well, hello," she replied. They exchanged a slightly awkward hug as she was holding the painting in one hand. He looked good enough to eat in comfy jeans and a navy blue polo shirt that showed off his muscular physique. His feet were bare, and something about that sent a shiver of lust straight to her center.

He stood back, and she walked into his home. The atmosphere felt slightly different, as though he was already inhabiting his space. How well this house suited him, she thought with a flicker of professional pride. She'd known it was perfect for him, and how right she'd been. He seemed much more relaxed now that he was out of the hotel and in his own space.

"This place suits you already," she said.

They walked into the living room, which looked very much as it had when they'd toured the house, with the owners' furniture. But there were a few touches that were purely Herschel—a photograph on the wall of him and his team in their spacesuits, ready to go out on a mission, and an old leather-covered globe. She wondered if that was how the world looked to him, so small and compact, when he was up in space looking down. The place smelled fresh, and she suspected a team of professional cleaners had already been through.

She presented him with the gift.

"Ah, you shouldn't have," he said. "You've already done so much."

For a second, Mila wondered if she'd gone too far in buying the painting, but no, it was thoughtful on two counts—one for Hersch and the other for Tessa.

Hersch opened the card first. She kept a stack of personalized housewarming cards that said Welcome Home with a picture of Carmel-by-the-Sea on the front and her printed details inside. Her position was she never knew when a happy customer would like to recommend her to a friend, so she always kept on hand housewarming and holiday cards that contained her phone, email, and website details. However, she'd added a personal message to Hersch's card. She'd thought long and hard and then written, *I'm so happy to have you in the neighborhood.*

She'd hesitated over how to sign off. With another client, she might have written *sincerely* or *truly* and signed her name, but after wrestling with it, she'd signed, *Love, Mila*. She put those same words on all kinds of notes and cards to friends, and if he was nothing else, he was certainly a friend. *Sincerely* would have been too formal.

He read the card and thanked her, setting it carefully on the coffee table, and proceeded to open her gift. She couldn't wait for him to see it. Would he love it as much as she did?

She had a long time to wait, because Herschel did not rip into a gift like she did. Again, that very careful, precise nature came through as he peeled the tape off each edge and then carefully unwrapped the painting. He held it away from himself and stared at it for such a long time she couldn't stand it another moment.

She blurted, "It's by Tessa Taylor. You were admiring her work at the plein air show when I first met you."

He nodded slowly, his gaze still focused on the painting. "I know. I'm just admiring the brushstrokes. She's a truly talented painter." He looked up at her, and she saw the warmth shining in his eyes. "I honestly cannot imagine a more ideal gift. I can't even decide where I'll hang this, because it will look right in every single room. It's so thoughtful. I love it."

She felt a rush of relief. He had seen the painting

the way she had. "I think so too. And you'll notice there isn't a drop of water in sight. I specifically chose a painting that only included trees."

He chuckled. "And I appreciate it. I've been here long enough to recognize that these are the Carmel cypresses. But she's made them seem so alive—as if you look at the painting long enough, they'll start moving with the breeze."

"You felt that too," she replied, so happy that he had seen the energy in the painting the way she had.

He stood then and, holding the painting in front of him, began to circle the room. A nice print was hanging above the fireplace. He took it down and put Tessa's painting in its place.

"Oh, it's perfect there," she breathed. Then louder, she said, "Just perfect."

He stepped back and nodded. "I will never look at this painting and not think of you. Thank you." He shook his head. "What kind of a terrible host am I? Let me get you something to drink."

He took the wrapping paper into the kitchen and put it away, and on impulse, she followed him. It was just nice to see him so at home. He opened the fridge, and she was impressed to see that it was already stocked with food. He pulled out a bottle of champagne and turned to her. "It's a housewarming party. We should celebrate."

He popped the cork while she fetched champagne

flutes from the cabinet. They were lovely crystal glasses that had belonged to the previous owners, but she suspected that at some point Hersch would swap them for something simpler. He poured the sparkling wine, and as they clinked rims, she said, "Here's to your new home."

And he said, "And to new beginnings."

Their eyes met, and she felt a shiver go from the top of her head to the tips of her toes. She took a sip, and the wine was cool and crisp on her tongue. Then she took another sip, possibly for courage. They went back to the living room, and she noticed that music was playing. Now she went to the framed photograph of him and his crew about to climb aboard the space shuttle. She couldn't help but recall the rescue effort she'd watched on YouTube.

She said, "I know you don't like to hear it, but you really are a hero. I could never have done what you did the day of your crash landing."

He seemed to take in her words and really consider them. "Going into space is easy. Just throw on the suit, eat freeze-dried food, and learn to sleep while floating. But I don't think I could have ever done what *you* did— own those waves, compete at that level, and come back so brilliantly from your injury. I think you're my hero."

If he was hosting a party for the two of them, he could have only one thing in mind, and Mila didn't feel like waiting around. She was far too keyed up. She moved toward him as though to kiss him, and at the same time, he moved forward as though to do the same, and they met in the middle. There was not a shred of hesitation in either of their bodies. They were full-on ready for each other.

Allowing their lips to meet, Mila sank into the kiss, and Hersch grabbed her waist, holding her firmly in his strong arms.

When they pulled away, she said, "I couldn't help noticing the box from that new mattress outside. Shall we try it out?"

He ran a hand down her hair and gazed into her face. For a second, she thought she'd gotten it all wrong, that he wasn't planning on seducing her tonight, but he said, "There's nothing I want more. I think I wanted you from the second I saw you. But I need to be honest with you. This can never be anything serious."

He was such a serious man anyway, and his expression was searching as he looked into her face. She felt shocked, as though she'd just unexpectedly flipped off her surfboard into freezing-cold water. *This can never be anything serious?* That was *her* line. *She* was the one who kept things casual.

Getting her feet back under her, she said, "Absolutely. That's perfect. Great."

But deep inside? She was irked. Why wouldn't he

want to be serious with her? What was wrong with her?

And then he kissed her again, and every thought about the future went out of her head. Even if they had nothing but this one night, she was determined to make the most of it, and when she was finished with him, he would never, ever again say, *This can never be anything serious*.

# Chapter Twenty

He took her hand and led her to his bedroom. Idly, she noted that the bedding looked great on the new bed—they'd chosen well—and that even in the short time that he'd inhabited this space, it was his. There was more of his art on the walls, and no doubt his clothes were already neatly folded in the drawers.

He moved toward her, took the champagne glass out of her hand, and put it on the nightstand, where it made a tiny *click*. He put his own glass beside it.

She breathed deeply. This was it. This was what she'd been waiting for since the moment she'd first laid eyes on him.

He pulled her in for another soul-searing kiss, his hands roaming over her hips, grazing her lower back. At the end of it, she was completely breathless. Every part of her tingled. He kissed her again, and she couldn't help herself. She ran her hands through his hair, over those gorgeous, muscular shoulders, down his back. She felt him hard against her chest, and every part of her began to melt and turn to liquid. She moved instinctually, her hips beginning to dance, and then she heard him groan. And now his hands found the rest of her, fingertips tracing circles up her back and over her shoulders, down her sides, and without any problem at all, he released the two bows at her shoulders and let her dress slide to the floor.

Then he stood back and gazed at her in her barely-there scraps of lace and said in a voice she'd never heard from him before, "I knew you'd be gorgeous, but I had no idea."

Then she reached forward, pulled his polo shirt out of his trousers, and yanked it up. He helped her, pulling it over his head so the Saint Christopher's medal caught slightly at the neck and then settled itself against his muscular chest. Before she could get to his belt, he was already divesting himself of his jeans, and then wearing nothing but a pair of navy boxer shorts, he came back to her and reached around for the clasp of her bra. The wisp of lace fell to the floor, and he dropped to his knees in front of her and slowly slipped her panties off and down her legs. She was trembling all over. Her legs could barely support her.

And then he kissed her. There. He gave her a little push so she fell back on the bed. He climbed up with her and parted her thighs. He made magic on her with his tongue. She climaxed so fast she barely saw it coming, her hips riding up as the wave took her.

While the aftershocks were still shaking her, she

cried, "I need you in me, now!"

For a man who was usually so methodical and so in control, he didn't need to be asked twice. He had his boxers off in a second, and that glorious body was moving up the bed. He reached for the bedside drawer, and she was happy to know that he had enough sense to think about protection. He sheathed himself with slightly trembling hands, and then he was kissing her, hard and commanding. It was a side of Herschel she'd never seen before, hadn't imagined he even possessed. And it was totally erotic. She wrapped her legs around him, and grabbing his hard, toned butt, she pulled him into her even as she thrust her hips up.

It was like nothing she'd ever experienced before. Afterward, she couldn't have said why. She'd been with plenty of men. But there was something about Herschel that was just different. They connected on every level. He thrust like a man who knew exactly what he was doing and understood a woman's body. She clung to him, actually struggling to keep up. Meanwhile, he kissed her, and she tasted her own pleasure on his lips, and then he grabbed her hands, putting them above her head, and they clung to each other as she climbed toward her pleasure yet again. For once, she was trying to hold herself back, but she couldn't. She cried out, and as she did, she heard him roar along with her.

She felt as though she was spiraling out of control,

and it was ages before she could catch her breath. He rolled off her and lay beside her, also struggling to catch his. After a while, he turned and tenderly kissed her shoulder.

In a husky voice, he said, "Usually, I'm a little more smooth and like to take my time. But I couldn't stop myself. I had to have you." He reached over and kissed the tip of her breast. "I should have taken more time with you and caressed your gorgeous breasts and all the other bits of you. But I was like a horny teenager."

Although she felt all warm and languid, she was so surprised that she laughed. "In case you didn't notice, I am plenty satisfied."

"But it was so quick," he complained. "I wanted to stretch it out and make our first time last."

She turned over and propped herself on one elbow. She loved how serious he was, even about sex. "I'll tell you what. You can stretch out the second time as long as you want. But I think we both needed that one to be hard and fast and glorious."

His eyes twinkled at her. "Glorious?"

"Are you fishing for a compliment?"

He looked slightly bashful. "Well, a man likes to think he's made a woman happy."

"Glorious," she repeated quite firmly. "And you have made me so happy, I'm going to let you do that again."

He didn't need a second invitation. This time, he

took plenty of time to caress her and kiss her breasts and her belly. He discovered the ticklish spot just beneath her earlobe and that if he kissed the soft skin on her inner wrist, she'd sigh.

In turn, she took her time exploring him, all those hard planes and ridges, and when they couldn't stand it anymore, she flipped him onto his back and rode him until, once more, they both cried out together.

When he came back to himself she looked right down into his eyes and smiled at him, knowing somehow he'd never again say to her this could never be anything serious.

This might not be long-term, but it was very serious.

\* \* \*

Hersch gazed up at Mila and saw her smiling down at him with her sea witch's eyes. And she was a sea witch, he realized, because she had spun some kind of spell around him that seemed to have captured his heart. He thought, *I could fall in love with this woman*, and that scared him more than anything, because he was so determined never to put someone he loved through the worry of losing him or the grief if he died.

But the sex had been mind-blowing. He'd never known a woman so utterly open and responsive. They'd made love twice, and he wanted her as badly now as he had when she'd first walked in the door in that sexy dress that hugged all her curves. Now he'd seen all of her, and their time together was better than he could have imagined. She wasn't a slight, delicate woman whom he was frightened he might hurt. She was strong, resilient—a woman who could give as well as she took, and he loved that about her.

Still sitting on top of him so he had a view of her glorious breasts, she said, "When I first met you, I thought you were kind of nerdy. But wow, do you know your way around a woman."

She surprised an embarrassed chuckle out of him, but he was also quite pleased. She was so open and frank. He'd never been one to talk about his emotions, and he wasn't ready to now, but he had them.

At some point he was going to have to face what this woman had done to him.

But not quite yet.

Instead, he piled pillows behind them and reached for a champagne glass while she scooched up so they were both sitting propped against the pillows. He passed her champagne and tapped his glass against hers again. The glasses were now only half full, but the bubbles were valiantly still racing up and down through the liquid.

"We've warmed my house, and we've warmed my new bed. And I'm pretty happy with both."

"I'm going to echo what you said earlier. To new beginnings."

They both sipped. And then, very deliberately, holding his gaze, she sipped champagne and held it in her mouth, then leaned over and sucked one of his nipples between her lips. He felt the bubbles of the champagne and the coldness, and then the warmth of her tongue licking at him, and amazingly he was rock hard again. He wouldn't have thought he'd had enough time to recover, but his sea witch could do anything to him. This time, it was she who took the glass out of his hand and put it on the bedside table along with hers, and then she proceeded to love him with her mouth until he couldn't stand it anymore, and he flipped her onto her back and regained control.

They might have gone on like that all night, but at some point somebody's stomach grumbled. He thought it might have been his. He looked up at her. "Are you hungry?"

"Starving," she admitted.

And so they got up, and instead of putting her dress on, she snuggled into his navy blue robe that had been hanging on the back of the door. He loved how she looked in it. It hung almost to her ankles, and she had to roll up the sleeves. He picked up his jeans and slipped into them, and then they went downstairs to the kitchen.

Herschel opened the fridge, and Mila remarked on the bounty within. He glanced at her. "My specialty is omelets. How do you feel about an omelet?"

"Sounds perfect."

She topped up their champagne and sat at his kitchen island, watching as he methodically and expertly washed his hands as though preparing for surgery, then chopped mushrooms, peppers, ham, and grated cheese, checking with her each time to see if she approved of the ingredients, all of which she did. When he opened cupboards to get down dishes, she said, "Have you already rearranged the cupboards? They look way more precise."

He nodded. "Of course. I didn't find the previous layout as efficient."

She laughed. "Normally, I would find that super weird, but actually I admire how orderly you are. Maybe because it's the exact opposite of me."

When the eggs went into the pan, he lifted the edges and rolled the liquid around just like a sous-chef, so that when they were cooked, they would be fluffy and perfect. While he was doing that, he also managed to slice a fresh avocado, melon, and fresh strawberries so that the final presentation was multicolored and beautiful. He wanted Mila to remember this meal forever, even if it was just an omelet.

When he saw her gazing at him, he was suddenly worried. "What? Did I forget something?"

She got up, walked around the island, and then kissed him. "I have never watched anyone make an omelet so beautifully."

Now the worry turned to bashfulness. "I like to cook," he admitted.

"And I like to eat," she replied.

While they sat side by side, the sides of their legs touching, she asked, "What foods did you miss most when you were in space?"

"Fresh fruit and vegetables, for sure," he said without a hint of hesitation.

She looked thoughtful. "What do you eat up there, anyway?"

"Packets of freeze-dried stuff. They're marked *beef stroganoff* or *chicken curry*, but really it's space food. Keeps the body nourished and going, but it's nothing to write home about."

She tapped her glass. "I guess there's no wine."

He shook his head. "There's tubes of things like orange juice, but you have to be careful. Because there's no gravity, if the liquid gets away from you, it floats away." He got out of his chair and mimed a drop of liquid and him chasing it as though it were a butterfly and his mouth were a net. His reward was Mila's gorgeous laugh, so carefree and infectious.

He sat and finished the last of his omelet. By the time he looked up at Mila, he sensed her mood had changed.

Licking the last of the melon juice from her lips, she said, "So, you're good-looking, great in bed, you can cook, and you have a pretty interesting job. Why aren't you married?"

He felt his face fall, and he knew he'd have to explain. "I sort of got close once, a long time ago, but it didn't work out. And now I'm glad it didn't, because I never want to leave someone I love behind when I go into space, knowing I might not come back. I've never wanted to leave behind a widow or orphans. My work is too risky. I can't have a wife and kids and then disappear into the stars one day... and never come home."

He hoped she'd understand him a bit better now.

Quietly, she said, "Is that why you told me this could never be anything serious? Because you'd be afraid to leave someone you loved behind?"

He nodded solemnly. He hoped that she would know now that it wasn't about not wanting her permanently in his life. It was that he didn't feel he could have *anyone* permanently in his life.

She looked sad and a little baffled too. "But there are all kinds of people who have dangerous jobs in this world. They get married and have families. Cops, firefighters, anybody in the armed forces. Hersch, life is risk. You could have the most boring job in the world—I don't know, an accountant in a shoe factory—and somebody could fall asleep at the wheel and run you over."

"You're right. I know you're right. But I don't think I could do it. I think if I had a wife and family that I loved very much, I might have to give up my job."

She looked stunned. "Why does that have to be *your* choice?"

"What do you mean?"

"Doesn't the woman who loves you get a choice in whether she's willing to take on those risks too?"

He'd never looked at it that way. Could he maybe have a relationship with Mila because she'd lived with risk every day of her professional life as a surfer? She might be one of the few people on the planet who could handle his career.

"How about you?" he asked. "You're beautiful, funny, an excellent Realtor, great in bed—which maybe I should have said first—and you're single. What's your story?"

She pushed her plate away and sipped champagne to give herself a moment. "The truth is, I haven't truly trusted a man since Travis."

Herschel reached out and touched her hand, feeling like the biggest klutz in the world. He'd known that Travis had left her after her accident. *Of course* she felt she couldn't trust men. "Some men can be trusted. Just saying."

Her eyes flickered up. "I know. I have a feeling I can trust you, can't I?"

As always, he tried to give an honest answer. "You can trust me to treat you right and do the right thing, but you can't trust me not to go off on a dangerous mission and die. I'm sorry to be so blunt, but there it is."

She bridled a little and retaliated by saying, "And you can trust me to be faithful as long as we're together, always up for a good time, and if either of us decides it's time to move on, there won't be any recriminations or tears. But you cannot stop me from going out on my surfboard whenever I feel like it, no matter how big those waves are, and maybe one day I won't come back. I like risk. I love that feeling of being in control, but only just, and of always knowing that I can ride the waves, but I can never control them, and they can turn on me at any second and swallow me."

"Okay," he said. "We have a deal."

"We do? What deal?"

"We'll enjoy each other until one of us can't do it anymore. How does that sound?"

There was something in her face he couldn't read, like maybe this should have been the perfect deal, what she always wanted from her lovers, not to feel tied down or constricted in any way, to enjoy each other until one or both of them was done. But now that he was offering it to her, she didn't want it anymore.

But if that was what she was thinking, she didn't admit it. She stood instead. "I agree. We have a deal."

Herschel tried not to laugh as Mila formally held out her hand and shook his while the too-big bathrobe slipped open, exposing the delicious slopes of her breasts. "Deal," he replied. Then he had no words left. He hiked her into his arms and carried her to bed.

After the initial start of surprise, she laughed and threw her arms around his neck. "I am no feather-weight," she said.

And she wasn't—she was all muscle, which he loved about her. His reply was to remind her that he worked out. A lot. And then she settled back in his arms and nibbled his earlobe and whispered things in his ear that made him half crazy with desire. By the time he had her back in his bed, it was even wilder than the first few times.

As though there was only limited time, and they had to squeeze every drop of pleasure from every moment.

# Chapter Twenty-One

Mila woke with the unfamiliar sensation of warmth at her back. For a second, she hazily thought she was looking after Erin's dog, Boswell, who, no matter how sternly she told him he had to sleep on the floor, always ended up in her bed when she looked after him. But as her eyes opened, and she came fully awake, she realized that not only was she not sleeping with Boswell, she wasn't even in her own bed.

And then it all came back to her. She'd fallen asleep in Hersch's arms. It was something she never did, certainly not the first time she slept with a man.

What was wrong with her? And then she realized that for the first time in her life, she was thinking about him as a *maybe*. Maybe she could do this. Maybe she could trust a man to be there for her. Maybe she could see herself with only one man for the rest of her life. The thought should have been terrifying, but instead, it was oddly comforting.

He was sound asleep beside her, and she paused just a moment to take pleasure in the strong lines of his face, the moustache that she was coming to love, and that Saint Christopher's medal glinting on his chest. A quick glance at her watch told her she had time to go surfing before she went to work. She very much needed to clear her head.

As silently as she could, she slipped out of bed. She found her dress, which the incredibly tidy Hersch had somehow found time to pick up and fold neatly. Beside it was her bra, but she couldn't find her panties.

She slipped on her bra and the dress and was looking under the bed for her missing underwear when a sleepy voice said, "I like that view."

She felt horribly flustered as she stood. Her panties were in her hand, and she tried to be casual as she stepped into them and pulled them up. He watched, hooking an arm behind his head, his eyes filled with lazy amusement.

"Do you have to go so soon?"

"Yes. I have waves to surf."

He glanced at the clock on his bedside table and crooked an eyebrow. "At six in the morning?"

"Oh yeah."

He started to roll out of bed. "I could put on some coffee."

She leaned over and kissed him. "Go back to sleep." She glanced at her watch, and he was right. It was just after six. "I looked at the surf report. It's going to be epic."

She hadn't looked, but she didn't care if the ocean was flat as glass. She'd take her surfboard and get out on the water even if she just floated there, trying to make sense of what had happened between her and Hersch.

The way he looked at her made her wonder if he was seeing more than she wanted him to. She was so confused. She'd never felt this confused.

"You can't go surfing without coffee. I've seen you. You have an addiction."

Darn it, he really did see too much. "I'll brew some while I'm getting my surf stuff on," she told him.

"What about breakfast? I can make you some breakfast. Maybe something to go?"

Now she realized there was a flicker of humor in his beautiful eyes. It was as though he knew how badly he'd shaken her and was enjoying it.

"No. I'm fine. I'll call you later." She kissed him quickly on the lips before rushing out.

When she reached her house, she sent Erin a quick message. *Coffee this morning? Need advice.*

Erin was also an early riser. Mila was tempted to tell her sister to grab her surfboard, but she needed an hour or two alone. Erin texted back in no time. Just one word: *Sure.*

The ocean wasn't that calm, nor was it the best surfing she'd ever had. However, she managed to get some good rides, and more than that—enough time on the ocean to calm the choppy seas inside her. When she rode in, it was close to eight, and to her delight, her sister was waiting right there on the beach. With two cups of coffee in her hands. Mila immediately flashed back to when Hersch had stood not so far away, also with two cups of coffee in his hands.

When she reached Erin and had taken her first slug of beautiful, reviving coffee, she said, "I thought we'd go to the coffee shop."

Erin shook her head. "You think I don't know you? I could tell it was an emergency."

Mila dropped her board, and they turned and began to walk together. "Not an emergency, exactly."

Erin shot her a look. "Is it about Herschel?"

She nodded. "You see right through me."

"I'm an investigative journalist. It's my job to see beyond the façade to the deep core of truth. Did something happen?"

"Yes. How do you know so much?"

"Because I've seen the way you two look at each other. And so has Arch. Frankly, we agree it almost scorches our eyeballs."

Mila jabbed Erin's shoulder. "You didn't say anything to Arch, did you?"

Erin looked shocked. "Of course not. But he said you guys were pretty weird around each other at his house the other day. He asked me if something was going on."

Mila groaned. So much for keeping her sex life private. A gull wheeled overhead, and the surf pounded as they walked on the sand. "Hersch had a housewarming party last night."

Erin's eyebrows rose. "I didn't get an invitation."

"I was the only one invited."

"Aha."

"The party went on until this morning, when I woke up in his bed."

"A*ha*," she repeated, this time with a wicked glint in her eye. "I can't help but ask—was it…?"

"The hottest thing I've ever experienced? Oh yeah."

It seemed to her that Erin was trying very hard to suppress a grin. But all she said was, "And this is a crisis why?"

"Because he's a maybe," she blurted.

Of all the people in the world, only Erin would get the significance of this comment. She actually stopped walking. "You're kidding me. He's an actual maybe?"

"Yes."

Erin was so shocked she had trouble keeping up with Mila's much longer stride. Finally, she scampered to catch up. "I can't remember when you've been a maybe about a man. You're always a no."

"Well, this time I'm a maybe. Only, you know what the crazy part is?"

"There's a crazier part?"

"For him, I'm a no. *This can't be anything serious*. He actually told me that."

Erin didn't laugh out loud, but Mila could see her shoulders shaking as she tried to control herself.

"I can't believe you're laughing at me while I'm having a crisis."

"You have to admit it's kind of funny. Talk about having the tables turned on you." And then Erin stepped in front of her with a devilish look in her eyes. She held out her hand and said, "I want you to pinkie swear that you'll give this guy a chance."

Mila was so frustrated now she wished she hadn't even called her. "You know I hate pinkie swears with you."

"Yes, I do. That's why I'm making sure you do one. Because I know you, and the minute you get even the slightest bit uncomfortable, you will run. If he's as good as a maybe now, then one day he might be a yes."

Of course that was what frightened Mila the most. What if he was a yes for her, and she was a no for him? She hadn't risked her heart in such a long time, she wasn't sure she could survive having it broken again.

Erin continued, "Anyway, he doesn't seem like the kind of guy who's flighty, you know? I mean, outside of space shuttles."

"Are you saying I'm flighty?"

"Well, you do have a tendency to take flight the

minute anybody gets the tiniest bit serious about you."

It was hard to argue with reality. "Well, this time he seems to be the flighty one."

"No. I don't think he is. I think there's something else stopping him."

Since she'd told Erin this much, she decided to share the rest. "He says he never wants to have to go on a mission while leaving behind a wife or children. He thinks it wouldn't be fair to them because his job is so risky."

Erin looked at her. "Are you kidding me? What about police officers and people in the army? They risk their lives all the time."

She was so pleased Erin could see the situation the same way she did. "I know! That's exactly what I told him."

Erin shook her head. "Sometimes I really don't understand men."

"Amen, sister."

"So, what are you going to do?"

"Well, I'm going to enjoy the fabulous sex, and…" She thought long and hard. "And I'm just going to enjoy the fabulous sex. And not worry about tomorrow."

Erin shot her yet another searching look. "Are you going to bring him as your date to the wedding?"

Frustrated, she watched a spaniel run circles around them. It had crossed her mind to do that very thing. "We're sleeping together. We're not dating."

"Maybe you should think about it. Then we could get to know him better. I mean, he seems like a really nice guy."

She let out a huge sigh. "He is. He is a really nice guy." She picked up the slobbery ball the happy spaniel had dropped at her feet and threw it. The dog raced off. "I'll think about it." Then she turned to her little sister. "Are you bringing someone?"

"I don't know. I usually take Clark, the *Sea Shell* photographer, as my plus-one, but obviously I can't bring a news photographer to my celebrity brother's secret wedding that the media aren't supposed to know about."

Mila could see her problem. Besides, Clark was a convenient plus-one. He was nice and dressed well and never, ever challenged Erin in any way. All the world could tell he was in love with her from afar, but he wasn't bold enough to make a move, so they were friends—and not even friends with benefits.

Mila was about to remind Erin one more time that Jay Malone was coming to Archer's wedding, and she was pretty sure he wasn't bringing a plus-one. His current hot underwear model was exactly the sort of person who would alert the worst of the paparazzi if she ever got wind of it. However, Mila was still mad at Jay for pushing his biopic idea at Hersch. He didn't deserve a nice woman like Erin on his arm. And Erin definitely deserved someone nicer than Jay—someone who listened to Mila, for instance.

While she'd been thinking about this, Erin's mind had obviously gone down a different track. "As a journalist, I feel really bad promoting the fiction that my brother's getting married in Scotland."

Mila turned to her in shock. "You're not going to sell out Arch to the *Sea Shell*, are you?"

Irritation was evident on her sister's face. "Of course I would never do that. I'm just saying, when they find out, I'll get in huge trouble. You know I will. This would be the scoop of the century for the *Sea Shell*."

Mila could see her point, but still, family was more important than any job. She thought about it, and the best she could come up with was that maybe Arch could let the *Sea Shell* have an exclusive photograph. She shared this idea with Erin, who looked less than impressed. Then she shrugged.

"It's not like I'll lose my job or anything. I just feel bad, that's all."

"I get that. Jay's been trying to get hold of me lately. I think he's hoping I'll put in a good word for him with Herschel. Which I never will."

Erin said, "You can see where he's coming from, though. It would be an amazing project. I mean, Herschel Greenfield is an absolute hero, and what a great part for Archer to play."

Mila felt the familiar irritation rise in her that came every time that project was brought up. "Yes, I know it would be a great project, but it's the man's life. It's his trauma, and I don't think he wants to see it laid out on a big screen."

Erin turned and looked at her. "You're taking this really seriously. Are you sure it's completely Herschel that gets you all worked up? Or is there still some of your own stuff about the accident that you haven't dealt with?"

She looked down and stabbed a toe into the sand. "Sometimes you're so smart I can't stand it. I honestly hadn't even thought of that. But maybe that's what's bothering me so much."

"If somebody came along and wanted to make a movie of your life story, how would you feel?"

"Mostly awful, I think. And I'm pretty sure that's how Herschel feels too."

"I'm sure you're right. I'm just thinking that maybe you should let him fight his own battles. He seems perfectly capable of doing so."

She took a last sip of coffee and with an exaggerated sigh said, "Okay. I should head back and get ready for the office."

They hugged good-bye, and Mila collected her board and walked home slowly. She hated to admit it, but Hersch and his steamy lovemaking had gotten under her skin, and her sister had gotten straight to the heart of her annoyance with Jay. What was it with her lately? She kept things in control—everything from her time to her love life. Now? She felt her control slipping, and she didn't like it one bit.

# Chapter Twenty-Two

Mila couldn't believe she had actually done a pinkie swear with Erin, like they were twelve years old. But then, secretly maybe she was happy to have a reason to be forced to give Herschel a chance.

Erin knew her as well as anybody did, and if she could see that there was something special between Mila and Hersch, maybe Mila should listen. Besides, it wasn't difficult to imagine spending a little more time with the sexy astronaut. She couldn't stop fantasizing about getting wild with him again in bed. He had surprised her in every possible way. He could take charge in the bedroom while also making sure to check in with her, and he was unbelievably sensitive to her needs.

A couple of times, she found herself just gazing out of the office window, forgetting what she was working on. She was that blissed out.

When Hersch called her a little later, she was shocked at the way her heart jumped when she saw his name flashing on her phone. Instead of putting on her professional greeting voice, she just answered with, "Hey."

"Hey yourself," he said, his voice all low and sexy. "I want to ask you a favor."

"Okay."

"Archer put me in touch with your dad, and he's lined up some local painters for me. I've got some paint samples like you suggested, but I don't know which colors I like. Do you think you could give me a hand today?"

Mila laughed. "Wow, you work fast."

"I like to be efficient."

She respected that. But still, he wasn't wasting any time. She checked her schedule and said she could be there by four. Then she plowed through her to-do list so competently that she did everything she needed to do by three-forty.

When she drove up to Hersch's place, she was surprised to see her dad's truck sitting in the driveway. She recognized a low stab of disappointment as it reached her belly. Part of her had hoped that the painting call was more of a booty call than an interior-design emergency. But she should have known better. Hersch was a man of his word—if he'd been calling for hot sex, he would have just said, *Come over and get back in my bed.*

She rang the bell, and after Hersch let her in and gave her a quick peck hello, he led her to the living room, where she found Howard Davenport admiring the view. When he saw her, he came over to give her a hug.

"I know she's my daughter, Herschel, but I have to say Mila did fine work finding you this beautiful home. It just seems to suit you."

"She's the best Realtor I've ever worked with," he agreed.

Mila felt a glow of pride because her dad wasn't the kind of person who gave out compliments he didn't mean. She was glad he'd noticed, too, that this house was perfect for Herschel. While her dad was going on about the fine bones and the quality construction, she snuck a glance at Herschel and saw that he was gratified by the Howard Davenport stamp of approval. It was all feeling a little bit too mutual-appreciation-society for Mila, who had to break the tension by cracking a joke.

"Dad, are you doing the painting now too?"

He shook his head at her. "I admit I wanted to get a gander at this place. I've always admired it. So I brought the paint samples over myself, and Herschel was kind enough to give me a tour."

She couldn't believe him. Was it the house he'd wanted to see, or had he just wanted to meet the famous astronaut? Either way, he was as nosy as she was. Or maybe she'd inherited that trait from him. Still, her dad also had a good eye for design and color, having worked on so many homes over the years, and somehow the three of them found themselves on Hersch's couch discussing color palettes and possibilities.

Mila was surprised that spending time with her dad and her new lover didn't feel weird at all. In fact, it felt entirely natural, the conversation easy and warm, as though Hersch was already part of the family. Between them, they came up with a color plan that she thought would work. Her dad opened the tiny paint cans and took the time to paint sizable squares of three colors on the wall. He did the same in the kitchen, the bedroom, and the hallway. All of them had agreed that it would be best to keep all the hallways the same color and add a little more variety to the main living rooms.

After Howie was finished, Herschel offered him a beer to say thank you, but after shooting a far too scrutinizing look at his daughter, he said he'd better not. Betsy wanted him home in time for dinner. And with a cheerful good-bye, he left.

As his truck disappeared down the drive, Mila watched with a mix of pride for having such a cool dad and happiness that she was finally alone with Hersch.

"I like your dad," Herschel said, coming to join her at the window.

She grinned at him. "Everybody loves my dad. He's the best." Then she sniffed the air. "Something smells really good."

He looked slightly bashful. "It's lasagna. I made dinner in case you wanted to stay."

She felt her nose wrinkle in disbelief. "You made lasagna? Like, from scratch?"

"Sure. I told you I like to cook." Then he paused, and she felt there was something he wasn't going to say. Then he changed his mind. "Actually, I have a confession."

Mila's heart began to thud. Obviously, all this was too good to be true. Was he about to put another caveat on their time together?

"Your dad told me it was your favorite meal. That's why I cooked it."

She laughed, relieved. And then her eyebrows rose of their own accord. "Wait—that came up in conversation how?"

Hersch looked bashful again. "I may have asked him. In the context of my wanting to make you dinner to thank you for finding me this perfect house."

"Right. Because he doesn't know about the housewarming party for two."

"That would be correct. And if I have anything to say about it, he'll never find out."

"Well, as it turns out, I am free tonight." She sighed blissfully. "And lasagna is my fave. I guess I have no choice but to hang around a little while longer." She shot him a coy smile.

They ate in the kitchen, and not only had he made

possibly the best lasagna she'd ever eaten, there was a gorgeous salad bursting with fresh fruit and vegetables to go with it, along with crusty bread from her favorite bakery. This was a man who knew the way to Mila's heart... by more than one path.

But for now, Mila put that thought out of her mind. She just wanted to relax, and she quickly found herself doing just that. They chatted about their days, and she told him a bit about a couple who were being completely indecisive, even after she'd found them the perfect house. He told her he'd met his neighbors, and they were very nice. It was just the kind of comfortable conversation that two people who spent a lot of time together would indulge in. She tried not to let it worry her. She'd pinkie sworn after all.

After she'd turned down a third helping of lasagna, he tidied up and then said, "Dessert?"

She put a hand to her full stomach. "I don't think I can manage it."

He gave her a very wicked grin. "Good. I was hoping you'd say that." He stepped toward her and began to unbutton her blouse. "Because I was hoping you'd be my dessert."

While the last of the evening sun streamed into the kitchen, he stripped her naked, hoisted her onto the cool stone of the kitchen island, and proceeded to work a sweet magic more delectable than any dessert.

★ ★ ★

Mila woke in Hersch's bed again. Strangely, she was less freaked out this time and allowed herself to stretch and study Hersch as he slept. He was naked, as was she, and his body in repose was a thing of delight— strong but peaceful, the new sheets twisted around his hard abs as if tying a bow. She smiled and then checked her watch. It was still early—plenty of time to surf. Not because she had to, but just because she wanted to. She felt full of energy, even though her body was languorous from another night of expert lovemaking.

Once more, she tried to creep around and get dressed without waking him, and once more, she failed. He opened his eyes, propped his head on his arm, and said, "You're up early. Again."

"Epic waves do not wait, my friend."

He yawned and stretched and got out of bed too.

"Why don't you go back to sleep?"

"Can't. I'm awake now."

On impulse, she asked, "If you're up anyway, why don't you come down to the beach with me?" She held back from asking him to surf, but the implication was there.

The moment stretched, and she could feel his fear fighting with his determination to overcome it. She actually saw him pull in a breath and straighten his shoulders.

He nodded. "Okay. I will. But for the love of God, let me have a cup of coffee first."

She was so delighted she'd have let him have eggs Benedict before they went surfing, but coffee was quicker. He disappeared into his workout room and emerged with a wetsuit.

Seeing her raised eyebrows, he said, "I got one for my Ironman competitions."

"Right." She had to remember that he was a strong and excellent swimmer, that his fear of the water was very new.

She suggested they take one car and head to her place first so she could change into her wetsuit.

As she pulled into her drive, she realized this was the first time he would see her little house. It was much more modest than his, but she loved it. She hoped he would see it the same way she did.

He asked if he could take a look around, then walked through her house, not like someone on a real estate tour, but like someone getting to know a person. He looked at the titles on her bookshelves—a lot of books on surfing and recovering from injuries, on positive thinking and sales techniques. There were a few serious novels in there, too, mostly because Erin pressed them on her, and then Mila would reluctantly start them and find herself so engrossed she couldn't put them down.

He glanced at her with a laugh in his eyes. "Your

bookshelf is a lot like you are."

"Really?"

"Sure. A lot of lightness on top, but some deep, serious stuff underneath. And always a belief that everything will turn out right."

She thought that was a pretty accurate description of her personality, and was impressed at how he'd pegged her so soon.

He rocked back on his heels. "The house suits you too. A lot of character, and it's as much a part of Carmel-by-the-Sea as you are."

Again, she was charmed by the way he'd phrased that. "The best view's in my bedroom."

He looked quite pleased to be invited into her bedroom. As they walked in together, and she saw it through his eyes, she said, "Of course, if you bought this house, you'd brick that window up so you didn't have to look at the view."

He winced. "Give me credit. I'm trying to get better."

She touched his shoulder, then gripped it reassuringly. "I do." As if to reassure him further, she gave him a steamy kiss, which made her want to rip his clothes off and push him onto her bed, but she stopped herself. It was time to surf and time for Hersch to get back in the water. The hot sex could come later. She picked up a board for her and asked if he wanted one.

"No board. If I get in above my ankles, I'll call today a win."

She agreed, understanding how important this was for him. She changed into her wetsuit right there in the bedroom, and he did the same. With some satisfaction, she noticed their kiss had aroused him as much as it had her. Then they headed out to the beach.

He was such a gentleman, he insisted on carrying her surfboard, which she found kind of sweet, considering she'd been carrying her own since she was five years old. She must have walked this beach, run this beach, and done cartwheels on this beach a million times. But she'd never walked it beside Herschel Greenfield.

When he put out his hand, she interlaced her fingers with his and was almost shocked at how comfortable it felt. As though they'd walked hand in hand for years, and yet, at the same time, it was all so very new.

She could sense Hersch already getting nervous as they approached the tide line. Rather than looking forward, he tilted his face toward the sky. She figured that was where he felt most at home. It was still early, still dawn, and the moon was a pale crescent. To distract him, she asked, "Do you know much about the stars?"

He looked puzzled by the question, but then pleasure overtook his expression. "I know a fair bit. Not as much as I'd like."

"Do you have a favorite constellation?"

Now he grinned. "Favorite constellation? But they're all perfect in their own way. The ancient Greeks gave us most of the names."

She nudged him with her elbow. "Hersch, don't answer me as a scientist. Answer me as a man who loves the stars."

"Orion," he answered without a moment's hesitation. "It's visible in both the north and south hemispheres and contains some of the brightest stars in the sky."

She grinned and then couldn't help herself—she leaned forward, tilting her chin a little, her mouth softening in invitation. When he kissed her, she felt the electricity, and the instant connection made her press her body hard against his. She just couldn't get enough of him.

When they pulled away, Hersch took a deep breath and said, "You sure are good at making me forget my fears."

She brushed his cheek with her fingertips, and then he kissed the tips of her fingers. They stood together at the water's edge. Hersch looked out, a grim expression on his face.

"Remember how well you did last time," she said. "You know as well as I do that your recovery is about putting the pieces together. I used to drive my surfboard down to the beach when I couldn't surf yet and just sit there with it and watch the waves. It was my way of reminding myself that I'd get back there one day. That's what you're doing. Just taking it one step at a time."

"When you're with me, I feel like it's possible." With that, he took a step forward without her. The water rushed over his feet, but he stood strong. This time, she let him take the lead and watched as he steeled himself and moved forward another inch.

"You're doing great," she whispered. "I'm right here."

Inch by inch, he kept going, and then to her delight, he made it in up to his knees. She strode out to meet him and took his hand. It was shaking. She turned him to face her and kissed him again, a passionate kiss that she hoped he would feel all the way through his being.

When they pulled away, he said, "I want to go in up to my waist, but I don't think I'm ready."

She wanted to hug him. "Don't push it. You've already smashed this week's record. Be proud of yourself. I know I am."

He shook his head. She could tell he was both pleased by and disappointed in his progress. She knew exactly what that felt like, and her heart went out to him.

"I'm going to head in and take a seat on that log over there. What I'd like most is to watch you surf. Is that okay? You look incredible when you're out there doing what you love."

She was delighted. "Of course. I've missed having an audience, and now I have a super sexy one."

* * *

Hersch settled himself on the log and breathed a huge sigh of relief. With Mila's help, he'd managed to go farther into the water than he could have imagined. He slipped on his sunglasses to shield his eyes against the rising sun and followed Mila's progress as she rode the waves. She was so beautiful and so brave. Right there, he made the decision to go to the beach with her every morning. He vowed that he would go deeper each time.

When she emerged from the water, he leaped to his feet and went to kiss her.

"You were amazing out there. Can you spend the day with me?"

"I wish I could, but I've got appointments this morning, then I'm tasting wedding cake and food with Tessa, my mom, and my sister."

"Tasting wedding cake?" He looked puzzled. "For Archer and Tessa? But they just announced their engagement. I'm sure I saw something as I was flipping channels last night about a wedding in Scotland."

She hesitated and then said, "That's only for show. They're really getting married here in Carmel, a really small wedding. Top secret."

"Good for them." He waited, wondering if she'd mentioned the cake because she was planning to invite him as her plus-one, but she didn't.

She threw her arms around him. "You did so well today. I'll see you tomorrow morning for surfing?"

He kissed her again, lingering longer this time, until she pulled away, breathless and laughing. "I really do need to go."

"Go now, or I can't promise that you'll make it to the menu tasting. Enjoy every bite."

She gave him a little nip on the lower lip. "I just did."

He laughed and then stood beside her on the sand, watching her, wanting her more and more with every second that passed.

*Is this what true love feels like?*

From somewhere deep inside, he felt the reply. *Yes.*

# Chapter Twenty-Three

Francesca's Catering was famous for both its catering and its discretion. The storefront was tucked away in a high-end outdoor shopping center about fifteen minutes' drive from Carmel. When Mila arrived, Crystal Lopez was standing in front of Francesca's window, speaking on the phone. Mila knew Crystal, as she'd been in Erin's year in high school and had been friends with Damien, two years older, for years. Back in high school, Crystal had been involved in organizing everything from school concerts to prom, so it was no surprise when she turned those skills into a living. Now, at thirty, she ran a successful event-planning business.

Crystal waved a greeting to Mila while giving someone instructions in Spanish. She gestured with her free hand to make a point, and the gold bracelets on her wrist flashed in the sunshine, as did the gold hoops in her ears. Crystal was gorgeous. There was no other word for it. She had long dark hair, which she wore in a ponytail today, huge dark eyes that could flash from tragedy to comedy in seconds, a full-lipped, sensuous mouth, and a lithe dancer's body. She wore loose black trousers and a fuchsia blouse. She ended the call and came forward. "Mila, hi, it's been ages."

They kissed cheeks, and Crystal said, "I hope you're hungry. We have lots of food to sample."

"I brought my appetite," Mila assured her.

Tessa turned up next, and after the quickest greeting, Crystal shepherded them into the storefront, scanning behind them as she did so. Mila knew she was looking for any paparazzi who might have followed Tessa.

They didn't even speak to the woman at the front desk, but walked through a door that Crystal opened. They were met by a stylish older woman all in black. "Crystal, it's lovely to see you again." She held out her hands and kissed Crystal on both cheeks.

This was Francesca, the famous chef who'd decided to move into catering. Mila knew Crystal had pulled strings and called in favors to get Francesca to take on a rush job, but nothing in Francesca's manner suggested she was anything but delighted to cook for them.

She showed them to a private room set up like a dining room and said Sergio would look after them.

When they were seated, each with a clipboard, pen, and menus of the items they'd be sampling, Mila noticed the two empty places at the table. "Where are Mom and Erin? Running late?"

Tessa shook her head. "Betsy had a crisis with a student, and Erin had a big story come in. She said she couldn't get away."

Mila scoffed. "A big story at the *Sea Shell*? Maybe the Dog of the Week got fleas."

Tessa smiled briefly, but Mila could tell she wasn't used to the teasing that went on among the Davenports.

"I've lined up a series of menus for you to try," Crystal said, gesturing to the clipboards. "After you and I talked, Tessa, I worked with Francesca to come up with a casually elegant menu suitable for a small garden wedding."

Obviously, Tessa was the one who would be making all the final choices, but she wanted more opinions. She probably felt a little out of her comfort zone here, but presumably among the three of them, they could find a menu that would work. Mila vowed to be as useful as possible. She didn't have a very busy day today, and she wasn't one to turn down delicious free food, though maybe she was slightly disappointed that she hadn't been able to spend the day with Hersch. She could just imagine how they would have spent it too.

As she looked over the three menus that included a cocktail hour, three courses, dessert, and a late-night snack, she found herself impressed. Everything sounded totally yummy and luxurious. Among the many offerings were mini crab cakes with avocado aioli, creamy lobster bisque, and filet mignon. She read the descriptions, salivating, and noted with pleasure how everything was farm-to-table.

"What do you think?" Crystal asked, and Mila realized she'd been waiting for a reaction.

She said to Crystal, "It all looks great. I'm assuming money's no object?"

Tessa immediately looked stricken, and the happy flush disappeared from her cheeks. She put a hand to her chest. "Honestly, I don't need an extravagant wedding. I thought your father's suggestion that we do hamburgers and hot dogs on the grill was fine."

Mila put an arm around her soon-to-be sister-in-law. "Don't mind me. Of course you want a beautiful wedding meal, and we're going to choose you one. That dig would have been a lot funnier if my brother were here. I'm used to teasing him, and sometimes I forget myself."

Tessa still looked worried. "I can't even imagine how much a wedding in Scotland is going to cost, and it's only a decoy." Then she lowered her voice. "Mila, Archer is talking about flying us all there on *private planes*."

She had to bite back a smile. Tessa's life was changing in a lot of ways. As she glanced down at the menus, she said, "At least let's make sure we pick the popcorn for the late-night snack. It's so perfect, Arch being a movie star and all."

Tessa and Crystal looked delighted by this idea, and without even trying, one decision had been made. Then Sergio, Francesca's son, arrived, all Italian and gorgeous. He presented the goat cheese and fig crostini, and all three of them found it delicious. While she tasted, Mila contemplated Tessa. The kind and warm-hearted woman who'd won her brother's heart was being tossed seriously out of her comfort zone. Decoy weddings and private planes, red-carpet events and paparazzi stalking her. It must be super stressful for someone who'd never been in the public eye before.

As she nibbled on the prawn and mango salad, she asked her, "How do you reconcile how much your life has changed? Do you feel like you're losing your identity?" As soon as she said the words, Mila realized she might have been too blunt. Truth was, she was wondering how much love could change a person.

Tessa wiped her mouth daintily with a napkin and seemed to genuinely consider the question. "I don't think I am losing my identity. I think I'm embracing a new one, that of Archer's wife. I'll still be me. Maybe I won't work as a caregiver anymore, because I'm selling paintings now, but I was always an artist, and it was Arch who made me see that. I think when I'm with him, I'm a better version of myself."

Mila thought this was a beautiful answer. She was still considering it when they moved on to tasting cake. As she bit into a chocolate fudge cake that had the most delicious chocolate and coffee icing she'd ever tasted, she continued to contemplate what Tessa had said. Finally, she had to ask, "But how do you know he's right for you? I mean, how do you actually know he's The One, out of all the men in the world that you could have met and married?"

Tessa put a star beside the chocolate cake on the checklist they were using and then said, "I don't know. I just really love him."

Crystal had been watching this interchange. "These are really good questions. Honestly, as a wedding planner, I wish more couples spent time thinking about these things. It's not whether you wear a veil or not that matters in the end. It's whether you chose a compatible partner."

Tessa laughed. "My wedding dress was the easiest choice I ever made. I'll be wearing Betsy's dress, and I couldn't be happier. But Arch is the person I want to be with. When I wake up in the morning, he's there beside me. It's the best feeling. And even if we argue sometimes, or he gets high-handed with me, or I have to remind him that I need time to paint, I know he gets me, and I think I get him."

Crystal and Mila exchanged a glance, and Crystal said, "Wow, that is true love. You're not being definitive. You're just trusting."

Tessa turned to her. "I think when you're truly in love, the trust is a natural part of it."

Trust. It was definitely the cornerstone of a good relationship. Was Mila willing to risk her heart by trusting again? "But what if your heart is wrong?"

Tessa looked over at her and obviously understood. "I get it. I was definitely not looking for love or marriage, especially since I'd been married before and not very happily, if I'm honest. But I think that even with whatever damage we're carrying around inside ourselves, if we're listening closely enough to what's truly inside our hearts, I don't think the heart can ever steer us wrong."

★ ★ ★

Having eaten a lot of tiny pieces of food and enjoyed her time with Tessa and Crystal more than she could have imagined, Mila checked her watch and then her email as they prepared to leave Francesca's. Her only client for tomorrow had canceled their appointment, citing a dental emergency. She felt bad for them, but pleased for herself. Now she could spend the whole day with her new lover.

Crystal said, "I'll tell Francesca what we've chosen. It's a beautiful menu. All this food is paid for. Why don't you take some of it?"

Mila spied the chocolate fudge cake and thought how much Hersch might enjoy it, so Crystal had the staff cut about a quarter of the cake, wrap it up, and put it in a box for her to take home. She waved away the rest of the food, but that chocolate cake was calling to her. She left first, got in her car, and as if on autopilot, drove straight to Herschel's place. Then, as she sat in her car outside his house, she thought, *What am I doing? I can't just show up on his doorstep with cake.* So she called him.

He sounded delighted to hear from her. "How did the tasting go?"

"Really well. In fact, I'm outside your house with a cake sample."

He laughed. "What are you doing calling me? Come on in."

She took in the cake, and they headed to the kitchen, which, second to the bedroom, was becoming their favorite room.

"I have more good news," she told him. "My only appointment tomorrow afternoon canceled. If you still want to spend the day with me, I'm free."

"That is excellent news."

"Almost as excellent as this cake. It's so good you have to try it." As she opened the cake box, he reached for forks, but she stopped him.

"I don't think we're going to eat this with forks."

He grinned down at her. "Okay, then."

Keeping her gaze on his, she reached in, scooped up a chunk of chocolate cake with her fingers, and fed it to him.

"Oh my, that is good," he said. "I never allow myself treats. Is this what I've been missing?"

"Mm-hmm," she said, pulling off a creamy cherry and popping it into his mouth.

"You're killing me," he murmured. Then, reaching for the box, he fed her a chunk of cake. She felt the icing melting against her lips and licked them slowly, seductively. She reached for him, not caring that she was smearing cake crumbs on his jeans. Before she knew it, he was slipping off her dress. She felt it flutter to the floor in a puddle.

"Nothing is sweeter than the taste of you," he murmured, licking her neck, then her collarbone, and then finally releasing her breasts from her bra and licking her nipples. She shivered with a pleasure so deep it felt primal. She let herself melt into his arms and moaned as he continued to strip her naked. Suddenly, he stood back and then dropped to his knees. With a sexy grin, he reached for the cake and smeared some icing on her navel. Using his tongue, he gently licked it off in circles, making his way down, farther and farther, until she was trembling, no longer able to support herself.

He scooped her up then and laid her back on the kitchen counter. She let her eyelids flicker shut and concentrated on the intense waves his mouth was giving her. Her body was sticky—from cake and from his mouth and from her own pleasure. There was something extra hot about him being fully clothed and her naked. She felt more worshiped than she ever had before, as though she were his Earth, and he was the moon, orbiting around her. It was heaven.

★ ★ ★

The next morning, Mila woke up Hersch.

He groaned. "What time is it?"

"Six a.m. That's when the waves are best."

He opened one eye, then the other. She kissed him, enjoying the tickle of his moustache that had become so familiar to her she could no longer imagine kissing a man without one.

"Tell me you're not going to make me go surfing with you this early."

"Come on, you did so well yesterday. We've got to seize the day."

He shook his head. "I'm pretty sure I injured myself."

She put her hands on her hips. "Hersch, you got in up to your knees."

"I think I stubbed my toe on a rock."

She pulled off the covers and slapped his rump. "You'll thank me afterward."

He groaned but was soon dressed and had coffee on. They ate a quick bowl of cereal with coffee. This time when they headed out, she grabbed a boogie board for him. He eyed it suspiciously.

"It's not surfing. You don't go in deep water. We're

just going to play like kids."

Then she put her surfboard back and grabbed a boogie board for herself as well.

While there were plenty of good waves out there, Mila resolutely turned her attention away from them, and she and Hersch ran up and down the beach, jumping on their boards and sliding like kids. Not even the dogs racing to catch balls were flying as high as Mila and Hersch on their boogie boards. She felt more carefree than she had in years.

After an hour, they were laughing, and Hersch was in above his knees now. She didn't think he'd even noticed. She kissed him, and he put his forehead against hers.

He said, "I'm so glad you're spending the day with me."

"Me too. You can consider it part of your welcome tour to the area. Part of the professional package of services I offer to my *very special* clients."

At the words *very special*, he grinned and pulled her in for another kiss. They went back to her place, and he helped her take off her suit.

"I think a little bit of chocolate cake ended up in the wrong place," he said and then leaned forward to lick the possibly nonexistent chocolate off the slope of her breast. They got in the shower, soaping each other up and enjoying each other with an urgency that surprised her. When they'd both climaxed under the streaming water, they turned off the shower and got out.

Then she opened her cabinet of wonders and treated him to an unscented sunscreen that was also a really good moisturizer. She took it upon herself to rub it well into his skin, explaining how important it was not to get a sunburn.

The next item on their agenda for the day was a bike ride down 17-Mile Drive. Of course, he had his own bike, and she had hers, so they donned helmets and headed out. It started out as a tranquil ride, as she pointed out to him some of the fanciest houses, more than one of which she'd sold, the Instagram-famous Lone Cypress, and the beauty of the coastline and forest. She loved showing off the gorgeous scenery and breathing in the sea-tinged air. But then she noticed he was riding a little faster than she was, and she was falling behind.

It sparked her competitive streak, so she picked up the pace until she was ahead of him. If Hersch was going to treat this like training, she would show him what she was made of. Her legs began to burn, and before she knew it, there were two very competitive people racing neck and neck, pretty much flying down the quiet road. They continued side by side, and soon the need to beat him rolled back to reveal an exhilaration that she'd found a man who could match her both physically and competitively. She was pretty sure he wouldn't pout if she won their race and then tried her level best to prove her point. However, he wasn't letting her win, no way. They reached the end of the drive, and by the imaginary finish line, they were both sweating profusely, their chests heaving with effort.

He turned and grinned at her. "That was amazing."

She laughed. "It was. I think you won by half a wheel."

He took a mock bow, and she laughed again. She was enjoying getting to know his more goofy, less serious side.

"I'll get you next time," she said, hoping beyond hope that there would be many more "next times" to come.

Hersch wiped sweat from his chin.

She asked, "Are you up for a hike? There are some amazing views I'd love to show you."

He raised his brows. "You're insatiable. Boogie boarding, cycling, and now hiking?"

"For some reason, I'm full of energy." It was true. Right now, she felt like she had enough energy to hike Mount Everest.

"Okay," he said. "If I ever get my breath back."

They both rehydrated when they returned to the car, and then she drove them to Garland Ranch Regional Park. It was a warm day, and she was in skimpy shorts and a sports bra under a wicking T-shirt that was already wet from the sweat of their ride. He was likewise casually dressed in shorts and a T-shirt.

However, Hersch being Hersch, he also carried a full backpack. When she quizzed him on what was in it, he told her water, snacks, medical supplies in case either of them had an accident, and a GPS device in case their phones stopped working.

Her jaw almost dropped. "You sure like to be prepared."

"Fail to prepare, prepare to fail," he said.

She carried a small bottle of water and a baseball cap to shield her face from the sun.

They set off, and as in the bike race, they were soon going at a pretty fair clip. They started by Carmel River, where the path was shaded by sycamore trees, then the trail veered sharply up, and they kept their fast pace.

She loved it. She loved not having to hold back or slow down. Even when she hiked with her sister or brothers, she often felt as though she was pacing herself, but not with Hersch. She could push as hard as she wanted, and he was right there with her.

They left the shade behind, and the sun grew increasingly warm. Soon, she'd gone through her bottle of water and was grateful when he handed her a fresh one from his pack. When the heat was too much, she simply pulled off her shirt, hiking in nothing but her sports bra and tiny shorts, and then he followed suit, stripping off his shirt so he was bare-chested. She had to stop glancing his way, because it made her mouth even drier, and all she wanted to do was stop and take him right here and right now.

They eventually reached the top of the trail, and munched apples he'd brought along.

When they got back, she took him to the farmers' market, and they both ordered three kinds of juice and then headed to the taco stand. "Everything tastes so much better when you've worked up an appetite," he said.

They found a grassy area and sat in the shade. He leaned against a tree trunk and tucked her under his arm so her head was on his chest. As she drank fresh juice and snacked on enchiladas, she wondered if she'd ever been this happy.

Hersch said, "I don't want this day to end. Do you have plans tonight?"

Mila toyed with a taco chip, buying herself a little time to think about what she was going to say next. Then, with both Erin's and Tessa's words about trust ringing in her memory, she said, "Arch and Tessa's real wedding is Saturday, two days from now. So far, it doesn't seem like any paps have gotten wind of it, but we have to be so careful. We're planning a family barbecue tonight to have some family time before the big day. Dad loves to get behind a grill and throw together hot dogs and hamburgers, and Mom makes her famous potato salad. It's traditional, but it means a lot to us."

"That sounds nice," he said, just a tad wistfully.

She turned to him. If she was honest with herself, she'd been thinking about this moment all day. She wanted to invite him to the Davenport home tonight and let him be part of their family tradition. But it was a big step. A huge step. She flashed back to him on the boogie board this morning. He and the water were a maybe, but she could see that maybe was making its way to yes. In the same way, her maybe about him was slowly but surely turning into a yes.

Finally, she said, "Would you like to come?"

He looked delighted with the invitation. "I'd love to. What can I bring?"

"Nothing. Dad will already have the beer and soft drinks on ice, and he'll have already bought the food."

He looked very serious. "Does your dad barbecue over real coals?"

"Yeah. I told you, it's not fancy."

He shook his head slowly at her. "We need to stop at the store, stat."

She merely raised her brows at him, and he said, "Where I come from, when you finish a meal like that, you have to have s'mores."

She had to hold back her laugh. "Now you're getting fancy."

"I want to make a good impression on your family."

When they'd cleaned up and dressed for the family

barbecue, they stopped at the corner store on their way to the Davenport home. She'd taken time to message the family group and let them know she was bringing Hersch, just to avoid any awkward exclamations. The replies were all positive—lots of thumbs-up, and of course Arch sent the heart symbol. She was hoping that the sibs might be a little more cool about things when she and Hersch arrived and act like she brought men to their family barbecues all the time, when in fact the only man she'd ever brought here was Travis, and that hadn't exactly turned out well.

But she was a different Mila now, and Hersch was nothing like her ex.

# Chapter Twenty-Four

Mila felt slightly nervous when they arrived at her parents' house to join the family for dinner. Before she opened the door, she turned to Hersch.

"Do we need a signal? If you're really not having a good time, maybe we should have a word you can say so I'll know to get you out of there."

His eyebrows rose. "You mean like a safe word?"

Immediately, she thought of all the kinky sexual positions they could be in that would involve a safe word and shook her head. "No. Well, not exactly. But my family can be a little much en masse."

He put an arm around her shoulders. "I think I'll be okay."

She realized that he wasn't as nervous as she was. In fact, he didn't seem nervous at all. He'd dressed in casual jeans and a relaxed white shirt, and he looked gorgeous. Moustache and all. She'd thrown on a black cotton dress and hoop earrings and let her hair hang loose down her back.

As she opened the door, she turned to look over

her shoulder. "Don't say I didn't warn you."

Tessa and Erin were in the main room with Crystal, unpacking wedding decorations. Hersch immediately went up to Tessa and said, "You need no introduction. Your painting of the Carmel cypresses is one of the things I love most about my new home."

Tessa turned pink with pleasure.

As Crystal shook his hand, she shot a puzzled look at Mila. Then she said, quite seriously, "You know this wedding's top secret, right? If word gets out—"

"You can trust Hersch, Crystal," Mila said. Did she really think she'd invite someone into their family who would blow a secret wedding operation? And then it occurred to her that she'd trusted Hersch from the beginning. She wasn't even sure she'd emphasized enough that this first wedding was a deep, dark secret, but she knew as well as she knew her own name that Hersch would never betray them to the media.

Herschel assured Crystal that he would keep the wedding in absolute confidence and was honored to be entrusted with such an important secret. That seemed to mollify Crystal, who said, "If anyone asks about the activity that's been going on around here, Howie and Betsy are throwing a wedding anniversary party." She went back to separating out the bows and balloons that had been delivered.

"Dad is loving the subterfuge," Erin said with a grin. She greeted Hersch with a hug and went to get him a beer.

In the backyard, Mila's brothers and dad were gathered around the fire pit. Each had a beer in hand, and the family resemblance was striking.

Betsy was setting the table. They'd pulled the picnic table and an extra fold-up patio table together, which they always did when there was a big crowd. Betsy was an old hand at catering for large numbers. She'd been doing it forever. She had a way of pulling together a dinner in no time and somehow making it work. She looked up when Mila called her name and put down the napkins she was folding to come forward.

Mila felt almost shy as she said, "Mom, I want you to meet Herschel Greenfield."

Betsy shook his hand and gave him her beautiful smile, but Mila could see she was appraising him as well. "It's a pleasure to meet you, Herschel. You're a man who needs no introduction. I remember how we were all glued to the TV during that terrifying rescue operation." She put her other hand over the back of his so his hand was sandwiched between hers. "I'm so glad you're with us today."

There were so many ways to interpret that. Mila gave her mom credit for being both genuine and tactful.

"Thank you very much for having me, Mrs. Davenport," Herschel said.

Her mom just patted his hand. "In this house, I'm either Mom or Betsy."

He laughed. "I'll choose Betsy." And then, so softly Mila barely heard him, he said, "For now."

Then she led him toward the clump of testosterone around the fire pit. The five Davenport men seemed to rock back on their heels and narrow their eyes at Herschel as though they'd planned to do it in sync. She swore that if one of them gave him a hard time, she'd plant her fist in his belly.

Then Howie came forward with his big hand outstretched. "How's the painting going?"

"I'm very pleased. Your crew are doing a great job."

Howie nodded, but she could tell he was proud of his work and his employees. "I told them to do an especially good job and do it quickly. Any friend of Mila's always gets special treatment."

Hersch said, "I think you're a good family to know. Everyone in town seems to pull special favors when a Davenport's involved."

Howie chuckled at that. "We've lived here a long time. Have deep roots in the community. It helps."

Hersch already knew Arch, and they clapped each other on the back like old friends. She watched as he met Finn and Damien, while Nick, her high-tech billionaire bro, sized him up. She was tempted to join the men to give Hersch support, until Mila felt a hand on her shoulder and found her mom leaning in. "Don't look so worried. They're not going to eat him."

"I think I'm more nervous than he is," she admitted. "We can be intimidating."

Betsy chuckled. "We can, but let's face it, Herschel Greenfield's dealt with worse."

Her dad was in his element. While the men, including Hersch, who had a beer in his hand just like the others, stood around, Howie piled things on the barbecue. In a loud voice, he said, "Who put tofu on my platter?"

Erin called, "I did, Dad. You shouldn't eat so much meat."

He made a rude noise, but added the tofu to the marinated chicken breasts and the hamburgers and the hot dogs that were grilling away.

* * *

Before long, they took their seats around the big tables to eat. Betsy sighed and said, "It's so good to have all my children at home at the same time."

In a booming voice, Finn called, "It's not every day that you and Dad celebrate your wedding anniversary." It was loud enough that every nosy neighbor in town could hear him.

Tessa had to cover her mouth to stop her giggles. Any nosy neighbor who'd bothered to peek over the fence might not have been fooled. The way she and

Arch were looking at each other, hands held tight, spoke of a deep and abiding love—one that would take any couple down the aisle. Although, Mila had to admit, anybody looking at her mom and dad would reach the same conclusion. Maybe they'd been married for going on forty years, but Howie could never walk past Betsy without touching her on the shoulder or leaning down to kiss her cheek or whisper something private in her ear.

Mila had always believed she'd never find love like that, but there was Hersch sitting beside her, his knee pressed against hers under the table where no one else could see it. She felt a warmth and connection with him that surprised her.

When they'd finished dinner, Betsy said, "All I have for dessert is a big tub of ice cream."

Mila said, "Actually, Mom, I think Herschel is taking care of dessert."

They all turned to him as though expecting him to run inside and bring out a big bakery box. Instead, he said, "Who wants s'mores?"

There was a burst of delighted laughter. Nick even looked up from his phone, where he'd been texting somebody, to say, "I haven't had s'mores in years. Is this for real?"

Herschel nodded in his serious way. "I consider it one of my culinary specialties. Who wants s'mores?" he repeated. Every hand around the table went up. He said, "If you don't mind, Howie, I'll use the rest of your hot dog skewers."

"Be my guest," Howie said, clearly enjoying himself.

Mila went to the kitchen and brought out the graham crackers, Hershey's chocolate bars, and marshmallows. He quietly got to work with the intense concentration he seemed to apply to everything while the family gathered around to watch.

Normally, they all would have roasted their own marshmallows, but there was something about the way Hersch operated that made it more fun to watch. Erin was the first to speak. "When I roast a marshmallow, it always catches fire. But you have this amazing ability to just brown the outside without the marshmallow either catching fire or falling off the stick."

Without shifting his attention, he said, "It's a simple matter of physics and thermodynamics."

It was such a funny line—about s'mores—and yet, no one laughed because he was actually serious.

He slipped the first perfect marshmallow off the stick and onto a graham cracker on top of part of a candy bar, then another marshmallow and another piece of chocolate. He topped it all off with a second graham cracker. With careful precision, he pressed the two crackers together, and like magic, the marshmallow began to ooze and the chocolate to melt.

To Betsy, he said, "May I offer you the first one?"

"I'd be honored," she said, equally formally, and then as they all watched, Betsy bit into it. She literally moaned with delight. "Honestly, Herschel," she said after she finished a mouthful, "this is the best s'more I've ever eaten in my life."

"I'm glad to hear it," he replied. It didn't seem to be the first time he'd received this very compliment. Tessa got the second s'more, and as full as Mila was from dinner, her mouth was watering by the time he passed her one. Soon, everyone was enjoying their dessert.

Finn had a smear of chocolate on his lip, and Tessa was licking marshmallow off her thumb when Archer asked, "Do they teach this in astronaut school? Because you're the bomb at s'mores."

"They do not. But like everything else, a decent s'more involves a healthy dose of science."

No one was drunk, but there had been a few beers put away. Arch suddenly said, "Wait. If I'm going to play you in the biopic of your life, I need to shadow you. Herschel, you need to show me how to make a good s'more."

Nick jumped up and yelled, "Screen test! Wait, let me get the camera." He dashed into the house, no doubt to find the good old camcorder that the family had been using for years. All of them had smartphones that could have made a better recording, but there was something sentimental and nostalgic about that old camcorder. While he was gone, Mila realized there weren't enough ingredients for everybody to get a second s'more, so she went back into the kitchen to get more supplies. Her mom followed her.

Betsy put on tea and coffee and said, "Honey, I've never seen you like this with a man. Herschel seems to fit right in with all of us. Do you think there's a future there?"

Mila leaned against the fridge, her hands full of chocolate bars. "A few days ago, he was a maybe. But now, I get these visions of us. He's inserting himself into my brain."

Her mom nodded. Mila loved that Betsy didn't put pressure on her kids. All she said was, "Thanks for telling me. You know I'm always here if you ever want to talk."

"I know."

They headed back out and handed Herschel the extra supplies. Then they all stood around, watching. Nick yelled, "Screen test for Herschel Greenfield and Archer Davenport." Then he looked around at everyone. "What's the title of the movie? *Herschel Goes to Space…*"

"*And Comes Back*," Mila yelled.

Nick nodded. "Great title. Snappy. A blockbuster already. Okay. *Herschel Goes to Space and Comes Back*. Screen test with Archer Davenport. Take one." And then he started the camcorder.

Herschel looked around as though they were all

crazy, and then his gaze caught Mila's, where she saw the twinkle of amusement. He played right along. Turning to the camera, he said, "Not everyone takes the sweet dessert treat known as a s'more seriously. But I urge you to do so. Using physics and the laws of thermodynamics, we can avoid such disasters as the flaming marshmallow that's hard inside and charred on the outside, chocolate that's brittle and doesn't melt, and—perhaps saddest of all—the marshmallow that slips right off the skewer because it's been overheated and the inside lacks the structural integrity to hold itself on the stick."

Beside him, Archer was hamming it up like crazy. He was imitating every move, and then he called, "Cut."

Everyone stared at him. "I'm a method actor. I can't play you without a moustache."

"Where are you going to get a moustache now?" Erin asked him.

Running into the house, he said, "I'm a resourceful actor. I'll think of something."

Deciding that something very exciting was going on, Buster bounded into the house with him, barking.

"Mom!" Arch yelled. "Where's your knitting box?"

With a shake of her head, Betsy went inside, and within five minutes Archer returned. He might have the services of the finest hair and makeup people in the world at his disposal, but tonight, he walked out with pieces of black wool taped above his lip. When he talked, the bits of wool fluttered around his mouth.

It was the most ridiculous thing Mila had ever seen, but by some effort of will, she managed to keep a straight face as Archer strode up to stand beside Herschel and said, "Now I'm ready."

Nick yelled, "*Herschel Goes to Space and Comes Back,* Take two."

As Herschel made the s'more, he talked about the relatively low heat needed to break down the gelatin in the marshmallow so that the air pockets would expand, making it larger and softer as it warmed. Then he explained how the heat would break the bonds linking the fructose and glucose molecules to sugar, developing more nuanced flavors. Finally, he talked about something called the Maillard reaction, which apparently was a chemical process that happened when certain amino acids came up against each other, causing the outside of the marshmallow to brown and giving it its characteristic toasty flavor. It was hard to keep a straight face, especially when Archer insisted on making his own s'more.

Her brother pulled out every big word he knew, rolling the word *thermodynamics* around in his mouth as though it were a big wad of chewing gum. But at the end of it, he was able to present Herschel with a pretty good-looking s'more.

Very seriously, Herschel inspected it before biting

into it, and then he said to Archer, "That's not bad."

Archer whipped round to face the camera and said, "It's not rocket science."

Now the pent-up laughter they'd all been holding in burst out. While Nick yelled, "And that's a wrap," Hersch and Arch were patting each other on the back, and Mila and Erin were doubled over with giggles.

Howie wiped tears of laughter from his eyes and said, "Somebody better make me another s'more. I've definitely burned off the calories from the first one."

In the middle of the craziness and laughter, Mila felt slightly lightheaded at how well Herschel fit in with her family. Then Archer said, bits of black wool still flapping on his upper lip, "I guess the women melt all over you like this chocolate on a s'more."

Hersch paused and turned to look right at Mila. "I only want one woman."

Archer probably hadn't caught the moment, because he was still studying his s'more. He said, "You know, if you ever wanted to give up the astronaut gig, you could open a stall at the farmers' market."

Tessa came up beside Mila and said gently, but with a tinge of excitement, "Arch and I were talking earlier. There's plenty of room for Hersch at the wedding if you'd like to invite him."

Mila stared at her. This was a huge deal. They'd worked so hard to keep the wedding small and private. "Are you sure?"

Tessa whispered, "Arch likes him. I like him. And he really fits in. I have a feeling we'll be seeing more of Herschel Greenfield."

She knew that Tessa had meant to make Mila feel better and perhaps to signal both her and Arch's approval of Hersch as a potential... what? Boyfriend? Partner? Husband? The whole idea was freaking her out. Instead of feeling warm and fuzzy, she felt slightly panicked.

After tea and coffee and listening to Howie explain all the sneaky moves he'd pulled to get everything ready and brought into the house for the wedding without raising suspicion, Mila whispered to Hersch that they needed to get going.

They said their good-byes, and all the women hugged Hersch, and the men slapped him on the back. It was like he'd always been part of her family.

But oddly, her anxiety had begun to rise.

\* \* \*

They walked the short distance to the car, and Herschel opened her door for her, always the gentleman. As they drove away, she said, "I think we should sleep at our own places tonight."

He was clearly surprised as he turned to her. "Why?"

It would have been so easy to make an excuse—she was getting a headache, didn't feel well, was tired—but she decided to be honest with him. He deserved the truth. "I'm kind of freaking out. It was scary how well you fit in with my family. All of them are begging for you to be The One for me. But you've made it perfectly clear that you're not going to go down that road because your job is so dangerous and you don't want to leave a family behind if something bad happens." She paused a beat. "Has anything changed for you on that front?"

He was quiet for a long moment as he processed her question. She loved that he was measured and didn't blurt out the first thought in his head.

"Something has changed, but it's still scary for me." He leaned over and put a hand on her knee. "You have nothing to be nervous about. I won't push." Then he grinned at her. "Like you don't push me deeper and deeper into the water. Maybe that's a metaphor for our relationship. Every time I go deeper into the waves, I fall for you a little harder."

Oh, why did he have to do that? Why did he have to say the perfect thing? She knew exactly what he meant. That was how she felt, too—as though she was being pulled deeper and deeper, and the water was already over her head, and she wasn't sure she could swim.

He pulled up in front of her little house and didn't seem put out at all that she'd decided to sleep alone. She kissed him and said, "I'm sorry. I just need some time."

"I understand," He kissed her again, and waited in the car until she was safely inside before he drove away.

* * *

Herschel had trouble getting to sleep. In the short time they'd been together, he'd become accustomed to sleeping with his arms curled around Mila or her head on his chest or her legs tangled with his. Everything felt better when she was in his bed, and now he wondered how he'd ever slept before she'd come into his life. It was scary how quickly and how hard he'd fallen for this woman who was suddenly pulling away. It wasn't that he didn't understand her feelings, because he did. Weirdly, he just didn't share them.

He'd always thought he didn't have it in him to have a wife and family who might potentially be left behind with broken hearts. But as he considered his feelings for Mila, he wondered if he had been lying to himself all this time. Maybe what he was really scared of was that someone would break *his* heart.

And now here was a woman who was capable of doing just that. For once in his life, he just couldn't see a clear path of action. There was no logic here, no science. He'd finally allowed himself to fall deeply in love with a woman, and she was the one saying it might not work.

It was quite an epiphany to have at thirty-five years old.

He put a hand on his chest, and his palm brushed the disk of gold. The Saint Christopher's medal had gone to space with him and back again. He had traveled so far, never risking his heart. His life, sure, but never his heart. Now it was too late. His heart was gone. He hadn't lost it—he'd given it away. Voluntarily.

What was he going to do if Mila discovered she didn't love him the way he loved her?

He was still staring at the ceiling, pondering this question, when someone banged on his door.

A glance at the clock beside his bed told him that it was just after two a.m. He tried not to feel hopeful—maybe a neighbor had a broken water pipe or something—but still, he raced down the stairs to the front door. Taking a deep breath and steeling himself for disappointment, he opened it.

As he'd hoped against hope, Mila stood on his doorstep. He let out his breath. She was wearing sweatpants, a T-shirt, possibly no bra, and a pair of flip-flops.

"I couldn't sleep," she said, gesturing at her clothes.

"Me either." He opened the door wider. "I was waiting for you." And he realized that was true.

Without another word, she walked into his arms. He closed the door, and they went straight to his bedroom. When they made love, it was so sweet and so intimate they didn't need words. If two bodies could say *I love you*, theirs did, until they fell asleep in each other's arms.

★ ★ ★

They woke up early the next morning. Well, Mila woke up early and jarred him from sleep as she jumped out of bed. He didn't mind in the slightest. It had nearly killed him the night before when she'd wanted to sleep in separate houses. He was the most thankful man alive that she'd shown up in the middle of the night, wanting and needing to be with him, just like he'd wanted and needed her.

"There's just time to go surfing before work," she said brightly. "Then tonight, the girls will sleep over at Mom and Dad's, including Tessa, and the boys will hang out with Arch. We'll go to Mom and Dad's in casual clothes and then dress up there."

Hersch tried to stifle a yawn and wake up fully. "Wow, this is definitely a clandestine operation. Good thing I signed that nondisclosure agreement."

"Very funny." There was a pregnant pause, but she didn't invite him to come, at least not to the wedding. But she did invite him to go surfing. He accepted, still nervous but confident that Mila would be by his side.

When they got to the beach, he realized that all the dread he usually felt had melted away. Mila was making this fun for him, and he followed her into the water with his boogie board. It was interesting that, even though both of them were still processing what it meant to be so serious about each other, it hadn't ruined their budding friendship and respect for each other one bit. Maybe that was the foundation of a long-lasting relationship.

Swallowing down any residual fear, he managed to paddle his boogie board out. He could still touch the sand at the bottom, but now he was up to his shoulders in water. He couldn't believe his progress.

Mila beamed at him and then said the words he was so longing to hear. "I am so proud of you." She kissed him firmly on the mouth, her hand stroking the back of his neck. "You're a superstar."

He stared at her, realizing it was the greatest, most important compliment anyone had ever given him. Forget space and moon landings. Mila's praise and Mila's kisses were better than all the stars and the planets in the universe combined.

In a rush, as though she had to get the words out before she regretted them, she said, "I know it's really late notice, but would you like to come to Arch and Tessa's wedding with me?"

He knew how much it meant that she had invited him. "Luckily for you, I had my suit freshly dry-cleaned. Just in case."

# Chapter Twenty-Five

Saturday dawned bright and clear. It was the morning of Arch and Tessa's real wedding, and everyone was busy getting ready. The previous night, the women had gathered at the family home to sleep, and all the men had slept over at Archer's. Traditional though it was, they were definitely sticking to the notion that the groom shouldn't see the bride before the ceremony, and it had just seemed natural that Tessa would start out at the Davenport home. She was such a part of the family, Mila was always forgetting that she wasn't her actual sister and they hadn't grown up together.

As expected, everyone was excited about this first wedding of a Davenport sibling. Mila found it interesting that they were all calling it the first, as though there would be more, despite all the kids holding out this long. Still, when she saw the happiness glowing in Tessa's eyes, she couldn't help but feel wistful that maybe one day she'd be sitting there having Erin do her hair and makeup and chatting nervously about how much she hoped she wouldn't screw up on her big day.

They'd all suggested she get her hair and makeup done professionally, but Tessa had steadfastly refused. "Nobody does my hair and makeup better than Erin," she said now, staring at herself in the mirror. "Remember what an amazing job she did for that red-carpet event with Arch? I'll let some professional make me over in Scotland, but for this wedding, I want everything to be real."

If it had been her wedding, Mila would have put herself in the hands of makeup and hair professionals, but she had to accept that she and Tessa were very different. Besides, Tessa could show up in a burlap sack and still look gorgeous. She was a beautiful woman anyway, but the glow of love and excitement in her eyes made her almost ethereal. Every time Mila looked at her, she had to smile.

Erin came over and whispered, "It almost makes you believe in love just to look at her, doesn't it?"

"I know," Mila replied. "And if she can feel like that about Archer, we can definitely do better than that."

Erin snorted with laughter. It was still hard for either of them to imagine any woman finding bratty Archer Davenport irresistible, though they'd had a few years to get used to it as he'd blazed across the big screens, making a career for himself as a heartthrob. She figured it was all in the way you saw a person. To millions of women around the world, he was gorgeous, sexy, and strong. To Mila and probably Erin, he was the annoying brother who'd teased them. Still, no matter what, any of her brothers would always have her back. As she'd have theirs. And now Tessa would be part of all that.

Betsy said, "You know Howie would be more than happy to walk you down the aisle."

Tessa's eyes filled with tears. "I know. And I appreciate it. But Margaret really wanted to do it, and when you think about it, she's the one who brought us together. I want to walk down the aisle toward Arch on her arm, just as I did that day on Carmel beach when I first met him. But I'm definitely looking forward to a dance with Howie later."

Betsy wrapped her arms around Tessa from behind, being careful not to muss her hair, and Mila looked at the two women reflected in the mirror. Her heart hurt with how much she loved them both. It made her think about family. "Are you okay that your sister's not going to be here?"

A shadow of sadness crossed Tessa's pretty face. "I hinted that maybe we'd do something small for our wedding, but the minute I started talking about the castle in Scotland, my sister shut down any idea of a small wedding and said that absolutely, since I was marrying a man of so much wealth, I should be sure to spend some of it on a big wedding. So, while I'm a little sad not to have my niece here, they'll be more than delighted to play a bigger part in the Scottish wedding." She glanced around and said, "I think of you all and Margaret as my family now."

Betsy tightened her hold and said, "And you are like another daughter to me. It warms my heart to see how happy you make Archer." Both women blinked furiously, and Betsy pulled away. "Before we spoil our makeup, let's get you ready to get married."

The dress that Betsy had first worn nearly forty years ago hung in perfect condition. The dry cleaner had managed to remove the stain so beautifully that no one could tell it had ever been there.

Mila teased, "So, that's your something old. Now you need something borrowed and something blue."

Tessa blushed furiously. "I went out and bought blue satin lingerie. It's the most money I've ever spent on any item of clothing in my life. So that's new *and* blue."

"Sexy blue lingerie? There's hope for you yet," Mila said.

"And obviously, the dress is borrowed."

"No," Betsy replied, looking surprised. "Honey, it's a gift from me to you."

Tessa looked both grateful and perturbed. "I'm honored that you would give me your beautiful dress, but if I don't return it, then I don't have something borrowed." She glanced at the women around her. "Isn't that bad luck?"

"I'm sure it's not," Betsy assured her, "but why don't I lend you those lovely pearl earrings you wore to the red-carpet event?"

Tessa lifted her hair to reveal the stunning diamond earrings Archer had bought her for a wedding present. They shone like perfect stars. "I have to wear the earrings Arch gave me."

"I have an idea," Mila said. "Give me one minute." She raced to her old bedroom. And, as she'd imagined would happen, Erin followed her.

Her sister was out of breath as she shut the door of the bedroom. "You don't have any ideas, do you?"

Mila shook her head. "Between us, we must have left something behind she could borrow."

Erin opened the closet doors while Mila went to her old desk and started opening drawers.

"Cowboy boots?" Erin murmured from inside the closet. "They'd make a strong statement."

"Cherry-flavored lip gloss?" Mila suggested as she pulled out her top drawer.

"But would you really want it back?" Erin asked.

Obviously not.

And then she found it and cried out with triumph. "Look. This is it."

Erin came over and gazed at the object in Mila's hand. "I gave that to you."

"I know. That's what makes it so special." To her surprise, Mila felt tears gather as she touched the silver bracelet with the secret message Erin had had engraved on the inside. *You're stronger than you know.* She'd given it to her after the accident, when she'd struggled so hard to get her life back. "I wore that every single day while I healed. And then, one day, I didn't need it anymore."

"And as Tessa starts her life married to a movie star and with a fledgling painting career, it's perfect for her."

The sisters hugged and then ran back to Tessa. As they told the story of the bracelet, every one of them got a bit teary. Tessa held out her wrist, and Mila slid the bracelet in place.

With the bride ready, it was time for her bridesmaids to get dressed.

Tessa had been the easiest bride as far as choosing bridesmaids' outfits went. Mila and Erin were the only attendants, and they'd each chosen a dress in a turquoise color that reminded them of the ocean on a sunny day. Erin's dress had a flared skirt and a full bodice that really suited her petite frame, while Mila, more on the statuesque side, had gone with a silk sheath with a deep V-neck. She wasn't one to hide her assets. She couldn't wait for Herschel to see her in it.

She heard a commotion outside and glanced out the window to see Howie and his sons, save for Archer, putting up the awning in the backyard. The awning was for two reasons. One, it would shield the guests from any strong sun, but two, it would keep prying eyes and drones from seeing what was going on. Mila was glad she wasn't a big enough celebrity that she had to worry about reporters buzzing her in helicopters on her wedding day. However, Crystal and her team were doing an excellent job of throwing everyone off the scent.

She'd seen the reports on TV and online about Archer Davenport's big wedding in Scotland and had watched Tessa become more and more comfortable under public scrutiny and the glare of the spotlight. She was impressed at how Tessa managed to keep her dignity intact, even when she was asked the most intrusive questions. When she thought of some of the women Archer could have ended up with, she was so glad he'd chosen someone so sensible and down-to-earth. And, even better, somebody who fit in with their family so well.

As she had the thought, she noticed there seemed to be an extra brother down there in the garden. It was Hersch. Without even turning her head, she said, "Mom, what's Herschel doing down there? Has Dad put him to work?"

Betsy joined her at the window. "I think since Archer wasn't available and Herschel already knew about the ceremony today, your dad decided he could use the extra pair of hands."

She did not believe that for a second. It was her

dad's way of bringing Hersch into the fold. She couldn't deny the fact that he was pretty handy with a hammer as he banged in tent pegs to secure the awning. As she watched the way his muscles bunched and flexed, her mouth went dry.

She made sure her hair and makeup were perfect and then slipped out to the garden. Herschel had a rivulet of sweat running down one side of his face as he straightened to face her. A slow grin transformed him from tired laborer to sexy date.

He took a moment to really study her. "I have never seen you look so beautiful. I thought you were pretty damn hot when you were covered in chocolate icing. But I had no idea."

Delighted by his compliment, she gave him a quick kiss. "I'm sorry my dad's put you to work already. I should have warned you, if he sees a strong pair of arms, he tends to find a job for them."

He chuckled. "I don't mind at all. I like your dad. I like your family."

Her voice caught a little bit as she said, "And they like you too."

He said, "This is such a high-tech security operation that I had to bring my suit disguised in a gym bag. It's hanging inside somewhere, and I'd really like a shower before the festivities begin."

"I think I can help you with that," she said.

She waited until he'd secured the last peg and tested his work thoroughly. That tent wouldn't come down in a hurricane. He put away the tools, and then she led him inside to the bathroom that she'd always shared with Erin. Fortunately, Erin was busy with the wedding party. She stepped in with him and, shutting the door behind them, locked it.

His eyebrows went up, and another slow grin spread across his face. "Are you planning what I think you're planning?"

"I was all ready for the wedding, but just seeing you out there made me all hot and sweaty. Want to work up another sweat before you shower?"

He came forward and kissed her slowly and deeply. His moustache brushed her lips. She could smell the heat on his skin and the healthy scent of perspiration. Then he said, "Better not crease that beautiful dress." With his gentlest touch, he helped her out of it and the underwear that cost at least as much as Tessa's wedding lingerie.

He said, "I want you so bad I don't think I can be gentle."

She grabbed him and kissed him. "Good." He took her up against the bathroom tiles. It was hot and fierce and exactly what she needed.

Afterward, she took even more pleasure in watching him soap up and then rinse off. Rubbing himself dry with a fluffy white towel, Hersch said, "I don't even know where my suit is."

She grinned at him. "It's hanging in my closet, of course."

Wrapped in towels, they scooted across the hall to her old bedroom, fortunately unnoticed. Hersch ran a comb through his astronaut-short hair and, to her delight, even combed his moustache. When he put on his suit, it was her turn to tell him how good he looked. She'd never seen him formally dressed, and she liked what she saw.

Once she'd dressed herself again and fixed her hair and makeup, she was ready.

When she went back downstairs, it was to a scene of organized chaos. Crystal took center stage, her instructions crisp and calm. With only an hour before the wedding, everybody chipped in, putting up decorations and balloons and making sure everything was perfect, from the teal tablecloths to the floral arrangements on each table. Mila's job was to put out the tiny gifts that Arch and Tessa had chosen for their guests. They were locally made candles. While Archer could have bought everybody something from Tiffany's, Mila loved that they'd gone with something simple and local. It was perfect.

# Chapter Twenty-Six

Margaret Percy was the first guest to arrive, looking magnificent in a green linen trouser suit and high heels. She'd had her hair done that morning and obviously taken pains with her makeup.

When Mila saw the high heels, she said, "Margaret, Tessa will have a fit if she sees you wearing those heels."

Margaret had been Tessa's patient before Arch broke his leg and needed a live-in caregiver. The eighty-something-year-old shot her a mischievous look. "Then you'd better not tell her. I wasn't going to walk that girl down the aisle looking like a little old lady. If I fall, somebody'll pick me up."

"I will," Howie said, coming in to give her a bear hug. "You know I've always got your back, Margaret."

She patted his cheek. "Don't I know it. It's a proud day for you, Howard Davenport."

"You can say that again. Today, I welcome a new daughter into my family. I couldn't be happier."

"And to think I introduced them," Margaret said,

not for the first time. Since she'd been sworn to secrecy about this wedding, she hadn't been able to crow to all her friends about being responsible for the love match. But every time she was with the family, she made sure that they all knew that this day would never have happened without her. The delightful thing was, it was true. Although Mila had to wonder, even without Margaret's introducing them, wouldn't Archer and Tessa have met somehow? Wasn't that what destiny was all about?

And then she thought about Herschel and how she'd seen him at the plein air show, staring at that painting of her, and from that moment, her life seemed to have taken a different turn. That had to be destiny, didn't it? And on this day, which was all about love and commitment, she had to accept the truth. She'd fallen in love with Herschel Greenfield. Deeply and forever in love. The thought scared her, but it exhilarated her too. As he'd said to her once, he was a man of the stars and sky, and she was a woman of the water. Yet somehow they were magic together.

While she was still having these thoughts, Herschel walked in. She could see him searching for her, and when their gazes met, he gave her a special smile, one she was pretty sure he saved only for her. There was an answering smile on her lips that nobody else ever got either. He came over and stood beside her. She passed him a glass of champagne.

Howie's brothers and their wives arrived together. Howie had wanted to invite all of his brothers and all their kids and all the cousins, but Betsy had talked him down to just the brothers and their wives. But they were all so big and noisy, they took up as much space as twenty people. Fortunately, the weather was nice, and they all picked up their champagne and headed outside. A string quartet played softly in the backyard, and thanks to Crystal and her staff and Francesca's caterers, everything went perfectly.

Francesca came and took charge of the food, which Mila knew was a great honor. Sergio and a young woman, both dressed in black and white, walked around with trays of canapés, all of which Mila had tasted. She was pleased to see that the crab cakes with the avocado aioli were a big hit, as were the other goodies she'd sampled.

Arch arrived, looking as good as she'd ever seen him and definitely happier than she'd ever seen him. He hadn't gone with anything wacky or theatrical for his wedding attire. He wore an elegant tuxedo, as did Nick and Finn. Damien was slightly less formal. His mother had tried to get him to shave, which had made them all laugh. Still, he'd cleaned himself up enough to wear a decent pair of trousers and a crisp white shirt.

Smith Sullivan and a glowing and gorgeous Valentina arrived soon after Arch and his brothers. Smith apologized, telling Crystal in a low voice that they'd taken a detour, as they'd suspected they were being followed by a pap. It happened often enough that Smith wasn't fazed. "Pretty sure we lost him," he said. "But he was driving an old blue Honda Civic."

Crystal nodded and picked up her cell phone. In a minute, she returned. "I've alerted security. They'll keep an eye out for that car, but don't worry. No one who isn't on the guest list will get near this house."

At a nod from Crystal, everyone took their seats. Nobody bothered about bride's side or groom's side, they just all sat together. And then Damien picked up his Martin acoustic guitar and began to play, along with the string quartet. It was time.

Crystal had arranged for a white gazebo, and Archer stood under it with the same minister who'd christened all the Davenport kids. He was a silver-haired man of seventy who looked so much the part he could have been cast in one of Arch's movies.

At Crystal's signal, Tessa came slowly downstairs, and Betsy slipped out to join Howie in the front row.

Erin, Mila, and Tessa had a final hug and all whispered at once, "Good luck," to one another.

"You won't need it," Margaret assured them. "Big smiles. Take your time."

"Exactly," Crystal agreed.

And then they were off. Erin first, because she was the tiniest, partnered with Nick, and then Mila followed with Finn. She caught Herschel's glance from where he was sitting, and she felt her heart actually swell. And then they reached the gazebo and turned.

There was a tiny pause, and then Damien and the string quartet struck up a rock 'n' roll version of "Here Comes the Bride."

Everyone stood to watch Tessa walk up the short grass aisle, which had been covered with a red carpet. The dress looked phenomenal, so classic and chic. Erin had done a wonderful job of enhancing Tessa's natural beauty with makeup. She was a stunning bride.

Mila glanced at Arch and thought she'd never seen such an expression on her brother's face. On screen, he'd pretended to be in love probably a hundred times—and was good at it too. But the reality of Archer Davenport deeply in love? He couldn't fake that. He glowed with happiness, and that glow was shared by the woman who was about to become his wife.

When Tessa reached the altar, Margaret kissed her cheek, and then Arch took her hand and whispered, "You look so beautiful."

"So do you," she whispered back, making Mila smile.

Tessa handed her bouquet to Erin and turned to give Arch both her hands.

The minister began to speak. He talked of love and commitment and all those other words that used to scare Mila so much, but somehow they didn't seem quite so frightening anymore. Love and commitment.

She'd thought for a while she couldn't do it, but maybe she was wrong. Maybe she just hadn't found the right person before now.

The minister paused and, turning to the guests, said, "Tessa and Archer wrote their own vows. I'm looking forward to what they have to say. I hope you are too."

Tessa went first.

"Arch, in the tapestry of my life, you arrived as a brilliant stroke of color on a surface I had left untouched, fearing the world would not understand the depth of my dreams. You saw in me not just a painter, but a soul with a vision, a voice yearning to be heard. You nurtured my hidden talent, giving me the confidence to embrace my true identity. Today, I stand before you, and I vow to be your sanctuary, a source of peace and inspiration, as you have been mine. I promise to support your dreams, to walk beside you as we navigate the ebb and flow of life, painting our future with strokes of courage, passion, and undying love. I choose you, Arch, as my partner, my muse, my husband."

Mila felt her eyes fill with tears. She was so proud of Tessa. Her voice was clear, and although her words were emotional, she had managed to say her vows without crying. In fact, she was pretty much the only one who wasn't. Even Mila, who considered herself not the mushy type, was sniffling and surreptitiously wiping the tears from her face. Good thing Crystal had thought to put tissues in each of their bouquets. She pulled one out, knowing that her tears weren't all for Tessa and her brother.

Her mind and her soul were completely full of Hersch. She couldn't hide from herself any longer. She loved him. She loved him with all her heart.

And then Archer began to speak. "Usually, when I talk about love, I'm spouting rehearsed lines that somebody else wrote." He took a shaky breath. "But these are my words, my real words and my true feelings, and I've never been so nervous about giving a speech in my whole life."

Mila's heart melted. Her big, tough, movie-star brother suffering a bad case of nerves? She found it charming and adorable. Erin had told her that she'd offered to help him write his vows, and he'd turned her down. Even though Erin was a professional writer, Arch had said it was really important that he come up with his own vows. Mila respected that. Archer usually had anything he said in public written for him by scriptwriters or PR people, so it was really something to hear him offering Tessa his love and his heart in his own words.

"Tessa, before I met you, the world knew me as Archer Davenport, the actor, a man celebrated for his roles under the spotlight. But with you, I found the role of a lifetime. Husband. When you came to me, you healed more than a broken leg. I discovered a love as profound and vast as the ocean that whispers our names. Today, I stand before you, inspired by the legacy of love my parents nurtured, a love that has weathered storms and celebrated triumphs for nearly four decades. I vow to you, Tessa, my heart, my strength, my unwavering support. You showed me the beauty of a love that seeks not the spotlight, but thrives in the authenticity of our shared, quiet moments. I promise to cherish you, to lift you up, and to be the mirror that reflects the boundless talent and beauty within you. I love you, and I ask you to be my wife."

The minister spoke the few formal lines that were required and said, "I now pronounce you husband and wife. You may kiss your bride."

Archer leaned forward, and Tessa tilted her face up to his, and he kissed her. The kiss lasted so long that Finn finally yelled, "Get a room," and they broke apart, laughing.

There were so many tears and so much laughter that Mila knew the event was a wild success. They walked down the short aisle while everybody stood and clapped.

The family gathered for photographs, and despite it being a special event, Finn still made a goofy face in most of them, as was his tradition. At their mom's request, he smiled normally in one, and she proclaimed that it would take pride of place on the mantel.

The rest of the guests began to mingle. Howie, the unofficial master of ceremonies, called for silence in his warm, booming voice. He said, "My son Damien has written you both a song." And then he looked around. "For any of you who don't know, Damien Davenport has famously never written a love song. This is his first one, so go easy on the kid, will ya?"

There was plenty of laughter and applause. Damien Davenport was one of the most successful singer/songwriters in the world. Nobody was worried that the song wouldn't be worth hearing.

"Thanks, Dad," Damien said, and then he settled himself on a chair with his guitar.

He played a few chords, and over them in his deep, gravelly voice, he said, "It's true, Dad. I've never written a love song before. But when inspiration strikes, you have to go with it. And when I see Tessa and Arch together, the only song I can write is a song about love. I hope you guys like it. It's called 'Colors of Love,' and this is for you."

*On the coast of California, under the golden sun,*
*A tale of love began so pure, it couldn't be undone.*
*A painter with her easel, in a world of her own,*
*Healed a broken man and gave him a home.*

*With every stroke of her brush, she painted dreams in the sky.*
*He watched in awe, as his heart couldn't deny.*

*Their love story unfolding, in colors bold and bright,*
*Under the California sun, everything just felt right.*

*Brushstrokes of love, in every hue and tone,*
*A masterpiece they've created, a world of their own.*
*From the easel to the heart, a beautiful start,*
*In California, they vowed never to part.*

Mila had thought the wedding vows were emotional, but she found herself crying all over again at the beautiful song Damien had composed. Halfway through, she found Hersch reaching for her hand, and they clung to each other until the closing chords ended, and then everybody broke into spontaneous applause. Damien, who wowed crowds everywhere, from London to Beijing to Sydney to New York, looked bashful as he bowed his head.

Arch and Tessa's love had touched each of the Davenport siblings in a special way.

# Chapter Twenty-Seven

The party continued as they sat down to eat the beautiful meal that Mila had helped choose. It was delicious, as she knew it would be, but she was still glad that everything was perfect for Tessa. Smith Sullivan made the first speech. He talked about how he and Archer had wooed a lot of women onscreen, but when the real thing hit, no rehearsal helped you navigate the new role of husband. His advice, given with a humorous smile, was to always accept that your wife knew best.

"Absolutely," echoed Valentina, who looked stunning in a blue silk dress.

Next was their mom. Betsy stood, gorgeous in a deep pink dress patterned with flowers. "What a beautiful day this is for all of us. Howie and I couldn't be more pleased to welcome you into our family, Tessa. You have been beyond wonderful in caring for our son, and though I would never have wished a broken leg on anyone, I'm glad it brought you and Arch together. You healed him, and you loved him. I thank you for that, and welcome you to our family." Then she turned to Arch. "Since you were a little boy, everything you touched turned to gold, but nothing in your life has ever shone brighter than your love for Tessa. I know you two are forever, and I love you both."

Everyone raised their glasses in appreciation, and Mila took a happy sip of champagne. Her mom took her seat, and her dad gently wiped her tears from her cheeks before standing himself. He smiled at his guests. "First, Tessa, as my beautiful wife just said, we all adore you. I'm so glad you're part of the family now. And Arch." His voice broke with emotion, and he took a moment to calm himself. "Arch, welcome to the married life. And well done falling for someone as lovely and perfect for you as Tessa. To see your child find their perfect fit is one of the greatest joys a parent can know. Here's to forever love!"

They all raised their glasses in a toast.

Nick, as the oldest brother, was next to stand. Mila could see that he was a bit embarrassed that his eyes had already filled with tears. He swallowed hard and said, "Arch, Nick, Damien, Finn, and I have always been such a tight-knit unit that I'll admit I thought when Arch got married, something might change. But now I see that we're all going to be closer than ever. Being witness to your love makes me realize that every time we bring a new person into the family circle, the love only gets bigger. It's a thrill to gain another sister." He grinned at Tessa. "Welcome to the madhouse... I mean, welcome to our family."

Everyone laughed and raised their glasses in another toast.

Arch rose and replied to the toasts, thanked the bridesmaids, joked about his brothers, and then thanked Tessa's parents, who he was sure were smiling down on this day. He finally turned to thank Betsy and Howie. "You two showed us all what a real marriage and real love look like. It took me a long time to find that kind of forever love, but when I met Tessa, I knew I was done for." To the assembled guests, he said, "Thank you all for coming and helping us celebrate this special day. Now, let's party!"

And then the dancing started. Arch led Tessa across the makeshift dance floor, and everyone watched in a happy hush as they moved in perfect harmony. After the song ended, Howie and Betsy stepped onto the dance floor, Howie partnering with Tessa and Betsy her son.

Mila was a little worried that Erin might feel like the only singleton, since Mila had brought a date at the last minute, and Erin hadn't. But to her surprise and secret delight, Jay Malone had also come alone. He'd been smart enough to realize that none of those underwear models he dated could be trusted not to blab the secret of this wedding to the paparazzi.

The minute the dance floor opened up, he went over to Erin and offered his hand. Mila watched her sister hesitate for just a second, then nod and get up. She didn't know what Jay said, but he made Erin laugh, and then she relaxed in his arms. And just for a moment, Mila wondered if…

Then she shook her head. She was getting overly romantic because she was at a wedding. Pushy Jay Malone and quiet, intellectual Erin? No. That could never work.

Herschel asked her to dance, and as she settled in his arms for their own first-ever dance, she discovered that they fit perfectly, and the astronaut had some real moves.

Damien danced with a couple of his aunts and Tessa, and then she saw him go over to Crystal. He obviously asked her to dance, and Crystal, still wearing her headset, made a gesture toward the cake. He shook his head and, reaching up, removed the headset. *Good for him,* Mila thought.

He led the still protesting Crystal out to the dance floor, where Mila was able to watch how much the two old friends enjoyed each other. It must be such a relief to Damien to be able to let go with someone he trusted, since they'd known each other long before he'd become famous. The more she watched them dancing, she more she noticed that there was real chemistry between the two of them. But Crystal didn't stay on the dance floor long, abandoning him to head back to her duties.

Damien danced the next one with Margaret, who had been waltzed around by each of the Davenport men in turn. Second to Tessa, Mila thought that Margaret was the belle of the ball. She only hoped she was as gorgeous and feisty and vibrant when she was that age.

Then it was time to cut the cake. When the big chocolate fudge cake came out, Herschel leaned over and whispered in her ear, "I'm going to need a very large piece of that cake to go."

Immediately, her thoughts turned to the night they'd spread chocolate cake all over each other and licked it off their bodies. She was never going to look at chocolate cake the same way again.

After everyone had enjoyed a slice of cake, Smith Sullivan came over to where Mila was standing beside Arch and Tessa. He said, "Great job on keeping the ceremony on the down-low. I noticed the well disguised security outside the house, but it wasn't needed. The ruse worked."

She was glad he didn't mention that he and Valentina might have been followed. It didn't matter now, and besides, it was probably just a fan who'd caught sight of Smith and decided to follow him. As she knew from her famous brothers, fans did stuff like that all the time.

Arch nodded with pride. "The decoy wedding worked. Between Crystal being a brilliant planner and everybody who came today keeping the secret, right down to the caterers and servers, I couldn't be happier."

"Are you going to have a honeymoon?" Smith wanted to know.

He nodded. "We're going to Damien's island in the Bahamas." He turned a teasing glance on his bride. "It's gorgeous, right on the beach, and fully staffed. Tessa's not sure about the butler and the servants, but I think she'll get used to them."

Smith laughed. "I know you're going to have a great time."

Tessa said, "Then we'll have our Scottish wedding. But I won't mind the fuss, because I've already had my perfect backyard wedding. And also, I can't wait to see Scotland."

"You're coming, right?" Arch asked. "There's not a schedule clash with filming?"

Smith put his arm around Valentina and looked down into her face to find her nodding. He tightened his grip slightly and said, "We're hoping to, but Valentina's been a little under the weather the past few weeks."

"You're not sick?" Arch started to say in alarm, then saw his best man's huge grin.

"You don't mean—are you—"

"Pregnant?" Valentina said. "Yes." She raised her champagne flute of sparkling water.

Arch grabbed her for a hug, being gentle, as though she might break. Then he gave Smith a big hug too. "I didn't think I could be any happier on this day, but this is the best wedding gift I could hope for."

"This is just wonderful," Tessa said. "And if you're not up to the Scottish wedding, of course we'll understand."

"I'm having a maternity wardrobe made," Valentina admitted. "I definitely plan to be there."

After the bride changed into a gorgeous pale pink dress, she and Archer said their good-byes, and everybody clapped and cheered as they left the house. They'd spend what was left of the night at their house in Carmel, and the next morning, they would jet off by private plane to Damien's island.

Smith and Valentina left soon after, holding hands.

Herschel and Mila continued dancing until she couldn't take it any longer—she just wanted to be alone with Hersch.

They left the house hand in hand. Hersch said, "That was amazing. One of the best weddings I've ever been to."

"I'm so happy they pulled it off," she said. "And I agree. I almost felt that my brother deserves Tessa, and most of the time, I don't think he deserves anybody."

Herschel chuckled. "Spoken like a sister. He's a

good guy. And she's a wonderful woman. If there were ever two people who deserved to be happy, it's Archer and Tessa."

She looked at him. "You should have made that speech. It would have made a great toast."

He shook his head at her. "There were plenty of toasts. Nobody needed mine."

"I hope it wasn't too Davenport-family for you?" she asked.

He seemed to think about her words. "It was plenty Davenport-family, but I happen to like the Davenports. Even Howie's brothers and their wives."

"Even if my dad put you to work?"

"Especially because your dad put me to work. It made me feel like I was one of you."

She was delighted he'd figured that out. Because the truth was, it had been Howie's way of letting Hersch, and probably her, know that he felt Herschel fit right in. Subtle her dad wasn't, but he was the most loving, bighearted man you'd ever meet. She didn't say any of that to Herschel, just reached out and took his hand. Then she said, "Your place or mine?"

"I don't care, so long as we're together."

She made a sudden decision. "Let's go to my place. Closer to the beach."

He gave an exaggerated groan. "You never give up, do you?"

"Herschel, you're getting more confident every

day. I don't want to break this winning streak."

"Good thing I left some board shorts at your place, then," he said. "I had a feeling I'd be needing them."

# Chapter Twenty-Eight

A beautiful full moon hung low in the sky as Hersch and Mila drove back to her place. He jumped out and ran around the car to open the door for her, which charmed her. Perhaps it was because they were still all dressed up, but there was almost a little formality to the way they treated each other. He opened the gate and held it for her to go through, and when she slipped the key into the lock and opened the door to her house, she held it politely for him to enter.

Her skin felt extra sensitive as he brushed against her on their way to the bedroom. She helped him slip off his jacket and hung it neatly in her closet, then she undid his tie and released it slowly from the collar of the shirt he'd so crisply ironed. She undid each button, kissing the skin she uncovered. He was patient with her for a while and then increasingly restless.

She tasted salt on his skin from all that dancing, and felt the heat from his belly on her lips, which made her even more hot. She kissed her way back up, and he was there, kissing her mouth, urgent and deep until she moaned low in her throat.

He turned her around and undid the zipper on her silk dress. He didn't even let it hit the floor, but carefully held it while she stepped out of it. He hung the dress neatly in her wardrobe. There was something kind of sexy about the fastidious way he looked after her things even when she could feel his raging need for her. Besides, it gave her a little more time to pose in her fancy, barely-there underwear.

When he returned from the closet, he looked her up and down. "You do have some very nice lingerie," he said.

She twirled slowly for him, letting him get a real eyeful, and then he kicked off his shoes, pulled off his socks, and slipped out of his dress pants. She walked right up to him and, with a firm but loving hand, tumbled him back on her bed. Finally, she had him where she wanted him. She slipped his boxers down and off, revealing how incredibly turned on he was. She climbed on top of him and kissed him, and then he flipped her onto her back and slowly and deliberately removed each piece of lingerie. After that, it was a little bit of a competition, her on top, then him on top, until they were kissing and laughing and worn out from teasing each other. When he slipped inside her at last, she felt that she'd remember this moment forever, and then he drove her up, up, and even as she tried to make the moment last, she was wrapping her legs around him, meeting him thrust for thrust, until it was too much, and she tumbled over the edge, crying out his name.

It had been the perfect day.

Just as they were about to go to sleep, he leaned over and whispered, "I love you."

Mila went from feeling utter bliss to alarm. She moved her lips but found she was tongue-tied. Even though she'd thought those words to herself at her brother's wedding, to say them out loud now felt dangerous, as though she'd be giving herself away.

Instead of responding, she kissed him.

He didn't call her out for not saying the words back to him, but she thought she caught a tiny glimmer of hurt in his eyes. The last thing she saw was the moonlight glinting off his Saint Christopher's medal.

* * *

Mila woke earlier than usual. It was just past five, the moon was still full, and the waves were huge. She nudged Herschel awake.

"Come on, let's go out and surf."

He opened one eye and said, "It's still dark out there. You can't surf in the dark."

"You can when the moon is full. Anyway, it will be light soon. Come on!" She couldn't quite understand this driving need to surf. Probably the fact that he'd said *I love you*, and she hadn't been able to respond, had something to do with it. She did love him, she knew she did, but to say those words out loud would make her so vulnerable. She just wasn't sure she was ready.

Going out on the ocean would clear her confused thoughts, and then perhaps she could say the words back to him. Until she had her surfboard under her and the wind at her back, she'd remain in this state of confusion.

So, she banged around the kitchen and made coffee, fueling them up for some very early exercise. If Hersch was brokenhearted about the way she hadn't said *I love you*, he was hiding it well. He put on his board shorts and joined her in the kitchen, draining his first cup of coffee and then preparing an insulated mug for each to take with them.

Soon, they headed out, him with his boogie board and her with her surfboard.

\* \* \*

When Hersch got to the water's edge, he was shocked at how big the waves were. Scary big.

"Are you sure about this?" he asked.

He could feel her energy and could have kicked himself for blurting out *I love you*. He hadn't meant to do it that way. He had meant to be cool and prepared. Maybe to say the words when he'd taken her away for a weekend in Paris or something, not throw them at her when they were both tired after watching her brother get married. What had he been thinking?

And now here they were in what felt like the dead of night, and she thought it was a good idea to go surfing on the biggest waves he'd ever seen? If anything happened to her, it would be his fault for putting her in the position where she felt she needed to surf. If he'd learned anything about Mila, it was that she worked out her problems on the water.

He really wanted to talk her out of this terrible idea of swimming out and meeting those huge, dark, soul-sucking waves. "Why don't we go get breakfast?" he suggested. "We could come back later when it's light."

Her answer was to laugh at him. "Give me an hour, then I'll go for breakfast with you."

"Okay," he said quietly. She put her mug in the sand for later and would have headed into the surf, but he pulled her to him and kissed her swiftly. "Be careful," he said.

She smiled that gorgeous smile of hers. "Don't worry. I've got this." And then she was off.

He knew that she worked things out surfing and that he'd given her a biggie to ponder, but he'd never seen her like this. She was swimming out toward those big, dark waves as though she wanted to dance with danger.

His heart was in his throat. He couldn't even sit down. He stood, walked to the edge of the water, and just watched. She was a dark shape against dark waves, and then the sun began to rise, casting a deep pink glow. She popped up on her board as easily and lightly as a ballerina leaping onto a stage and began to ride the waves. She was glorious, so beautiful it made his heart ache, and he watched her coming in toward him, so grateful she was safe. But she didn't come all the way in. He realized with dread that she wasn't finished.

She jumped off her board while she was still pretty far from shore and swam back out again. Half a dozen times, he waited for her to come all the way in, and each time she went back out for another ride.

Day was dawning, and he couldn't take much more of this tension. He could see her more clearly now, and it seemed to him that she was barely in control of her board. Yet, when he was certain a wave would toss her, she somehow managed to stay on its back and ride.

Now he watched helplessly as she rode a big one, one of those that always scared him, where it curled right over like a big mouth trying to gobble her up. He could hardly bear to watch, yet he couldn't tear his eyes away.

She seemed so small and defenseless in the curl of the wave. "Come on, come on," he said aloud, his heart pounding. "Come out of there."

And as she did, his worst fear was realized. The greedy mouth of the wave snapped its jaws shut.

And she disappeared.

A few seconds later, he watched her board pop up, but she wasn't on it.

He didn't even think. He dropped his coffee and sprinted into the water, calling her name.

Back when he'd been an Ironman, the swimming was the strongest leg of the event for him. His muscles remembered exactly how it felt to drag himself through the water with efficient strokes and at high speed. He kicked with all his strength, dragged himself forward with his arms, panting with the effort, half blinded by the waves, choking on seawater. Not knowing what else to do, he headed for her surfboard, where he could still see it bobbing. He was nearly there when a head popped up.

"Mila!" he yelled.

She looked slightly disoriented as she turned to-ward him. "Hersch?" And then she yelled again, "Hersch! You did it. You're swimming!"

He didn't even know what she was talking about. "I thought I'd lost you."

And then they reached each other, and she threw her arms around him, and he threw his arms around her. He kissed her cold lips.

She was trembling.

He was trembling.

He kissed her again, and they clung to each other.

She said, "You'll never lose me. I love you."

And then they both grabbed at her board, and it

supported them as they wrapped their arms around each other and kissed with the kind of deep love they'd never dared to express before.

He took another deep breath and said, "I love you too. I never should have said it last night. I wanted to make a big romantic thing of telling you, but the words just slipped out."

"I liked hearing it," she admitted. "But you startled me. I already knew I loved you. I was just scared to tell you."

In that moment, Hersch realized they were still in deep water, and panic began to set in. His teeth were chattering, and the beach seemed a long way away. "Can we go in now?" he asked.

"Of course," she said softly. "Let's go home."

★ ★ ★

When they got back, they showered until they were all warmed up and then cuddled in her bed, sharing coffee and just enjoying being in love and being with each other.

He leaned over and said, "I'm not going to scare you by asking too soon, but get used to the idea that one day I will. And before I even ask, I want you to think about how you'd feel marrying someone with one of the riskiest jobs on or off the planet."

She rolled over and kissed him, and the smile bloomed all over her face. "Haven't you noticed? I am a bona fide risk-taker. We'll make it work."

He reached over and ran his hand down her hair, tucking it behind one ear. "Bad things can happen. I've had to make my peace with that in order to be an astronaut."

She shook her head at him. "Love is risk. The biggest risk of all. I never thought I could find a man like you. I never thought I could love this deeply. And loving you this way, I understand that one day you could be in a rocket, and it might not go well. You know that I could be on a wave, and it might not go well either. But that's why we're perfect for each other, because we understand and accept that risk."

He pulled her close to him until her head was resting on his chest, and she could hear the slow, steady beat of his heart. He said, "You know, I had an epiphany the other day."

She glanced up at him. "You did? Epiphanies don't happen every day."

Hersch smiled. "This one was pretty profound. I realized that I'd been fooling myself. Maybe all my grand talk about not wanting to marry and have children wasn't about leaving anyone behind. Maybe I was the one who was afraid of being left behind."

They stared into each other's eyes for a long time, and then she kissed him tenderly. "I love you. That is all I know, and right now, it's enough."

He said, "And that's everything."

# Chapter Twenty-Nine

When they walked into Betsy and Howie's house for the post-wedding breakfast, Mila couldn't believe how efficient Crystal and her staff had been. It was hard to find any evidence that there'd been a wedding there yesterday. There were still a couple of nice, big flower arrangements, and to her delight, still a bit of chocolate cake left that she'd have to find a way to take home. But apart from Archer and Tessa not being there, it was just like one of the usual Davenport family breakfasts. Erin was cutting up fruit. Finn was frying bacon. Howie had put on his big barbecue apron and was asking everybody how they wanted their eggs.

Mila got involved making pancakes, and Betsy said to Herschel that Tessa's job was squeezing the fresh orange juice, but since she wasn't there, could he possibly take over? So he piled in with the rest of them while they talked about how amazing the wedding had been, all the fun things that had happened, how happy the bride and bridegroom had looked, how proud Margaret had been to be the instigator of the whole thing.

Then Jay Malone arrived.

Erin looked surprised and flustered to see him. She said, "I didn't know you'd be here for breakfast."

He came in, all bluster, and immediately went up and kissed her cheek. "Miss me?"

She shook her head and went back to chopping melon.

Jay boomed out in his big voice, "I got the kids to the plane this morning. As she was boarding, Tessa made sure to tell me how grateful she is to you and the family and how perfect the wedding was."

"It really was," Betsy said with a sigh. "I can't wait to plan the next one."

Mila glanced up at Hersch and found him looking at her with a very intimate smile.

Erin must have caught the moment, because she said, "I have a feeling you won't have to wait too long."

Then Jay looked from Mila to Hersch and back again. "Are you kidding me? Our man Herschel finds true love? Could there be a better ending to your life story? Come on, Hersch, tell me you're in for the biopic."

He glanced around at the family. Nick was snickering, and Finn was shaking his head. Even Betsy had to turn away to hide her laughter. Finally, Hersch answered, "Sorry, Jay. The movie's already been made."

Mila snorted with laughter, and behind her, Erin giggled. Howie let out his booming laugh. Jay looked around the kitchen and shook his head slowly. "No. You did not make one of those cheesy home movies."

It was Nick who answered him, grinning from ear to ear. "We sure did. Come on, you've got to see this man make a s'more on film."

While Jay was still protesting and Nick was fetching the camcorder, Erin walked over to Mila and hugged her. "I'm so happy for you."

"We're pretty happy too," Mila said.

Over breakfast, Jay continued to argue that the biopic was an excellent idea. Finally, to everyone's surprise, Herschel said, "You know, Jay, you could be right. Maybe if I'm willing to share how devastating that accident was, how I developed a fear of the water, and how I'm working to overcome it, maybe I can help other people too."

Jay was so used to arguing for the movie and being shut down that his fork stopped halfway to his mouth with a piece of bacon and a chunk of egg on it. "Really?"

Herschel glanced at Mila, who suddenly saw all the reasons why it could be a good idea and nodded.

"I think so," Herschel said. "Let's wait till Arch is back, and we can talk about it some more." He looked at Nick. "I'm sure Nick will back me up, but Archer did a pretty damn good screen test. His moustache was particularly authentic."

Now they all cracked up again, and Nick showed the home movie to Jay, who had a good laugh along with the rest of them. "Okay, it's a joke and a home movie filmed on an out-of-date camera, but you have to admit, there's some serious chemistry there. I was riveted."

"Like I said," Hersch said, "I'm willing to discuss the project when Archer gets back. I wouldn't want anyone else to play me."

"You have good taste."

Mila said, "I need to know who will be playing me." She threw out the name of every stupendously gorgeous and smoking-hot actress she could think of.

Jay started to laugh. "Don't worry, Mila. Whoever plays you will not only be a powerhouse, she'll be gorgeous."

"I still want casting approval."

Jay laughed, and then his expression turned more serious. He said, "You know I've been trying to get hold of you, Mila. Leaving messages. I think you've been avoiding my calls."

She felt kind of bad. Especially now that he'd tackled her in front of her whole family. "I thought you were calling to get me to talk Hersch into letting you do your movie."

"No, I wouldn't do that. I can talk to Herschel myself. Mila, I've spent years visiting all of you here, and every time I fall more in love with this place. I want you to find me a house here in Carmel-by-the-Sea."

As Mila gave him a delighted smile and said, "I'd be happy to," she heard the *clink* of Erin's fork dropping to the tabletop.

As they left the house, everything felt different. Now that Mila had told Herschel she loved him and he'd admitted that he wanted to marry her, she felt that a whole new chapter was beginning for her. And for him. He seemed much happier too.

She said, "Are you sure about that biopic? Don't let Jay bully you into anything. I've been defending you against the idea since the day we met."

"No. I mean, of course it's embarrassing to have the whole world see my private fears, but, Mila, maybe if I told my story honestly, it could help people. That's all I've ever wanted to do. I've spent a long time trying to help the world with Alzheimer's research. Maybe now it's time to offer a story that might help somebody else overcome their trauma."

She loved him so much. She threw her arms around him and kissed him. "You are the best man I know."

He kissed her back, then pulled away. "Come on. There's something I want to show you."

"What is it?"

He wouldn't give her even a hint. Instead, they got into his car, and he drove her to his place. She quirked an eyebrow at him. "If you're planning to show me your etchings, I've already seen them. And they are very nice."

He chuckled. "Close."

Now she really was curious. He unlocked the front door and made her wait in the hallway while he ran forward and fiddled with something. She was already smiling with anticipation when he said, "You can come in now."

As she walked into the living room, she cried out with delight. Hanging on the big wall in the living room was Tessa's painting of Mila in the curl of a wave, dancing with the ocean.

"It's the picture that brought us together," he said, his voice full of emotion.

She felt kind of choked up. "When I first met you at the plein air show, I got the feeling this picture terrified you."

"It did. And then I got to know you, and now I feel different. You're my sea witch, and this painting reminds me of how glorious you are. You changed my life, and being with you on land, and even on sea, makes me happier than I ever thought I could be."

She was half blinded by tears as she ran forward and threw her arms around him. "I love you, Herschel Greenfield." She laughed. "It was so hard to say the words the first time. Now I can't stop."

"Never stop," he said, kissing her until she had no words at all.

# *Epilogue*

Erin Davenport loved to surf. Oh, she'd never be the champion her sister was, but she had the technique and, like Mila, like all of them, had been surfing since she could walk. Her dad had put each of them on the end of his board and taken them out for little rides as soon as they were old enough. Mila had always been fearless. She rode those waves like she owned them. Erin was a little more respectful of the power of the ocean. She liked to think she didn't so much ride the waves as ask their permission before getting on their backs.

It was early morning, and the Davenports were surfing together. It was a great day. Archer and Tessa were back from their honeymoon, looking completely relaxed and totally in love. Damien was goofing around happily between gigs. Even Nick, who was usually busy with app development, had left his work at home and was clowning around with the rest of them. Finn, the largest of them all, had swum farther out than anybody.

But Hersch was the one she was watching. Herschel Greenfield, who'd been so traumatized by his near-death experience that he'd been frightened of water, was learning how to surf. And he wasn't half bad either. She'd watched Mila teach plenty of people to surf, mostly kids, and she was a good teacher. But Herschel was definitely her prize student. It probably didn't hurt that when he did something spectacularly good, he got a big, smacking kiss. She suspected Mila's other students had to make do with a word of praise or maybe a piece of candy if she had some on hand.

Erin had never seen Mila so happy and carefree. It did her heart good. She tried to believe that one day there might be somebody out there for her too, but she was only a reporter for a small-town weekly. She wasn't a bright international star like Damien or Archer. She wasn't a statuesque and successful Realtor and former surf champion like Mila. She was the girl next door. The quiet one. Maybe her destiny was to be an aunt to all the nieces and nephews she imagined were on the horizon. And she'd be fine with that. She thought of all the Victorian novels she'd read about women who were devoted aunts. Maybe that was her destiny.

And then a loud and unwelcome voice intruded on her thoughts.

"Hey, is there room for one more?"

She didn't have to turn her head to recognize the

voice. Jay Malone, Archer's agent, the loudest, pushiest man she'd ever known. He came up and slung an arm around her. They'd known each other more than ten years, so he treated her more like a kid sister than a grown woman.

"Hey there, short stuff. Race you to the waves." And then he pounded into the surf, got on his board, and started to swim out to join the others.

*Short stuff?* Was that how he saw her? Erin didn't have much of a competitive streak, but in that moment, she decided to show Julius "Call Me Jay" Malone exactly what she was made of. She'd show him short stuff.

She ran in, jumped on her own board, and swam as though there were a medal at stake. As she overtook Jay, she saw his eyes widen in surprise. She reached the break ahead of him, which pleased her immensely. Then she sat on her board, waiting for the next set of waves.

He set up not too far from her. While they bobbed atop the water, he gazed toward the row of expensive houses on the beach and said, "One of those has my name on it."

She rolled her eyes. He was so annoying. "Not one of them is even for sale."

"Erin, if there's one thing I've learned in life, it's that if you want something badly enough, you can usually get it."

And then he gazed at her with an intensity that made her breath catch. There was one thing she knew for sure. Jay was single-minded and didn't stop until he got what he wanted, whether it was the best deal for one of his clients or a woman he'd set his sights on.

For an awful moment, Erin wondered if he was setting his sights on her. If so, he was going to be very disappointed.

But the moment passed as a set of waves headed toward them and caught Jay's attention. "Come on, short stuff," Jay yelled to her, popping up on his board. "Race you to shore."

As she jumped up on her own board and felt the wave lift her, she began to dance. Obviously, her momentary impression had been wrong. A man who called her *short stuff* and challenged her to surfing races didn't have romance in mind. Which was excellent news, as she couldn't imagine a worse match for any reasonable woman than Jay Malone.

Then she and the wave picked up speed, and she forgot all about Jay as she gazed ahead at Carmel-by-the-Sea, her home and, in her opinion, the best place in the world.

★ ★ ★

# ABOUT THE AUTHORS

Having sold more than 10 million books, Bella Andre's novels have been #1 bestsellers around the world and have appeared on the *New York Times* and *USA Today* bestseller lists 93 times. She has been the #1 Ranked Author on a top 10 list that included Nora Roberts, JK Rowling, James Patterson and Steven King.

Known for "sensual, empowered stories enveloped in heady romance" (Publishers Weekly), her books have been Cosmopolitan Magazine "Red Hot Reads" twice and have been translated into ten languages. She is a graduate of Stanford University and has won the Award of Excellence in romantic fiction. The Washington Post called her "One of the top writers in America" and she has been featured by Entertainment Weekly, NPR, USA Today, Forbes, The Wall Street Journal, and TIME Magazine.

In addition to writing "The Sullivans" series, "The Maverick Billionaires" series, and "The Davenport" series, Bella also writes the *New York Times* bestselling "Four Weddings and a Fiasco" series as Lucy Kevin. Her sweet contemporary romances also include the USA Today bestselling "Walker Island" and "Married in Malibu" series.

If not behind her computer, you can find her reading her favorite authors, hiking, swimming or laughing. Married with two children, Bella splits her time between the Northern California wine country, a log cabin in the Adirondack mountains of upstate New York, and a flat in London overlooking the Thames.

**Sign up for Bella's New Release newsletter:**
**bellaandre.com/newsletter**

**Join Bella Andre on Facebook:**
**facebook.com/authorbellaandre**

**Join Bella Andre's reader group:**
**bellaandre.com/readergroup**

**Follow Bella Andre on Instagram:**
**instagram.com/bellaandrebooks**

**Follow Bella Andre on Twitter:**
**twitter.com/bellaandre**

**Visit Bella's website for her complete booklist:**
**www.BellaAndre.com**

Nicky Arden (aka Nancy Warren) is the USA Today Bestselling author of mystery and romance who had sold more than 5 million books so far! She's originally from Vancouver, Canada, though she tends to wander and has lived in England, Italy and California at various times. Favorite moments include being the answer to a crossword puzzle clue in Canada's National Post newspaper, being featured on the front page of the New York Times when her book Speed Dating launched Harlequin's NASCAR series, and being nominated three times for Romance Writers of America's RITA award. She has an MA in Creative Writing from Bath Spa University. She's an avid hiker, loves chocolate and most of all, loves to hear from readers! You'll often find her in her private Facebook group, Nancy Warren's Knitwits.

**Newsletter signup:**
**nickyarden.com/newsletter**

**Nicky's Website:**
**www.NickyArden.com**

Printed in Great Britain
by Amazon